DR. OFF LIMITS

LOUISE BAY

ISBN – 978-1-910747-75-9

BOOKS BY LOUISE BAY

Hopeful

The Empire State Series

Gentleman Series

The Wrong Gentleman

The Ruthless Gentleman

The Royals Series

The Earl of London

The British Knight

Duke of Manhattan

Park Avenue Prince

King of Wall Street

The Nights Series

Indigo Nights

Promised Nights

Parisian Nights

Faithful

Sign up to the Louise Bay mailing list at
www.louisebay/mailinglist

Read more at www.louisebay.com

ONE

Sutton

In just five days' time, I'd be working at one of the most prestigious hospitals in London, answering to the name I'd worked hard to make mine: Doctor Scott. The thought was very likely to hospitalize me with a panic attack between now and then.

"How are the odds looking?" Parker asked me.

"Not good." I winced at the tightness of the strap around my chin. I fiddled with the fastenings of my helmet and instantly the harness that I'd just been strapped into started to bite into my thighs. Normally being in the outdoors, in the midst of trees the height of skyscrapers, breathing in air as fresh as it got in London would be a welcome change from studying at my desk. Not today. As I took in the crisscross of wires between the trees and the so-called bridges between them that I was expected to walk along, I decided this kind of change, I could live without. "The likelihood of me having a panic attack just went to ninety-two percent."

"But we got down to forty yesterday," Parker said, her tone a teenager who'd been told her curfew was 9pm.

"*Yesterday* involved an open-top bus, an uber-enthusiastic tour guide with a passion for the fire of London, and mimosas. Today is different territory. In every sense."

My best friend was well aware of my anxiety when it came to starting at the hospital. She'd witnessed the years I'd spent studying. The long days that ran into longer nights. The nonexistent social life, sacrificed to the study gods. The way I used to send up a tiny prayer that my clients would cancel their haircuts so I could cram in an extra forty-five minutes of study. Over the years, enough of my prayers were answered that I passed each stage of my journey on the way to being a doctor. My new job had been a long time coming, the culmination of every second of hard work I'd put in over the last seven years.

"I thought a ropes course would be the *height* of distracting," Parker argued. "Pun intended."

"Not from my imminent death, it's not."

"I suppose I didn't think about that. You want me to go first?"

I shook my head. I always found it was better not to know how difficult things were about to get or you risked chickening out before even trying. If I'd known what I was going to face studying to become a doctor back when I was cutting hair and discussing people's holidays six days a week, I would have never filled out that first application form. For many of the years since, it had been beyond hard, but if I'd known how hard it was about to get, there were a thousand times I would have given up. Naivety and blind ambition were a powerful combination.

One of the instructors clipped my harness onto the twisted metal rope and ushered me forward. "Keep moving.

There are arrows showing you the direction you're heading and instructors placed regularly along the route."

"You all dressed in black in case we fall from fifty meters, die, and you don't want to look like you're ready to break out the party tunes?" I asked.

He squinted. "Wow, quite the optimist, aren't you?"

"Just asking," I replied.

"We dress in black so we don't distract anyone with bright colors."

"Sure," I said noncommittally.

"And no one has died on this ropes course," he added.

The elephant on my chest decided to stand and take a stroll. "No deaths" might seem like a low bar for a safety record, but I'd take what I could get.

"Not today anyway." He gave me a little shove off the platform where we were standing, onto the first "bridge" to the next tree. The so-called bridge was a series of wooden slats spaced about fifty centimeters apart and connected by chains that tinkled in the wind. A more fanciful person might say it sounded like we were in the home of the fairies. I knew it was probably a fake soundtrack played to drown out the sound of screams.

I took a step forward onto the first plank and grabbed the horizontal wires placed either side of my head.

"All those years ago when you first considered training to be a doctor, did you always know you'd get to this point?" Parker asked.

"What, staring into the jaws of death?"

As I took the next step, I realized I was only about a meter above the ground—for now. A broken toe was the most likely scenario if I fell and the safety harness didn't do its job. I took the next few steps more confidently, and found it wasn't as bad as I thought it would be. The slats were a comfortable distance apart. We weren't too high up and things felt pretty sturdy—the same way I might have described my life after getting on my feet again following a rough few years. I had a job, a roof over my head, cereal in the cupboard, and milk in the fridge.

I stepped up onto the next platform and turned as Parker started on the other end of the bridge.

"You okay?" I asked her as she reached me.

"I will be when we're done here." She grinned up at me. "But at least you're thinking about your imminent death rather than starting work."

"Every cloud has a silver lining," I said. She knew that I hated that phrase because it was total rubbish. Every cloud didn't have a silver lining. When a door closed another one didn't magically open, and I wanted nothing to do with any ill winds. I hated those kinds of platitudes. I liked reality. And reality was that life was hard. And to get anything in this life took hard work, dedication, and sacrifice.

"Okay, onto the next," I said, following the arrows. "This one looks a little higher but not too bad." The slats on the next bridge were arranged in a more haphazard way—some crossed, some small, some big. With a little more confidence, I stepped across the bridge and my threatening panic attack receded slightly. That was until I was just about to step up to the platform and the entire bridge started to shake.

I screamed.

Had the metal ropes holding my harness clip fallen down? I turned my head—it was just Parker stepping onto the bridge before I'd finished.

"Is that safe? Us both being on the bridge at one time?" I asked the instructor right in front of me.

He offered his hand and I took it, letting him hoist me

up onto the platform. "It's perfectly safe. A hundred people on this bridge at the same time would be perfectly safe."

I wasn't sure a hundred people would fit, but I wasn't going to be one of a hundred that went on that bridge to find out.

"Next, you need to use that climbing wall to reach the platform above and commando crawl across the net to the next platform."

I bent my head so I could see where he was pointing. About five meters above us, the next section was not only higher, but you weren't upright. People were crawling over a rope net, forced to look down. "Who designed this thing? Sadists?"

"Some people like to push themselves," Parker said, coming up behind me. "Like you. You're always pushing yourself to do better."

"The difference is I like to push myself at a desk in front of a computer. There's no mortality risk involved." I grabbed onto the pebble-shaped blue plastic holds on the climbing wall and started my ascent.

"Then dinner on Saturday night should be right up your street."

I groaned. "Noooo."

"It's dinner. And it will be hellishly distracting. I've seen a photo. You're not going to be able to look at anything else or think about anything else while you're sitting opposite this guy. Also, your arse looks fantastic from down here. You need to show it off more."

I reached the top of the climbing wall and inelegantly pulled myself up onto the platform. I rolled to safety and just lay there on my back, wondering if there was an easy exit and whether Parker would forgive me if I abandoned her. "This, for the record, is a terrible place for a date."

"Saturday night is in a restaurant. With chairs and everything. And although there's a lovely view, there's a lift. No harnesses required."

"Sounds like all my dreams come true. But no. I'm not going on a date. The last thing I want to do is get involved with anyone at the moment. I'm about to start as a foundation doctor at one of the best hospitals in the country. I don't want to be distracted from Monday. I want to be completely and utterly focused on my job. It's going to be difficult enough to just survive the next two years without trying to keep a relationship alive."

"You're going to be just fine."

"I need to prove myself. I can guarantee you there will be plenty of doctors there waiting for me to fail. Getting into medical school the way I did is already controversial. I don't need to be proving anyone right."

"I don't see how working your arse off can be controversial. I know loads of them are from Oxford and Cambridge and all that, but you all had to sit the same exams."

I didn't say anything. There was no point. Parker was right—the snobbery that existed in medical circles about where you went to school and university and who your parents were didn't make sense and wasn't fair. I'd learned a long time ago that life wasn't fair. Complaining about it didn't help.

"Anyway, your job starts on Monday," Parker continued. "The date is Saturday night. I'm not introducing you to your future husband or even boyfriend. He's a hot way to spend an evening, that's all. And he's leaving for Medecins Sans Frontieres the week after next, so even if you wanted to be distracted by him again, it won't be an option."

I sighed. Parker was right—I should enjoy my last weekend of freedom before exhaustion and shift patterns meant that weekends didn't exist for me anymore. "I'm going to have to crawl across this net backwards, I think. You've seen enough of my arse today." I crouched down and dangled my legs over the edge of the platform, trying to find a foothold on the net.

"Fantastic technique," the instructor called over at me. He was kidding, right?

"You see? You get it right without trying," Parker said.

"I'm trying to spare you the sight of my bottom, not be a ropes-course whiz."

"You surprise yourself. It will be the same on Saturday night when you come to the end of the dinner and realize you've had a wonderful evening and haven't thought about Monday at all."

I groaned. "Stop trying to convince me." She knew better than to take any notice of what I was saying. I wanted to be convinced. The problem was, when I wasn't working or studying, I felt guilty. Like downtime, fun, or relaxation wasn't something I deserved. Parker was the person in my life who reminded me that I was allowed to be human sometimes.

"It might be the last time you have sex for two years if you're so intent on being relationship-free while you're at the hospital."

Maybe I should reach out to a guy in another hospital who was also just starting out and we could have an arrangement of no-strings hook-ups for the next two years. At least that would be entirely consistent with my dating history so far. I'd never found time to indulge in relationships when I was trying to keep a roof over my head. I had to keep focused on my future.

"I thought you said Saturday night was dinner. Not sex."

"It might turn into sex. I mean, this guy is seriously hot."

"If you showed me his picture, maybe I'd change my mind."

"No," she called after me. I could tell by the strain in her voice that she was lowering herself onto the net. "It's a blind date. That way it takes up more of your headspace as you think about what he might be like. It's more distracting. What have you got to lose? It's one night of your life."

"I'll tell you what I've got to lose—a night in with Nick and Vanessa Lachey and a bunch of Instagram-influencer wannabes. God I'm going to miss Netflix."

"Exactly. You'll have much more fun with a hot doctor you never have to see again."

I had to admire her persistence. She was genuinely trying to do what she thought was best for me. As always. Now she was so happy with her fiancé, Tristan, she felt my life needed a little man-injection. I couldn't blame her for that. It was just delightful to see her so in love. And she'd put so much effort into this week of distraction, I felt bad saying no to her.

"Tell you what, if we get to the end of the day without ending up in hospital and we can work in a mimosa at some point, I'll go on the date with your mystery man." Truth be told, I was a little curious to meet someone who was going to do Doctors Without Borders. Though I couldn't imagine doing it myself, I liked the idea of spending time with someone who hadn't taken the traditional route. Maybe this ex-hairdresser would find something in common with another doctor. For a change.

TWO

Jacob

If an hour went by without one of my four little brothers calling or texting, it was a good day. Anyone would think I sat in a darkened room, just waiting for one of them to need me, rather than held down a demanding job at the Royal Free, one of the best hospitals in the country. I ignored the call from Beau and stuffed my phone back into my pocket.

"Good evening, Dr. Cove," Dina, one of the receptionists from A&E, said as I passed her in the corridor. I smiled, nodded, and then thanked heaven that when she'd told me she'd like to suck my cock at last year's Christmas party, I'd politely declined. Not because she wasn't gorgeous. And not because I hated blow jobs—was that even a thing? No, it was because I didn't want to pass a line of women who'd had my dick in their mouth in the hospital corridors, sober and under the glare of the fluorescent hospital lights as my shoes squeaked on the freshly-mopped linoleum floor.

Call me old fashioned.

"Keep your private life private." It was almost a mantra

in our house growing up. My father wasn't around much when I was a kid, but he was quick to bark out pieces of advice here and there. I could always count on him for a *could be better* or *why wasn't it one hundred percent*, whenever I presented him with an imperfect test score. He didn't seem to be so easy with the advice with my other brothers, but the one thing he'd said to all of us was, "Keep your private life private." He'd said it when each of us had gotten into med school, every time any of us got a job, and if any of us got into trouble—no matter whether it was relevant.

There was a lot of my father's advice I didn't agree with, but I'd always lived by his private life mantra. A friend I'd gone to school with ended up leaving the Royal Free last year because he'd fucked too many nurses and junior doctors. He'd gone for a promotion and was told he had *too much baggage*.

There was no rule about fraternization in the hospital. Or maybe there was and everyone ignored it. The medical staff spent far too much of their lives in the place for sex and even romance not to happen. Hooking up with someone at work was easy. And when you were exhausted from the long hours and demanding work, and wanted to blow off some steam or have some human contact with a person who wasn't sick or dying, it made sense that you'd reach for someone close.

But not me.

Partly because of my dad's advice and partly because . . . well, because of my last name. I was a Cove. First-born son of doctors Carole and John Cove. That last name brought a profile. I was never just "Jacob" or "Dr. Cove." I was always "Jacob Cove, yes that Cove," or "Dr. Cove's son" or "Cove—was your mother Carole Cove?" It was a label I was used to and not one I wanted to swap for

Jacob Cove, the guy who'd dated everyone in pediatric medicine. Or Jacob Cove, the disappointing son of the Coves. I didn't want people I had to see every day and give instructions to and take instructions from, to know intimate details about me and my sex life. I didn't want the Cove name associated with anything other than being game-changing doctors. I was ambitious and I wanted to be a groundbreaking doctor in pediatric cardiology or even the advisor to the government on child health. I never wanted to be denied a promotion because I'd slept with the wrong person or too many people. It wasn't worth it. When people heard my name, the association should be with excellence. Not sex.

My phone buzzed in my pocket and I pulled it out. A message from Beau.

Pick up. I need a favor.

Nothing new about that. Before I had the chance to reply, his name flashed up on my screen.

I answered as I strode through the exit doors to the stairs and started to head down. Beau was the most tenacious of us all and that was saying something. "The answer's no," I barked into the phone.

"You haven't even heard me out. It's not even that bad."

"I beg to differ. If I'm helping you, it's bound to be bad." Beau was mischievous. A stint doing Medecins Sans Frontieres would do him good.

"I'm serious. All I need you to do is eat some mouth-watering food and drink some wine that might even be good enough for your sophisticated palate." He must really need my help if he was dishing out compliments.

"Out with it. What do you need?"

"I need you to go on a date for me. It's just dinner and drinks. No big thing."

"A date? Are you my pimp now?"

"I'm not setting you up. A friend set *me* up—gorgeous girl apparently. I'm totally pissed off I'm missing it. I don't want to let anyone down at the last minute."

I paused at the door to the ground floor so I could finish our call in privacy. "This sounds suspiciously like a pity date. Why—"

"No, seriously, it's not at all. She's really pretty by all accounts. And she's a doctor. You can talk shop. She's at Tommy's, I think. New to London or something. Her friend said something about it. I can't quite remember. I can't go because . . ." He started to laugh. "You're not going to believe it, but I'm in hospital. I think I've broken my nose."

"What?" Why was he laughing?

"Had rugby practice this afternoon. Took an elbow to the face."

Only Beau could laugh about getting his nose broken.

"Is it going to affect your trip?" He was due to fly out in a week.

"No idea," he said. "I guess we'll have to see if it's broken first. But no way I'm going to be out of hospital in time to make the date."

"The date is tonight?"

"Yes, why do you think I've been calling you non-stop for an hour?"

Shit, I had just finished my shift. I was exhausted. I just wanted to check in on one patient then head home and go to bed. "Can't you ask Zach?"

"He's in Norfolk."

I'd forgotten he was spending the weekend with our parents.

"One of your mates then?"

"Like I'd trust any of them."

It was a good point. I sighed, finally accepting I wasn't going to get the early night I'd been hoping for. "You're going to owe me big for this."

"You're the best big brother I could wish for. You're meeting her at the top of the NatWest Tower. Her name's Sutton. Eight forty-five. Anyway, it's all on me. I've given the restaurant my credit card. If it were any other brother, I'd tell them not to do anything I wouldn't do, but for you that's a given. Go wild."

Before I had a chance to ask for Sutton's last name, he hung up. I'd kill him when I next saw him.

"You heading home?" a woman asked from behind me.

Dina appeared from nowhere and I pulled my mouth into a smile. "No such luck."

She tilted her head. "Shame. I need a lift."

"Good luck. I have to see a patient."

I hated being late but there was no way I wasn't going to stop to see Barnaby. He'd been an inpatient for nearly two months now and was the oldest of five children. His parents didn't have time for daily visits.

I turned into ward six and saw Barnaby staring out the window. I leaned across the nurses' desk. "Anyone been in to see Barnaby today?"

Annette, the nurse in charge, shook her head and scrunched up her nose. No one liked it when the kids didn't have visitors.

He wasn't my patient, but Barnaby had been on the ward for so long that it was impossible not to notice him as I came in to check on my own patients.

From my back pocket, I pulled out a credit token for the vending machine. I'd put twenty quid on it before I'd picked up the call from Beau.

"Barnaby, mate," I said, striding over to the end bed. "I

found something with your name on it." I wafted the credit token in his direction.

Barnaby scowled back at me. "What is it?"

I shrugged my shoulders. "Try it in the vending machine."

"It can't be mine. I didn't have one." I was pretty sure Barnaby's parents didn't have much money.

"You're right. It's mine, but I need to give up junk food —you know how it is, old man that I am. So . . . have it."

He glanced at me and then the card. I tossed it on his table.

He nodded. "Thanks."

"What have you been watching?" I nodded toward the TV.

"Nothing," he said.

I glanced at the clock over the nurses' station. It would probably take me over half an hour to get to Tower 42 and it was nearly ten past eight now. Why did Beau have to choose a restaurant in the City to take his date when the West End was so much closer?

"Don't tell anyone I told you, but Peaky Blinders is on BBC iPlayer and it's good. Trust me."

"I don't have any headphones," he said. "I couldn't watch it if I wanted to."

Poor kid.

"Oh, let me get you some. We have plenty of spares." I turned. I wasn't sure where I'd find any headphones at all, especially not in the forty seconds I had before I needed to leave. I sped down the corridor toward the supplies cupboard. Maybe there'd be some lost property. Angie, a healthcare assistant coming off shift overtook me. She smiled and waved her hand, the tinny tick, tick, tick from the earbud waving loosely by her waist catching my attention.

"Hey, Angie?" She stopped and turned around. "Can I buy your headphones?"

She pulled out the ear bud that was in her ear. "What?"

"Your headphones. How much?" I grabbed my wallet from my back pocket.

Angie frowned at me. "They're not special. They cost me about five pounds. Why do you want them?"

I didn't have time to explain. Pulling out a twenty-pound note, I said. "Would you give them up for twenty pounds?"

She shrugged, handed them over but didn't take the money. "Just give them back to me tomorrow." Angie earned minimum wage.

"Please let me buy them from you."

"You can have them," she said.

I stuffed the purple note into her hand and she handed them over.

"You're strange, Dr. Cove," she said in a tone that told me she didn't really care—she was just going with it.

"Thanks so much," I said and raced back to Barnaby.

Maybe I'd make it to the restaurant on time after all.

THREE

Jacob

Security at the NatWest Tower was like getting on a flight—complete with bag scans and metal detectors. I'd been to my fair share of nice restaurants, but they'd never come with a full pat-down.

When I finally made it to the forty-second floor, I was three minutes late. I hated that.

"Table under the name Beau." Beau had said Sutton was a doctor. Hopefully she was young enough not to have heard the Cove name. It was a stupid hope, but maybe she'd do me a favor and pretend. I didn't want to spend the evening listening to how she thought my parents were awesome. They *were* awesome, but I didn't need to hear it from a perfect stranger. As much as I loved my parents and was proud they had such phenomenal reputations, it sometimes felt like I'd never grown up. They were always there—in interviews for university and when I was applying to hospitals. At Christmas parties and leaving dos. The first thing strangers wanted to talk to me about was my parents.

It was a lot to live up to. And a lot to put up with. Sometimes I wish I'd been an architect.

"I think we're having dinner together," a woman called from behind me. I turned to find a beautiful woman staring up at me expectantly, and my entire body flushed with gratitude that my brother had broken his nose. Her long, chestnut-brown hair was pulled back from her face in a casual way and she had a beauty spot on her right cheek. Her smile was wide and warm and right then, I knew I needed to buy Beau a drink next time I saw him.

"You must be Sutton," I said and I leaned forward to kiss her cheek.

"It's quite the rigmarole to get up here," she said. "I thought I was going to be late."

I swallowed a chuckle. We had both made it up by five past eight. If there hadn't been a security check, we would have both been early.

"But I hear the view is worth it," she said.

"That's definitely true," I said, not taking my eyes off of her.

She blushed and I put my hand at the small of her back as the hostess led us into the dining room.

"Whoever told you that was right—the city looks fantastic," I said, taking in the views. The restaurant was floor-to-ceiling windows. The sun had almost disappeared completely, leaving a hazy pink on the horizon and allowing the lights of the buildings surrounding us to glow like stars.

"It's sensational," Sutton said and I couldn't help but smile at her enthusiasm. "We're right in the middle of the City, but it's so peaceful."

We took our seats, sitting at right angle to each other, the table arranged so we could both see the view. It felt intimate, regardless of the fact Sutton and I had just met. Our knees touched and I moved out of the way so she didn't feel awkward. She caught my eye, obviously wondering, like I was, whether we should acknowledge the contact.

"Can I get you a drink?" the hostess asked us.

"Sutton, what would you like?"

She chewed the inside of her cheek before she said, "I'll have whatever you're having."

"Well I'm not working tomorrow," I replied. I didn't add *and my brother is paying*, because I didn't want her to think I was just here for the free meal. Doctors in the NHS weren't well paid, but I could handle dinner and drinks in any restaurant in the world, and the private jet to get there, thanks to a side hustle I'd had as a student. She wasn't to know that though.

"Me neither," she said. "And I've never been known to say no to a margarita."

Margarita wasn't exactly my drink. But why not? "Two margaritas, please."

"You're a doctor, right?" Sutton asked as she watched the waitress head off with our order.

I nodded. I was pretty sure she didn't know my last name, because I'd met her more than two minutes ago and she hadn't mentioned my parents. "And you are as well, I hear?"

"Sort of . . . Actually, I've got a proposal for you."

"So soon? We've not had any drinks yet."

She gave a small laugh and her shoulders dropped visibly. She was nervous, which was kind of endearing. Her swept-up hair revealed her long neck, its graceful curve making me want to reach out and touch her.

"I mentioned the doctor thing first, and I shouldn't have. I'm about to start the foundation program. If it's okay by you, can we not talk about being doctors, or medical school, or hospitals or anything like that? I just can't think about it. I'm as nervous as a long-tailed cat in a room full of rocking chairs."

A long-tailed cat? I wanted to laugh but the look on her face told me she wasn't joking. I shrugged. "Fine by me." Her proposition was unexpected—for most doctors, their work was their lives and the idea of not mentioning medicine for an entire evening would feel like walking the Great Wall of China in twenty-four hours—absolutely impossible. To me the idea was intriguing. The Coves talked about medicine all the time, and it had been the same since I could remember.

"There should be a forfeit for breaking the rule," she said, an unexpectedly playful glint in her eye.

"Not messing around, I see. What kind of forfeit?"

She gave a one-shouldered shrug and for the first time, I was conscious of her exposed skin in an electric-blue, one-shouldered top. It was the one time in my life blue seemed sexy and didn't make me think of hospital masks.

The hostess returned with our margaritas in oversized glasses. Orange peel sculpted into weird shapes decorated the sides.

"We've started on the margs," she said. "Maybe a tequila shot?"

Sutton was already more intriguing than I'd expected. I knew for certain that tonight was going to be fun. Beau had missed out.

"Done. The ban starts . . . now." I raised my glass.

She lifted hers in response, the challenge in her eye drawing my attention. She was a fighter. I could see it in her and there was something extremely attractive about that.

I took a sip of my drink but Sutton paused, the glass still offered up in celebration. "You know, I'm not sure I have anything to talk about, if I'm not talking about medicine."

I made the sound of a buzzer. "One tequila shot, coming right up." I caught a passing waiter and ordered the shot. "Very poor play by you, if I may say so. You failed coming out of the gate. You've got to try a little harder from now on."

She laughed and took a sip of her margarita. "Fair enough. So, your turn. Tell me about yourself."

The waiter presented the tequila and I indicated it was Sutton's.

"Not until you take your shot."

She set down her margarita and picked up the shot glass. Before I had a chance to wish her luck or tell her she couldn't sip it, she downed it.

I took another sip of my drink to cover the look of satisfaction that must have been plastered all over my face.

"You were saying," she said, without missing a beat, a grin threatening at the corners of her mouth.

"I have four brothers."

She raised her eyebrows. "Wow. Are they all . . . Wow."

I chuckled. "Are they all what? Pains in my arse? Affirmative."

"Little brothers?"

"Unfortunately. What about you?"

The glimmer that had been in her eye since she'd been challenged to take her shot dimmed a little. "I have some stepsiblings I've never met. They live in Texas."

"Medicine is a hard business to be in and maintain relationships."

"Ding, ding, ding, ding. Looks like we need more tequila for our lucky winner," Sutton said, beaming at me.

"Hey, that doesn't count. It was a general observation."

She tutted. "Reneging on a deal—very unattractive. Didn't catch me doing that, did you?" she said, challenging and charming in equal measure.

I held her gaze. "I'd hate for you to think I wasn't attractive." It was true—I wanted her to be as attracted to me as I was to her.

I called another waiter over and ordered another shot. Maybe I should have just ordered a bottle. The way we were going, we'd both be trashed before the starters.

I took my shot, tried not to wince, and then topped up both of our water glasses. I didn't want tonight to be over before it had begun.

"Okay. We're even now," I said. "Let's start again. What about hobbies?"

We ordered food when the waitress returned, but it was one of those situations where I couldn't wait to hand the menu back and return to my conversation with Sutton.

"Let me think what I can say . . ." Sutton said, picking up where we left off. "I like to shower, travel on public transport . . ." She winced like she was really thinking hard. I tried to stifle a laugh. To anyone outside of medicine, she might have come across as boring, but I knew that stage she was at—there really wasn't anything other than work and study. "I'm exaggerating. When my anxiety is really bad, I like to go to libraries or art galleries. I'm not sure it would qualify as a hobby because I'm not there for the books or the art—it's just calming. Or maybe my body is forced to calm down because nothing would be more embarrassing than an anxiety attack in a place so quiet."

I watched her full lips push together and pull apart as she spoke. She wasn't wearing lipstick. Other than some makeup around her eyes, she didn't seem to be wearing any. I started to think through the implications, like the fact that no lipstick would come off on me or my shirt. I wondered how her one-shouldered top unfastened. Was there a zip at the side or was it stretchy? Did she have a bra on or was she naked . . .

"Don't you agree?" she asked. "Have I bored you to death?"

I shook my head, trying to pretend I hadn't zoned out and started to imagine her naked. "Not at all." My tolerance for alcohol had fallen in recent months, but surely, I could manage more than one shot. "Maybe next time you get a two for one: decompress *and* see some art, or borrow a book —depending on your chosen venue."

"Maybe, but I've got a good thing going. Why ruin it? Zoning out in a place like that helps me if I have a problem to solve and I'm stuck or . . . you know, I just need some peace. Anyway, your turn," she said, taking a sip of her margarita.

What did I have to tell anyone? "I spend a lot of time in Norfolk. My parents moved there after they retired, although we had a holiday house there where we'd spend summers as kids."

"You're close with them?"

"I've always been close with my mother. She's the center of our family."

"And your father?"

I sucked in a breath. "Yeah. I mean, I love him and—" Why hadn't I just answered her question with *yes, we're a close family*. It would have been the truth. Even if it wasn't the whole truth. "He has high standards. Growing up, sometimes it was hard not to feel like I was falling short."

I glanced up from my margarita glass to find Sutton's soft, open, and somehow familiar gaze. Something about her made me feel like I'd known her my entire life. As if there was no point in hiding anything from her, because she already knew the core of who I was.

She gave me a small, reassuring smile. "And your brothers?"

"I complain about my brothers—they really are annoying most of the time—but hanging out with my family is my favorite thing to do, outside the thing we can't talk about."

"That must be nice. Things are better now with your dad."

It wasn't a question, more an observation, and an accurate one at that. My relationship with my father had transformed over the years. I was never sure if the change had come from his side or mine. Had I grown up or had he finally seen me as a capable man?

"And you still love medicine?" she asked.

I raised my eyebrows. Without blinking she raised her hand to catch the attention of the waiter and ordered three more shots. "I want you to answer and then I want to follow up if need be," she explained.

"Yeah, I still love making a difference in people's lives. I love the diagnostic side. I love the interaction with the patients. Even when it's just a simple thing—a broken leg or congenital torticollis—I'll never get bored of the feeling of being able to reassure someone that it's not as bad as they think it is."

"I get that."

I smiled at her. "I want to ask you more questions."

"I want to too, but I'll enjoy it at first and then something will send me into a spin and I'll be hightailing it out of here, looking for the nearest library."

I laughed. "Fair enough."

The waiter came back with two shot glasses and the

bottle and told us to enjoy our night. We poured out and drank two shots each before our starters arrived.

"Can we get a bread basket as well?" Sutton asked. "I need to soak up some alcohol or you're going to have to carry me out of here."

That didn't seem such a bad option. But not yet. There was more I wanted to get to know first.

Our food arrived just before we transitioned from relaxed to drunk. Saved by the carbs.

"Tell me about Norfolk," she said. "Is it your library?"

I sighed and thought about it. "You know what? I think it has been. There have been times . . ." I tried to think about how to say it without talking about medicine. I couldn't take any more tequila. "Points in my career have been incredibly stressful and . . . I haven't told anyone this, but my parents live just outside a village up there, right on the marshes. It's a beautiful place and it's easy to do nothing there, you know?"

She nodded like she knew exactly what I meant.

"There are coastal paths all around there, and I used to enjoy walking them to try and walk off the stresses of the job. During one walk I discovered an old rowing boat that seemed to have just been abandoned in the marshes. I was hungry, so I climbed in and took out a snack and sat there under the sun, eating my protein bar. Anyway, it was windy because it's the coast and it's Norfolk, so I decided to lie down in this boat to escape the wind. And I just lay there, thinking about . . . everything. And nothing. I watched the different shapes of the clouds pass overhead and wished I'd paid more attention in geography—there are so many different clouds. I listened to the sounds of the sea, the wind through the reeds and the grasses, the gulls, the seals in the distance. It was almost like some kind of de-stressing chamber. I got up hours later and felt . . . amazing. Ever since, going to Norfolk has been like pressing a reset button, if you know what I mean."

"I like the idea of a reset button. I'll have to go on the hunt for this boat. I can't spend hours lying down in a library or an art gallery without the police being called. Believe me, I've tried."

I laughed. "The weird thing is that I went back to that boat for years after that first time. Each time it had the same effect. And then one day, I went looking for it and it had disappeared."

"Maybe the owner claimed it."

"Maybe. It just felt . . . This is going to sound—no, forget it."

She slid her hand over mine. "Tell me."

We locked eyes and I could tell she was genuinely interested in my story. Not the story of Jacob Cove, son of Carole and John Cove, or the oldest of five Cove brothers or Dr. Cove. She was just interested in me.

"It felt like the boat had done its job for me and because I was over the part of my career—in my life—that I really needed it . . . It kind of disappeared."

She nodded. A comfortable silence wound between us.

"Like it was magic or something." She didn't say it in a jokey way—not in the way of a jaded scientist being told that because she was a Taurus, she was destined to feel x or y. She said it like she accepted entirely how I felt about that boat—like it was slightly magical. Like it had been healing for me when I needed it for as long as I needed it.

"To anyone else it would sound stupid—"

She shook her head. "Don't say that. The day we stop believing in magic—just a little bit—is a sad day." She withdrew her hand but I leaned my knee against hers, wanting a continued physical connection with her. She didn't move away or flinch, just looked up at me and smiled a smile full of fondness, like we were old friends.

"I agree," I said. "Science is full of magic."

We grinned at each other like a couple of idiots. The more I saw her smile, the happier I felt.

"I didn't want to come tonight," she confessed. "But I'm really glad I did."

I took a sip of margarita because if I allowed myself to respond straight away, I was pretty sure I'd get arrested for being ridiculous. "Same," I said. "I don't know what I was expecting but it wasn't . . ."

"I wonder if you'll see the boat again. Or something else like that will come into your life at the right time." She was so beautiful, I wanted to jump up and tell the restaurant to come see how glorious she was.

"Who knows. Maybe if you get thrown out of all the London libraries and art galleries, you might need a new spot to ease your anxiety and *you'll* find a rowing boat."

She narrowed her eyes as if she was really thinking about what she was saying. "You might be on to something. Perhaps I need to be outdoors."

"It's worth a try."

Somewhere during our conversation, our plates had been collected and replaced with our main courses. I ate mine as slowly as possible. I didn't want tonight to end. I knew she thought I was leaving the country next week. She thought I was Beau. There wasn't supposed to be any connection beyond tonight. If that was the case, I had to make our time together last as long as possible.

FOUR

Sutton

Tonight wasn't supposed to go like this. First, men weren't as gorgeous as Beau outside of films. It just didn't happen. Secondly, men who were remotely good looking weren't *also* sexy and attentive, and they didn't talk about magic rowing boats.

I had to give Parker her due: I wasn't thinking about anything other than what was right in front of me tonight. And what was right in front of me was Beau. It was just so . . . easy between us.

"What do you like to do when you have a day off?" I asked. I wanted to know everything about him. Surely he couldn't be as amazing as I thought he was. There must be a personality disorder or criminal record I could tease out of him.

"Not much. My brother Nathan isn't a medic. He and I like to kick around business ideas. Then he tries to convince me to give up my job and go into business with him."

I wanted to know more, so I paused. People liked to fill

silences. Life as a hairdresser had taught me that much. But he didn't take the bait and the silence stretched between us like strings of mozzarella fresh from a bite of a favorite pizza.

"He obviously thinks you have a talent for business," I said, eventually.

He shrugged. "I had a lucky break at university with a business idea. He thinks I have untapped potential."

"A business idea? Tell me more." Beau struck me as the kind of guy who could effortlessly turn his hand to anything. Life just seemed like a breeze to someone like him.

He shook his head. "Nope. Can't do that. It's in the area we can't talk about."

"Intriguing," I answered. "The only problem is, my imagination is always much more vivid than reality."

He laughed and I wondered whether he'd just come back from holiday. Was that his natural skin tone, or was he one of those men who fake tanned?

"Yes, I've got it. You invented a mind-reading computer!"

The corner of his mouth nudged upward. "If I had something like that, I think I'd be using it on you right about now."

Beau didn't need to know how many times I'd mentally undressed him tonight, how I'd wondered whether all his brothers were as handsome as he was, whether or not his large hands were an indicator of the size of his other organs.

"That would be embarrassing," I said.

By the expression on his face, he knew exactly what I meant. "Same." Heat seemed to roll off his body and curl around me, almost like I could feel him despite him not touching me.

I'd never felt so comfortable with someone I was so completely attracted to. It was as delicious as diving into warm chocolate, but an almost imperceptible voice reminded me nothing was so easy. It must be a trick.

Easy or difficult, it didn't matter. Beau was off to Africa next week. I didn't need to think beyond this evening.

"Okay, tell me something you like to do in London when you're not working."

He looked away and cleared his throat. "I used to go swimming."

I nodded, wondering how to follow up with that. "I can swim," I said and then felt like a total idiot. "I mean, I used to swim a lot when I was younger. Before I started med school. Now, the closest I get to the water is listening to a recording of waves lapping on the shore on my meditation app while I mix myself a cocktail."

"Well there were definitely no cocktails in the bathing pool on Hampstead Heath. Or tides come to that."

"You used to swim in a pond on the Heath?" I asked. "Like outdoors in the cold?" That was the most sinister thing he'd said all evening.

"It feels surprisingly good. The dopamine hit is intense —stimulates the vagus nerve, and obviously, it's great for circulation. I trained for an Iron Man at one point and used to be a member of the club."

I started to laugh. "An Iron Man? Of course you did." My mental undressing had revealed rock hard muscle under his shirt.

"You don't believe me?" he said, still smiling.

I didn't think either of us had stopped grinning like lunatics since we'd sat down. He was relaxed and warm and so much fun. And of course, handsome. This was the best date I'd ever been on. How could I not smile?

"I don't think you're lying. It's just you're . . ." I was going to say he seemed to be the perfect man, but I wasn't dishing out compliments like that to a perfect stranger. "You know, you seem to have it all together."

He laughed. "I'm thirty-six. I'm supposed to have it a little bit together."

I frowned. "So that does happen then? There's a point in your life when you start to think, 'I got this.'"

"I didn't say I *got* anything. Just that I had my life a *little* together."

We locked eyes. I wanted to stroke his face and feel his lips against mine, but despite the tequila, I held myself back. "I think you seem . . . solid." I started to laugh. "I mean that as a compliment."

Gah, he was so handsome. The way the right corner of his mouth lifted slightly higher than the left, gave the impression he wouldn't take offence no matter what I said. He was just so sure. So steady. "Solid? Not exactly a top ten compliment, is it?"

"You know what I mean. Like . . ."

"I'm all hard muscle?"

"Well, I didn't exactly mean that, but . . ." I scanned down his arms and across his chest and pretended I didn't notice when he flexed his biceps, stretching the cotton of his shirt. "The shoe fits, my friend."

I ran my tongue over my top lip and then reached for my water glass, trying to cover up the fact that I'd basically been licking my lips at the thought of Beau's naked body. As I leaned forward, he pressed his rock-*solid* thigh against mine.

"The shoe, the clog, the over-the-thigh boot. They all fit."

"I like you," he said. The words fluttered over my skin like feathers, covering me in goosebumps.

I nodded. "I like you too."

The waitress interrupted us. At some point, we'd abandoned our food and our plates had been cleared. "Can I get you guys anything else?"

Beau looked at me. "You want another margarita?"

"Absolutely not," I replied.

"Just the bill, thanks."

"Yup," I said, trying to sound casual. "Just the bill." Absentmindedly, I traced a line with my index finger from his knee up his leg.

"Do that again and I'll strip you naked and eat you out in front of the entire city." His voice was deep and gravelly. As I met his gaze, his ice-blue eyes had turned grey, like a storm was brewing.

"Okay," I said, but I couldn't decide whether or not to touch him.

"I can't sit here without kissing you for another second. Let's get out of here."

Apparently the feeling was mutual.

FIVE

Jacob

Becoming a doctor took discipline. Studying. Long hours. Sacrifice. But none of it required more discipline than not touching Sutton for the twenty minutes she and I spent in a cab on the way back to her place.

I knew that once I touched her, it would take an earthquake to stop us both. The sexual tension had been slowly simmering all night and was now threatening to boil over. The feeling was so thick, you could almost gather it up and tie it into bows.

The cab pulled to a stop and I tapped my phone against the card machine.

I'd been so focused on not touching Sutton that I hadn't realized we were heading to Hampstead. At least I wouldn't have a long trip home, whenever that might be.

"This is me," she said as she took steps down to a basement flat. "It was the only thing I could afford where I didn't have to share."

Thank fuck we didn't have to worry about waking her roommates. I was determined to make her scream.

She unlocked the door and we stepped inside.

We were alone. Finally.

Her heavy breaths hypnotized me as her breasts pushed up against the fabric of the blue top that had fascinated me all evening. I stepped toward her and she stepped back.

"Can I get you a drink?"

I shook my head.

"You look like you're about to devour me. It's both completely unnerving and surprisingly hot." She backed down the corridor into her bedroom and I followed her.

I laughed, and it relieved a little of the tightness in my shoulders and chest. "I am about to devour you. I hope you're ready for it."

She stopped and nodded. "I'm ready."

I wet my lips, holding her gaze, wondering where to start. She tilted her head, displaying her long, graceful neck, and I stepped closer, forked my fingers into her hair, and pressed a chaste kiss to her jaw.

I took in her warm scent of summer flowers, delicate like sweet peas and something feminine I couldn't quite place but fit her perfectly. Three seconds ago, I was wound so tight I was about to snap. Now it was just the two of us in the dim light of her flat, feeling her breaths against my skin, finally able to touch her. It was as if I'd dived into a pool of feathers. Time had lost all meaning. The urgency had abated. I might have snapped, but she'd broken my fall.

I held her head up so our eyes met. "Hey," I whispered.

The corners of her mouth lifted and she parted her full lips. My stomach lilted like her half-smile had me in free fall.

"Hey," she replied, a rasp in her voice. I wasn't sure if it was lust caught in her throat or the knowledge that this was where she was supposed to be had relaxed her to the point of being sleepy.

I wasn't meant to have taken this woman to dinner tonight, but I couldn't shake the feeling that somehow the universe had arranged itself to put me in this exact spot at this exact moment. I was sure she felt it too.

Her palm slid up my chest, and her fingers found the edge of my jaw. I closed my eyes, drinking in her touch. We were both fully clothed. We both knew what was going to happen next, but there was this part before that, that I wanted to string out and make last like the glow of embers before they burst into flame. It was the simmer before the boil, the hazy glow just before sunrise—the moment before The Moment that I didn't want to rush through.

"Undress." I took a step back and sat on the bed behind me. "I want to watch." *I want to savor every second with you.*

She hesitated at first, as if deciding whether she was going to comply. Thankfully, she moved her hands to her waist and undid her jeans. She paused again and glanced up from under her eyelashes at me.

I nodded, encouraging her to take the next step.

Slowly, like she was trying to torture me, she peeled her jeans off her legs, revealing nude lace underwear that tortured me with what lay beneath. She straightened, transferring her weight from foot to foot as I stared between her legs.

"More," I said, my voice taking on a deeper, darker tone.

She paused then shifted, her hands skimming her stomach, and pulling her blue top up and over her head. Discarding her clothes, she ran her thumb under the strap of her nude lace bra as if she were trying to make sure it was positioned correctly.

It was—I knew like I could feel it, like my thumb was where hers was, like I was feeling the fabric and her flesh. I had to suppress a groan.

My attention was caught by the dusky pink of her taut nipples pressing through the lace of the bra.

"Take it off," I said, running my hand over my growing erection. "I want to see all of you."

She watched my hand and pressed her teeth into her bottom lip as she reached around her back. The snap of her bra clasp sent my impatient blood rushing to my cock, urging me to fast forward to what was next.

She closed her eyes. "I feel stupid."

"Don't," I said, getting to my feet. "You're fucking mesmerizing."

She lowered the straps of her bra and let it fall to the ground.

"Beautiful." I took a step toward her, cupped her face, and pressed my lips against hers. I exhaled in relief that I was finally kissing this woman. She tasted as sweet as she smelled. Ours wasn't the kiss of two people who'd just met, fumbling and learning one another's bodies. It was more like the kiss of two people who'd known each other their entire lives and fit together perfectly.

Her hands crept under my shirt and I broke our kiss. Her touch on my skin was all I wanted. I pulled my top off and bent to kiss her again, groaning at the sensation of her sharp nipples and hot skin against me.

This woman was beautiful.

After what felt like hours of kissing, I lifted her and she wrapped her legs around my waist. She pressed kisses onto my neck and jaw while I turned and lay her down on her bed. I was never nervous. Not at work, not with women, but right now? Right now, a fine tremor raced down my spine.

I stood, took off the rest of my clothes, and pulled out a condom from my wallet.

"It feels like this isn't the first time we've done this," she said, gazing up at me.

I nodded as I tossed the condom onto the bed. "I know."

I crawled over her and dipped for a kiss, trying not to shudder as she skated her fingers up my arms.

I worked my way down her body, licking, sucking, pressing, enjoying her sharp breaths and the buzz under my skin that increased with every second. I paused my exploration at the edge of her underwear and licked a line above the seam from hip-bone to hip-bone. Sliding my fingers between her legs, I pushed underneath the fabric and couldn't help but grin at the sodden material. I ran my knuckles up her folds and pulled off her knickers in one swift movement. Maybe it was the way she arched a little off the bed; maybe it was her groan, or the scent of her pussy, but my vision blurred and I knew my patience had worn thin.

I grabbed her hips, pulled her to the edge of the bed, kneeled and drove my tongue through her folds, greedy to devour her, just like I'd warned. She skimmed her hands over the top of her head as she shifted, her hips undulating, creating a rhythm with my tongue. Her breaths came out in a series of staccato bursts as if she was walking a tightrope and was desperately trying to stop herself falling.

"Oh God, oh God, oh God," she chanted, her words coiling around us, cocooning us in the moment.

She pulsed against my tongue and I pushed into her, groaning at the thought that it wouldn't be long until I was driving into her, chasing my own orgasm. It wouldn't take long. One sweep of her fingers against my cock at this moment would have me spilling into her hand. I was going to have to try to control myself.

I replaced my tongue with my thumb, traced up to her clit, and she broke apart underneath me.

I was so close to following her over the edge—just her sounds, the pitch of her breasts, her fingers pressing into my scalp—it was almost too much for me to bear.

I rocked back on my ankles, smoothing my hands down her thighs as she floated down to earth. She guided me back over her, sleepily taking my face in her hands and pulling me to face her. Instead of kissing me, she licked her wetness from my mouth. I had to hold my breath, as she diligently worked to clean me up, worried that I'd miss a nanosecond of what might have been the most erotic moment of my life.

She finally pressed her lips against mine. I was done waiting.

"You ready?" I kneeled up between her legs and snatched the condom from beside her.

She opened her legs, wider. "And waiting."

Fuuuck. I was going to come before I'd gotten the condom on.

I couldn't tear my gaze from hers as I ripped open the foil. I leaned over her, nudging into her. It felt like a moment to be savored. To be remembered. Like this was my first time or something.

We locked eyes and I knew she felt the same.

Slowly, tortuously, I drove into her, trying to block out the pressure, the drag, the fucking bliss of it all. She arched against me and wrapped her hands over my shoulders. She gasped as I buried myself to the root and instinct took over. Two hundred thousand years of evolution and all I could think about was fucking her, coming in her, owning her.

"Sutton," I groaned in a plea.

Her brows pinched and she nodded. She knew what I was asking without me having to say the words. It was the permission I needed to let my instinct off the lead.

I plowed into her, driving deeper and harder and faster, just wanting to take more and more and more until I had all of her. I dipped my head, took a perfunctory kiss from her lips as if I were refueling.

Her nails dug into my shoulders and the flash of pain seemed to ramp up every sensation I was feeling. My orgasm strained, desperate to be released.

Fuck.

I didn't want this to be over this quickly. Not that I couldn't fuck her again, but this time, the first time—I wanted to savor it, make it last, stretch it out like molten toffee.

Fuck. Fuck. Fuck.

I had to stop or it was going to be over too soon.

I stilled inside her, but the sensation of her surrounding me was too intense. "I need a minute," I said, pulling out and rolling to my back. I needed to think about scrap metal and paving stones—something inert and inane. Anything but the hot slide of her pussy and the bite of her fingernails. Anything but the parting of her lips and the smooth softness of her skin.

She turned on her side and propped her head up on her hand. After a beat, she said, "It's like you've undressed me body and soul." I swallowed as she trailed her fingers from my stomach to my chest. "It feels like you're in my head, reading my mind, knowing me."

That's exactly how it felt. This wasn't just sex with a woman I'd met a few hours ago. We had a connection. Lying here together had *significance*. She pushed herself up and hooked her leg over my hips, positioning herself at the top of my thighs. She began to move, rubbing herself at the root of me. She stopped and tipped her head back.

"This," she said. "What you do to my body . . ." She shook her head. "It shouldn't be like that."

It was like my thoughts were coming out of her mouth. Like she was feeling every sensation I experienced, every notion buzzing through my mind.

She lifted herself and I grasped the base of my cock. As she slid onto me, she took long, deep breaths as if she was going to boil over.

I knew that feeling.

She started to move, slowly but with confidence, somehow knowing exactly how much I could take. I circled my hands at her tiny waist, and watched in awe as she moved against me.

I pulled one of her nipples between my thumb and forefinger and in response she circled her hips, intensifying the sensation at the base of my stomach.

How was it possible to be so into someone that I'd only just met?

I cupped her breasts, let them fall, then smoothed my hands over her hips, slowly transferring responsibility from her to me as I began to rock her backward and forward in slow, intensive movements that felt so good I wanted to call in sick for a week, just so we could do this—twenty-four hours a day.

This time, my orgasm didn't appear out of nowhere, threating to go off in a nanosecond. This time, my climax called before it told me it was coming, then sauntered toward me like it had all the time in the world. The buildup was slow and steady and inevitable. There would be no holding back this time.

"Sutton," I boomed.

She tipped her head forward. "So close."

She squeezed me as I moved her hips and I was lost. Electric sparks jumped between us and she shuddered beneath my fingers, like her entire body was convulsing in pleasure. I pushed up into her, holding her hips tight, needing to be so deep that I'd never come back. The tendons in my neck and every muscle in my body all joined to focus on pouring myself into her.

"Fuck," I bit out. The room seemed to melt away, leaving Sutton the only thing in focus.

Her body was limp under my hands and I guided her forward, onto my chest as I continued to rock in and out of her in small movements to make the aftershocks last as long as possible.

"Don't go," she whispered. "Not yet."

"No chance," I replied.

SIX

Sutton

As I arrived at reception in the hospital, I took a deep breath, put my hands on my hips and pushed out my chest like I was Superman. The posture was apparently proven to boost confidence.

What I'd needed yesterday was a magic rowing boat. What I'd had was a soft bed, an iPad, and a pile of TED talks. It wasn't quite as good, but I'd spent the day nursing a hangover and discovering small, oval bruises the size of Beau's fingertips all over my body while learning, courtesy of TED, that body language could alter your feelings. Beau had left at dawn, cursing the appointment he had first thing and, like a gentleman, had texted me a couple of hours later, wanting to come over later that night.

I hadn't answered. Ignoring his message hurt more than it should. I'd gone into last night knowing that he was leaving. And of course, I was starting a new job and the last thing I wanted to was split my focus. Still, a part of me wished our situations were different. Saturday night we'd been so in synch and the sex had been so . . . different to anything I'd experienced before, that if the circumstances weren't what they were, I might have actually texted him back. But I had to play the hand I'd been dealt, not the one I wished for. Keeping a clear head for today was more important than more time with Beau.

I was going to be starting my foundation program alongside others who were five years younger than me and been to some of the best schools in the country. I doubt any of them had been hairdressers before they'd turned to medicine. Maybe some of them had worked on the side and accumulated debt to get to this point, but most would have been funded by the bank of mum and dad. That's how things were in medicine.

I was an outlier.

Somehow, I'd made it and we were all on the same program. Now I just wanted to make sure I didn't stand out like the sore thumb I was. I needed to keep my head down and fly under the radar, focus on the job. I took a breath. I wasn't sure if the superhero pose was helping or just making me feel more self-conscious.

"I saw that TED talk as well," the blonde girl beside me said.

I tried my best not to wince. "Did it work for you?"

She shrugged. "Not that I noticed. Vodka is more reliable."

"Before work?"

She laughed. "No. That's the only downside—the dulling the senses part. Not ideal for the first day on the job. You part of the foundation program, too?"

I nodded, glancing at her smart shift dress and sensible heels. I'd worn jeans and trainers because the joining letter said we'd all be issued scrubs when we arrived. Maybe I'd got it wrong. "How many of us are starting today?" I asked. "Do you know?"

"I heard fifteen."

"I heard twenty-five," a woman behind us with curly red-hair whispered. We shuffled sideways to make space for her.

"Twenty-five is a lot," I said.

"It's a big hospital. What rotation are you hoping for?" she asked, glancing between me and the woman beside me.

I shrugged. I'd not even thought about it. "I'll be happy with anything."

"I want surgery," the second woman replied.

The woman behind the desk pointed us in the direction of a waiting room, and the three of us shuffled inside. The room had a small window and dark grey, plastic chairs set out around three small tables. We took a seat at the table nearest the window.

"I don't want surgery until I have more experience," the TED-talk woman said, picking up our conversation from earlier. "I hope it's one of my last rotations. I think I want to specialize there, so I want to be in a position where I'm as strong as I possibly can be."

"You'll need it for a surgical specialty," the other woman said.

I hadn't even begun to think about specialties. I was taking it one step at a time. "I'm Sutton," I said. "And you are?"

"I'm Gilly," TED Talk said.

"Veronica," the other woman said.

"You've heard about the competition?" Gilly half whispered.

"Obviously," Veronica said. "But I also heard it's not

just based on technical knowledge and application this year."

"What else could it be based on?" Gilly asked.

I'd clearly missed something in the joining instructions. What were they talking about?

"What competition?" I asked.

They both looked at me like I was in the wrong place. I had a feeling I'd have to get used to that look.

"The competition between first-year foundation doctors," Gilly said. "They say it's informal, but the winner always ends up as a consultant at the Free. It's like an all-access pass to whatever future they want."

I had to stifle a groan. A competition? Like survival wasn't enough.

"But how do they judge people across specialties?" Veronica asked. "It can't be fair."

"Okay, I shouldn't be telling you this, but apparently, the foundation doctors have to report to a different consultant on each rotation," Gilly said. "That lead consultant is responsible for making sure you get the experience you need. They also assess you. Every rotation, the lead consultant picks a 'best of the rotation' and then each of the rotation winners are assessed and one is picked as the overall winner."

"Should they really be getting doctors to compete with each other?" I asked. It seemed counterintuitive to encourage a spirit of competition.

"FY1s—Year One Foundation doctors—this way please." A black woman in scrubs waved us all to follow her. I was grateful to be out of the back and forth between Gilly and Veronica. They seemed to know a lot more about what the Royal Free had in store for us than I did.

"I'm Dr. Wanda Jones. Please line up, give me your

name, collect some scrubs—they're here, divided into vague size order, though they won't fit you. Adjust your expectations accordingly. Go and change and meet me back here."

"Are you sure we all have to wear scrubs?" Gilly asked.

"Completely sure," Wanda replied. "Hospital policy since Covid. If you don't like it, you're welcome to leave."

"I just bought an entire new wardrobe," Gilly complained.

"You should have read your joining instructions more carefully," Wanda replied.

"This isn't the army. Maybe I could speak to someone in charge?" I got the impression Gilly was used to getting her way.

"That would be me. What would you like to speak about?"

Gilly blushed and joined the back of the queue. There were twenty-five of us lined up to report for duty. From what I saw, there was an equal number of men and women, and I would put money on them all being younger than me. I was going to have to try to use it as an advantage. I had maturity. Life experience. Eye bags.

The guy in front of me gave his name, and I stepped to the front of the queue. "Sutton Scott," I said.

"Good to have you here, Sutton. Your locker number is 97. Please collect your scrubs, change, and meet me back here."

It did feel a little like I'd enrolled in the army, but it had been clear on the joining instructions that we were going to wear scrubs. They also asked us to wear trainers. I guess Gilly had only skimmed the letter or thought the rules wouldn't apply to her.

Once we were changed, we had our photos taken for

temporary security passes. Then we were ushered down three floors to the lower basement and into a lecture theatre.

Somehow, Veronica caught up to me as we took our seats. "You mind if I sit here?"

"Not at all," I said.

Veronica's red hair was a mass of curls and she wore a serious expression at all times. But she seemed friendly enough and I was grateful to know the names of a couple people here.

"I think this is just an introduction to the hospital and some health and safety," Veronica said. "Tomorrow we start technology training."

How did she know all this? I had read the joining instructions. Technology training? What did that involve? The use of robotics in surgery? I didn't expect to be dropped in at the deep end like that, but at the same time I was excited. This was what I'd been working toward for years. This was what I dreamed about when I zoned out while my clients talked about their holidays and ex-boyfriends, about their plastic surgery and their dog's personality shift since their castration. I'd heard it all. Twice. People confessed the strangest things to their hairdresser. Over the course of time, even without knowing a single personal detail about me, my clients came to see me as their friend.

Veronica must have seen the expression of excitement on my face. "You know," she said. "So we're familiar with the computer system, the phones, and the tablets."

"Oh," I replied, not covering my disappointment very well. I'd been excited to start to see patients as a doctor rather than a medical student and keen to prove myself. I supposed the next few days would be the administration to allow us to practice. It made sense but it was also a little disappointing. As much as I wasn't looking forward to long shifts and late nights, I was used to working hard and keen to do so again. I wanted to get my hands dirty.

"How do you know all this?" I asked.

"My brother did the same thing two years ago." She put her finger to her lips. "Don't tell anyone. I want to psych people out by being two steps ahead."

Looked like the competition had already started.

Wanda sat behind a table on the floor of the lecture theatre, and everyone found their seats in a space that could easily fit a hundred people.

"In front of you is the timetable for the next two weeks," Wanda said. "You won't start with your department until you've finished orientation." I groaned internally. Two weeks?

Hands around the lecture theatre shot up.

"If any of you are about to complain, think again. You might think these two weeks are a waste of your time, but let me tell you, it's better than you not understanding the computer system and having to take up the valuable time of doctors and nurses on the ward. We want you to be able to order prescriptions, understand what to do in various types of emergency situations. We want you to understand and memorize the layout of the hospital, key personnel, and every other detail we come at you with. Until then, you are a hazard to the rest of this hospital."

"I have another question," a guy with a baseball cap said.

"Take the cap off," Wanda said. "And save your questions until I've finished."

"You don't know what I was asking—"

Wanda continued without waiting for Baseball Cap to finish his sentence. "At the end of two weeks, you'll be split up into five specialties. During each rotation, you'll work under one of our consultants. That doesn't mean you'll be working with them all the time, but the Foundation Lead will be responsible for your training during your four months in that rotation. If you don't think you're getting the experience you need, you speak to them. If you have any issues related to your medical or surgical experience, you speak to them. You do not bother them with issues outside what is medically or surgically related. Anything in connection with salary, admin, technology—anything outside medical or surgical—you come to me. Am I clear?"

I nodded.

"The five consultants will be here after lunch to give you brief introductions to their departments and what they expect of you. Before that we have some health and safety training. Stand by as we get things set up."

Murmurs filled the lecture theatre and people began to chat among themselves.

"Do you think she's going to mention the competition?" Gilly said from behind us. I hadn't even realized she was sitting there.

"That's what I was going to ask about," Baseball Cap said from across the walkway.

"I love a competition," Gilly said. "I don't care if it's a hopscotch race or an eating contest, if there's competition, I'm in."

"Same," Baseball Cap said. "I heard there's no trophy or anything—just an understanding throughout the hospital that you're the best. And apparently it lasts your entire career. I heard she was a winner." He nodded toward Wanda, who was talking to a stocky white man with a chin that jutted out like Buzz Lightyear.

"That's what I heard too," Gilly said. "That you stand out for the rest of your career."

I didn't care about winning this competition. In fact, I wanted to lose. I didn't want to bring attention to myself or have anyone asking any questions. No one needed to know I was older. Or an ex-hairdresser. Or that I had left school and been supporting myself since I was sixteen. I just wanted to mind my own business and do the job I'd wanted to do for so long. That would be tough enough.

WE FILED BACK in to the lecture theatre from lunch break and all took the exact same seats as we'd been in this morning. Maybe I should have stayed on site to have lunch and gotten to know some of my colleagues, but I'd needed to find a library or an art gallery. There was a small library in the hospital, but I needed to get out of the center of my anxiety. Luckily, there was a library just up the road. I was pretty sure I'd staved off a panic attack by spending twenty minutes in autobiographies and memoirs.

I opened my notebook, ready to take down anything about the five doctors we would be introduced to this afternoon. Every person who studied medicine had their own intricate systems and devices to memorize things as well as the mnemonics and more commonly used devices that medical students had used for generations, like APGAR and P-THORAX. Most of them had come easy to me, but I had a brain block when it came to people's names, so I would think of an object or person that reminded me of them. Wanda was a cricket ball: hard, powerful, and would break you into pieces if it came at you. When I looked at her, I imagined her bowling a fast ball at me and making a W shape in the air. Veronica was a mattress, the springs curly, red and stuffed full of information. When I saw her, I imagined her jumping in the middle of a bed and making the mattress shoot up at either end, making a V shape.

I glanced up to see Wanda stride back into the room. I took out my pen and wrote the time and date in the top right-hand corner of the page. As I was writing, a murmur passed through the room. Veronica elbowed me and I looked up from where I was scribbling notes. People were filing into the room. It must be the consultants that were going to head up our rotations.

"That's Lowenstein," Veronica said. "I've got to get a placement on his team." Dr. Jed Lowenstein was one of the most famous surgeons in the country. He regularly used robotics as part of his practice and training under him would be a dream come true.

"And who's that hottie?" Veronica whispered. "Oh my God, is that Jacob Cove? I heard he was good looking but wow, in the flesh, he's beyond gorgeous."

"Who?" I asked. As soon as the question left my lips, I locked eyes with the man who'd taken me to dinner Saturday night, the man who'd made me come so often all I could do on Sunday was eat cheese and crackers and watch TED talks.

My breath settled in my lungs, and my heart rate dropped as if it had just given up. There was no point in going on anymore. I was pretty sure I was about to pass out.

"Did you say *Jacob*?" I asked. Parker had definitely told me his name was Beau.

His gaze looked far more serious than I'd experienced on Saturday. I wasn't sure whether it was shock or anger I could see staring back at me. Without a doubt, he saw complete disbelief in my eyes.

My heart seemed to kick back into gear, racing from a

standing stop. What was he doing here? And why was Veronica calling him Jacob?

Someone whispered in his ear; he pushed his hands into his pockets and looked away. I tried to look away. I really did, but I couldn't. My heart had picked up speed again but my brain was stuck in a dark room, unsure which way was up.

"The hot blond one," she said. Yup, she was definitely talking about the guy I'd spent the night with on Saturday. "You've heard of the Coves. He's the eldest son."

The eldest son? Of *the* Coves? Everyone in this lecture theatre had heard of the Coves. They were the most famous couple in medicine. John Cove was off-the-charts clever and had changed his specialty and research interests numerous times throughout his career, rising to the top in each one. It made him the most revered Chief Medical Officer the British Government had ever had. Carole Cove was the most famous surgeon in the UK. She'd done transplants and had been one of the first in the country to pioneer and refine keyhole surgery. She was incredible.

"And he *works* here? He hasn't left or he's not about to leave or something?" The only reason I'd agreed to a date on Saturday was because *Beau* was leaving for *Africa*. I would not have agreed to have dinner with a man who was sticking around London—especially one who was going to turn out to be working at the same hospital as me, as my superior.

"Of course he works here. He's in pediatrics and pediatric cardiology—spans across the two. He made consultant super quickly. Working under him will be a treat, in more ways than one."

"What did you say his name was? Beau?"

Veronica laughed. "No, I see I'm not the only one who has been ogling the Cove brothers online. They're a medical student's equivalent of One Direction, aren't they? Beau is younger than Jacob. Jacob is the oldest, but a complete trail-blazer, just like his parents. All the brothers are doctors except one."

She must be mistaken—I'd gone to dinner with Beau, not Jacob. I'd gotten drunk with Beau. I'd had sex—a lot of sex—with Beau. Had I asked him his last name?

I pulled out my phone and quickly scrolled through the messages we'd exchanged over the last twenty-four hours. Had he said anywhere what his name was?

In our messages, Parker very definitely had told me my date was with someone called Beau. She didn't mention a Jacob.

"And he works here?" I asked.

"Yes. I told you, he's a consultant in pediatrics and pedi-atric cardiology."

"A consultant?" I asked, my tone bordering on hyster-ical and my cheeks heated as people turned to see who was losing it. Shit, had I inadvertently slept with my superior? Why was he pretending to be Beau?

"Shhh," Veronica said. "Yes, he's a consultant. And a gorgeous one at that. Look at him."

I didn't need to look at him to know he was gorgeous. I'd sat across a dinner table with him for an entire, deliciously easy evening. He'd made me laugh and think and then after dinner he'd cleared my mind of absolutely everything. He'd ensured I wasn't thinking about anything other than him and the way his body moved over mine, the way his hands, his lips, his everything felt against me. He'd sent every one of my senses into hypersonic overdrive. None of Saturday night would have happened if I'd known he was a consul-tant at the place I was starting work.

I was trying to fly under the radar—pass through the

foundation program without drawing attention to myself. Sleeping with a consultant wasn't going to help my cause. Hospitals were cauldrons of gossip and speculation. I wanted to keep my head down and *focus*.

Shit, I hope he hadn't told anyone. He didn't seem to be a man who bragged, but who the hell pretended to be someone else for an entire evening? Shock started to give way to anger. Who the hell did he think he was, tricking someone into bed with him? Not that he actually tricked me. Or at all. It was just if I'd known who he was—why hadn't he told me? I slapped my forehead with the palm of my hand. He hadn't had the chance to tell me anything about his job. I'd banned him from saying anything at all— not without the forfeit of a shot of tequila.

I quickly typed Parker a message asking her why I'd had dinner with a man called Jacob Cove when she'd told me my date was meant to be some guy called Beau. Presumably Beau had been the doctor going abroad next week. Rather than Jacob who was very much, and very inconveniently, right in front of me.

And then it dawned on me: The five doctors who had just filed into the lecture theatre were the consultants responsible for our rotations in their departments.

Jacob was going to be my boss.

My boss who'd seen me very drunk. Very naked. And very loudly screaming his brother's name as he made me come.

SEVEN

Jacob

I always told myself that, despite disagreements with my brothers, I loved them all and always would. I always knew we'd withstand the general banter that cut a little close to the bone and occasional serious arguments that so far had only once turned physical with Nathan over a naan bread.

But not anymore.

Beau fucking Cove was dead to me.

I pushed my hand over my head. What the actual fuck was happening right now? Flashes of Saturday night swept through my brain. Her scent—that fucking scent she had that was impossible to place but was feminine and sexy and had driven me wild all evening as we sat next to each other in the restaurant. Her legs as they smoothed against mine, her lips, shiny wet from my kisses. Her hair and the way I used it to anchor her head so I could watch her as she came.

Fuck.

Beau's annoying face flashed up on my phone—a response to the message I'd just sent him asking him why the fuck the woman I'd taken to dinner on Saturday night was staring back at me as one of the new doctors starting the foundation program at my hospital. I cancelled the call, wondering about the likelihood of dying of a stress-induced heart attack at thirty-six. My phone lit up again.

I dipped into a supplies cupboard and answered it. "I can't believe you would do this to me. You know what Dad always says about keeping our private lives private, and it's like my *only* rule. I've never broken it despite the countless times I might have been tempted."

"Jacob," Beau said, trying to interrupt me, but I wasn't about to let him.

"You could have just told whoever your friend is that you couldn't make it. You could have just been fucking honest. No, you have to put my integrity on the line. You have to put yourself and your fucking feelings first because no one else fucking matters, do they?"

"Jacob?" Beau said again.

"Well that's it. I'm never doing anything again for you. If you're set on fire, don't expect me to piss on you." I felt better for getting it all out.

"I didn't know she was starting at the Royal Free. I promise you."

"But I bet you didn't ask either." Beau never thought about the consequences of anything he did. "I'm sick of your baby brother bullshit. She's now in a compromised position and so am I." I didn't tell him how I'd been positioning myself for the past two years to take over the running of the foundation doctors program from Wanda. Everyone knew it was a test to see if you were leadership material. Everyone who did a good job running that program—and frankly some who only did a mediocre job— ended up heading up departments at this hospital and others in London. Beau thought he'd just made a silly mistake when in reality, it had potentially career-threatening consequences. I couldn't be fucking a doctor on the program when I was trying to take over running the program.

"I'm taking it from your complete overreaction that the night didn't end at dinner. It's not my fault if you couldn't keep your meat and two veg in your jeans for the night."

"Excuse me, I didn't realize I needed to check in with you before I slept with someone. If I'd thought for a minute that she was working at the Free, there's no way I would have touched her."

I didn't know if I was angrier at Beau for putting me in this position or myself for actually liking Sutton. I'd even messaged her on Sunday and been hoping to see her again. There was no way that could happen now.

I took a breath. Beau was annoying and selfish sometimes, but I should have checked which hospital she was starting at and taken my shot of tequila. This mess wasn't Beau's fault.

"Look, I'm sorry," Beau said. "I wasn't trying to fuck up any weird rules you have about work."

"They're not weird rules. They're professional boundaries. But it's not your fault. It's mine. I should have been more careful."

"You're literally the only doctor I know who hasn't fucked someone at the hospital they work at."

"Doesn't mean it's right. You know what Dad says."

"Dad's a hypocrite. He met Mum at work."

"I know, but his advice isn't wrong."

"Relax, Jacob. You always give yourself such a hard time. Like I said, if I'd known, I would have told you. Didn't she tell you where she was doing her two years of foundation? Didn't you mention where you worked and then she said—'Surprise! Me too'?"

I sighed. If only. It was a perfectly reasonable question and on any normal night, what Beau was describing was exactly what would have happened. "It didn't come up."

Instead we'd spent the night *not* talking about medicine or where we worked. And that had been refreshing and fun and something I wanted to do again with Sutton. But there was no way it could happen now.

"Has she done something to make it embarrassing or something?"

"No, nothing." The shock I'd seen when I'd caught her eye told me as much. There was no way she could have known. "I've gotta go. I'm in a supplies cupboard and I've got things to do. This isn't your mess. Sorry for losing it."

"It's not as bad as you think it is."

It never was for Beau.

I had to find Sutton and ask her to keep things that had happened between us strictly private if she hadn't already said something to someone. Wanda had them still in the lecture theatre filling out three gazillion forms. I'd have to be casually passing when they filed out.

EIGHT

Sutton

Wanda dismissed us for the day. Despite the fact it had been hours since Jacob was introduced as one of the five leads of the foundation program, my heart was still beating like I was two miles into a marathon. How could this be happening? How on earth could *Jacob Cove* be the man I kicked out of bed on Sunday morning? That he was a consultant at the Free was bad enough, but he was a *Cove*. That family had real power. One word from him and I was sure that my participation on the foundation program would be over.

"I can't believe we get to work with a real live Cove," Veronica said as we shoved our notebooks into our bags.

"You know he's practically off-the-charts clever. I heard he had an IQ of one hundred and seventy," Gilly said from where she was sitting behind us.

One hundred seventy? That was insane. "No way." I'd spent the evening with him. He was funny and confident and normal. He wasn't so clever I couldn't comprehend our conversation.

"Apparently his mother is even brighter," Gilly said. "Such an incredible family."

The guy sitting next to Gilly grinned like he was imagining Jacob naked. My stomach churned at the memories of Saturday night. He was just as good as everyone was imagining. "And he's totally hot." He obviously knew instantly who we were talking about.

We all filed out and a group of us gathered just outside the lecture room. A couple of other women joined us. "Did I hear you all talking about Jacob Cove? He's definitely the McDreamy of the hospital."

"Except Patrick Dempsey has nothing on our McDreamy," Veronica added, practically salivating.

I bristled with irritation at the way they were talking. Jacob wasn't a piece of meat. He was a normal person who used to lay in rowboats for hours to de-stress. He was a man who knew his way around my body like he'd made me. And if I heard another word about him from any of these women, I might blow a fuse.

"He's not Dr. McDreamy," I said and five pairs of eyes turned and focused on me.

"You have a better nickname?" Gilly asked. "McSteamy?"

"What about Off Limits?" I suggested. "In real life, Meredith Grey would have probably been slut-shamed. In real life, a foundation doctor doesn't end up with the hot, rockstar consultant. In real life, doing the boss is a good way to lose your job."

"Wow, Sutton. Way to kill our buzz," Veronica said.

"I'm just trying to be practical. We need to think of him as unavailable. Doesn't do any good to be mentally undressing our boss. As women, we want to be judged on our capabilities and merits, don't we? And like it or not, it's the woman who always gets judged if they have an affair with their boss."

"He's not my boss," Veronica said. "And it's not like he's married."

"But he's more senior to us," I said. "With a lot of sway and influence." What did I care if these women wanted to lust after Jacob? They were only human. And if they were talking about him and someone else, it meant they weren't talking about him and me—and why would they? Jacob and I were strictly a one-time deal. No one was going to find out. Even if he hadn't gone to Africa, I was going to pretend he had.

"Doctor Scott?" A familiar voice asked from behind me. My cheeks burned hotter than the sun and my breath halted abruptly in my throat as I realized who the voice belonged to.

I pushed back my shoulders and spun around to come face-to-face with Dr. Off Limits himself. I bit down on my inner cheek—Christ on a bike, he was tall. "Yes?" I tried to sound relaxed and confident. Except he knew that was exactly the opposite to how I was feeling.

"Follow me, please."

I could feel the stares from my colleagues gathered in the lobby of the lecture theatre. I wanted the linoleum to open up and swallow me down. What the hell was he doing, singling me out like this?

I caught up with him and said, "Stop right now and show me something on your phone."

He stopped. "What?"

"Get your tablet out and show it to me but be careful that the screen is pointed to the wall." My eyes were about to bulge out of my head. We couldn't be seen casually chatting.

He hesitated.

"Please just do this," I said. "Trust me."

Lucky for me, he got out his iPad and began to point at the blank screen.

"Don't single me out like that," I said. "Don't speak to me. Don't even look at me. I don't want anyone to know anything about what happened on Saturday night."

"And a lot of Sunday morning," he added. I glared at him.

"Sign up for some kind of operation that will make you forget," I said. "And don't ever speak to me about anything other than work. For the record, you just called me over because the hospital had misplaced some of my personal information. Are we clear?"

He nodded.

"Good. I'm going to leave now. I hope I don't see you soon."

I was practically shaking as I walked back to the group. I was going to have to hold it together a little longer so I could explain why Jacob had called me over to him. Then I was heading back to the library. I was due for a lie-down between towering stacks of books. It had been that kind of a day.

NINE

Jacob

I'd been acting impulsively and irrationally and I didn't like it. I don't know what I'd been thinking going up to Sutton in front of her new colleagues. We were supposed to be strangers. She'd been furious and rightly so. But that didn't change the fact that we needed to have a conversation—a *rational* conversation—about our situation.

I leaned against her front door frame and knocked. No answer. Then I knocked again. There was a rustling of keys followed by the door creaking open a crack. The chain was across the door and I could see Sutton's one eye peeping into the hallway like a hot, pint-sized Cyclops.

"We need to talk," I said.

"We absolutely do not need to talk," she replied. "That's exactly what I was trying to explain earlier when you made a scene in front of every new foundation doctor at the hospital."

"A scene? Really? I just wanted to talk to you. Seeing

you was a shock." Saturday night had been so good. So completely unexpected and so much fun. She'd been so relaxed and funny and herself. It was like she'd turned into a different person. I hated myself for causing it.

She closed the door and I waited as she unchained the lock and we came face-to-face. "You better come in."

"Thanks." I followed her into her living room. I hadn't remembered it being laid out like this on Saturday. We'd probably headed straight to her bedroom.

"You want a drink?"

I shook my head.

"Sit over there on that chair." She pointed to one of those Ikea chairs that looked like an adult baby bouncer. I grinned at the thought that she was being so assertive. Was she scared she wouldn't be able to keep her hands off me or something?

I took a seat and realized we were actually in her bedroom. And her living room. She was sitting on her bed.

"Why didn't you tell me you worked at the Free?" I asked, trying to put a cork in all the memories from Saturday threatening to fly out into the small room. God, I'd had a good time. The dinner had been so great. I'd been weirdly open with her and told her things I'd never told anyone, let alone a near stranger. And then back here, after dinner? It had been fun and so fucking sexy. It had been the kind of sex that sobered you up—not because it was bad but because it was so fucking good and your body understood on a molecular level that you needed to remember it. It was sex that was to be put in the archives, kept and pulled up at various times for the rest of your life. It was the kind of sex that made you feel like a fucking god.

"Me?" she said, incredulous. "Why didn't *you* say

anything? I hadn't even started my job. You were meant to be going to Africa next week doing Medecins Sans Frontieres. And your name was *supposed* to be Beau."

I pushed my hand over my head and tried to fight back the memories of her fingers smoothing over my scalp. How she'd cried out about how it felt between her legs. Fuck, I could feel the stirrings of an erection.

This wasn't the time. The mood she was in, she'd probably cut it off.

"I filled in for my brother," I said. The thought of Beau helped negate my growing lust.

"You *filled in*?" she asked. "You weren't renting a car."

"I know, but he broke his nose, and he didn't want to let down your friend . . ."

"Parker," she added.

"Parker. He was doing her a favor—"

"Listen, I don't need someone to go on a date with me as a favor."

Of course she didn't. Why was everything I was saying coming out wrong? "I didn't mean it like that. I just—look, if I'd known you were about to start at the Free, there was no way I would have said yes to the date."

"Yeah, well if I hadn't thought you were going to be thousands of miles away in a few days, there was no way I would have slept with you," she said.

Her words were like an icy wind, chasing a chill up my spine. I winced. I hated the idea that Saturday night wouldn't have happened if she'd known who I was. I mean, if I'd known who she was, I would have had to walk away, but that would have been my choice.

"I don't want a boyfriend," she continued. "And I sure as hell don't want the added hassle of wondering whether people are looking at me differently or treating me differently because I slept with one of the consultants." She buried her face in her hands. "And not just one of the consultants. A Cove."

"Fuck," I shouted.

"Exactly my thoughts."

I took in a deep breath and tried to steady my breathing. I was so pissed off at Beau. I was so pissed off at myself. And I was really pissed off that despite all that and despite my hard and fast rules about not messing about in the work-place pond, I really, really wanted to kiss her. Right now. I wanted to stalk over to her, push her to her back, strip off those leggings, and plunge straight into her and listen as she begged me to make her come.

But I had to shake that fantasy right out of my head. It wasn't going to happen. I wouldn't let it.

"Look," I said. "If you don't want anyone finding out and I don't want anyone finding out, we can agree not to tell anyone. I'm going for a promotion—ironically, heading up the foundation program. If they know I slept with one of the doctors on the program, there's no way I'm getting that job. And if I don't get that job, that means—oh never mind. You don't need to know. But we're both screwed if it gets out that we've . . ."

"Screwed?" she added, and I couldn't help but smile. She was most definitely still the woman I'd spent Saturday night and Sunday morning with.

Our eyes locked and I could feel her body heat from a meter away. I knew how those hands felt on me. How that mouth fit my cock. I knew what I could do to her body. Something told me I hadn't discovered the half of what she was capable of doing to me.

"Right," I said, pulling myself out of the haze that I'd

descended into as a result of being so close to her. "Can we agree that no one needs to know about this then?"

"Agreed," she said, holding my gaze again.

We were silent for one beat, then two.

"You didn't reply to my text," I said. I shouldn't have said anything. I should just leave now. I'd gotten what I'd came her for—I was reassured that she didn't want anyone to know about us. And I'd been able to give her the same reassurance. She'd agreed that we'd both keep it a secret.

There was nothing left to do here.

I should go.

"I was hungover when it came through and I was starting a new job the next day," she replied. "I didn't have a chance. And now . . ."

We both knew how the sentence ended. Now she was never going to reply to that text because continuing anything between us was completely impossible.

She got up off the bed and headed for the door. I followed.

"For the record, I had a really good time," I said, pushing my hands into my pockets.

"For the record, I did too." She paused. "Except I don't want that on the record."

"No," I said, "There's no record of anything happening between you and me."

"Exactly," she said. "Because nothing happened." There was a tinge of disappointment in her voice that made my insides ache. She knew how good Saturday had been—how could she not? She wanted it to happen again as much as I did. It was just impossible given the circumstances.

"Nothing at all," I said, holding her gaze, unable to look away. "It's like this flat doesn't even exist." I stepped toward her—after all, I was heading to the door. It wasn't like I wanted to get closer to her—close enough to touch, kiss, fuck. We were so close that I could almost taste her hot, sweet scent, feel her breath curl over my skin. "If it doesn't exist, I'm not . . ." I paused, took in her expression to make sure I wasn't overstepping because we'd just spent the last however-long saying how Saturday night was a huge mistake. Now here I was, about to be happy to make the exact same mistake again. But I could hear it in her short breaths and see it in her slightly parted lips, she wanted this just as much as I did. I moved closer, dug my hand into the back of her hair, and licked her bottom lip, side to side like she was tequila, salt, and lime all mixed into one. She groaned and slipped her leg between mine. I was instantly hard. I dove my tongue into her mouth, desperate to taste her, possess her, wanting to understand if how good it was on Saturday was about the booze and the darkness or whether it was about her and me. Now we were both sober, and unlike my self-control, the daylight was still hanging on.

Whatever I'd felt with Sutton wasn't fueled by booze. If anything, she tasted better now—sweeter than before. Her tongue met mine as her hands smoothed up my chest and around my neck. Fuck. I wanted to pin her to the door and strip her naked. Every nerve ending in my body was on a code red and I could practically feel the adrenaline marching into my bloodstream. I pushed my hips against her, forcing her back, and reached for the hem of her t-shirt. I wanted more of her, needed to feel my flesh against hers.

Just as I found the bottom of her shirt, she pushed against my shoulders with both hands. "Stop," she called out breathlessly. "Just stop."

I took a couple of steps back. It was like I escaped an undertow and had managed to come up for air.

"Shit," I said, pressing the heels of my hands into my eyes. "What the fuck is happening to me?"

"You should leave," she said. "I can't . . . I don't know what it is you have going on with you and what kind of witchcraft you're messing with, but I can't be around it."

At least it wasn't just me who felt it. I wasn't sure if it was witchcraft, chemistry, or if she was a magnet and I was every piece of iron that ever existed.

"You need to stay away from me," she said.

I nodded. She was right. I did need to stay away. Far away. The closer I was, the more I had to fight against her pull.

"This didn't happen," I said.

"My flat doesn't exist," she said. "We don't know each other."

I nodded. "Agreed." She opened the front door and I stepped out into the hallway.

"For the record, I wish it wasn't like this," I said.

"For the record, me too." She shut the door behind me. I stayed rooted to the spot as she turned the locks, slid the chain back on, and bolted me out.

I knew leaving was the right thing to do. For both of us. But at that moment, I just wanted one more night. I'd even take an hour. I headed back up the stairs to the pavement, fighting the urge to go back for one more kiss. I'd won the battle, but it didn't feel like a victory. Something told me it wouldn't be the last internal struggle I'd had over Sutton. Despite my intellectual grasp of the situation and how impossible anything more between us was, my gut told me we weren't done. Our connection remained and wouldn't be easily extinguished. I shook my head. It was just lust talking, right?

It didn't mean anything. I just wanted what I couldn't have.

Maybe.

Whether this draw I had to Sutton was real or imagined, it didn't matter. We both knew we had to keep away from each other. For good.

Like day and night, we were inextricably linked, but couldn't exist together.

TEN

Jacob

For the first time in a long time, my day started at five so I could make it to the Heath to swim in the men's bathing pond. It was what I'd needed to reset my brain and drain my mind of thoughts of Sutton. The cold from the fresh water had done its job and a healthy dose of oxytocin had funneled into my bloodstream. My vagus nerve was up and dancing. This morning I'd been firing on all cylinders as a result.

I didn't need Sutton when I had cold-water swimming.

I'd finished the morning rounds and was about to head to lunch when my phone buzzed in my pocket. For a second I thought it was Sutton. Of course it wouldn't be. I swiped up on my screen. It was my brother Nathan. He was confirming our dinner at his place later in the week. I typed back a reply, shoved my phone back in my pocket, and headed to the cafeteria.

The doctors in the hospital shared a cafeteria with the patients and their visitors, but the doctors had a separate room where they could eat. It meant we could discuss issues and cases among ourselves without having to worry about breaching confidentiality. The only problem was that the room was small for a hospital the size of the Royal Free.

"Jacob," a woman called from behind me, just as I was sliding macaroni cheese onto my tray.

"Macaroni cheese? Really?" It was Hartford, one of the other doctors in the pediatric department.

"I was cold-water swimming on the Heath at five thirty this morning. I earned this calorie-laden-baby."

She laughed. "Okay, I'll let you off as long as you have something green with it."

"I'm all over the broccoli." I picked up a spoon and scooped some onto my plate. "How are things going? Is it me or does it feel like we have things under control?"

"It's definitely you." She picked up her tray and headed to the tills. I followed her. "I don't feel like I have things under control at all. I'm close to drowning."

After she paid, she waited for me as the cashier rang up my lunch.

"Want to brainstorm a little?" I asked. "Maybe see if we can shuffle stuff around?"

She smiled up at me. "You'd make a great head of pediatrics when Gerry retires, you know."

I rolled my eyes and picked up my tray. "Well, he's not retiring for a thousand years, so there's little chance of that, is there?"

"You wouldn't go somewhere else though, would you?"

The thought hadn't occurred to me. I'd done my foundation program at the Free. I'd learned almost everything I knew here. I'd never considered moving. "I've no plans to."

"That's good to hear. Gerry is an inspiration. You know, he's not just a good doctor, but he's a talented scientist and a

compassionate human being who cares about his patients
and his staff. You'd be an excellent successor. And from
what I've heard, you're on the right path."

From what she'd heard? How this hospital liked to
gossip. Gerry was at least five years off retirement and the
search for a successor wouldn't begin until he announced a
firm leaving date. Taking on the head of the foundation
program for pediatrics was the first step on the ladder to
position myself as a successor, but the next step was taking
over the entire program. Then there were some research
papers I was working on. Each piece was a carefully positioned domino I was setting up to create the end result I was
aiming for.

"Enough about me," I said. "Let's talk about why you're
feeling overwhelmed."

Hartford pushed open the door to the doctor's dining
room and the noise hit us like we'd pushed through the
sound barrier. "There are never enough seats," Hartford
said, almost hissing.

Six large, round tables filled the room, each with room
for six but seats for eight. It was a squeeze at the best of
times.

"There's one," I said, nodding toward the table in the far
corner. As soon as I said it, I regretted it, because there was
Sutton. She had her back to me but she was unmistakable.

I'd managed to spend most of the morning without
thinking about her and our kiss the night before. How her
tongue tasted sweet, like apples. How the vibrations of her
moans had travelled right to my cock. How the feel of her
hands on my neck and chest made me transform into some
kind of neanderthal who had to fight back the urge to toss
her over my shoulder, flip her onto the bed, and fuck her
until I was asleep or dead.

Hartford headed over to the space opposite Sutton. But there wasn't another seat at that table. Maybe I could catch up with Hartford later and I'd take a seat at the next table where one came up. Unluckily for me, as Harford set her tray down, the doctor to Sutton's left stood.

It had taken cold-water swimming, but I'd managed to set the thoughts aside for a few hours. All it took was the back of her head to bring them all racing back to me. She had her hair up in a messy ponytail, just like when we'd had dinner together, and when she moved to speak to the person on her right, she revealed just the slightest sliver of her elegant neck and that beauty spot on her cheek. If I hadn't walked in with Hartford, I would have walked straight out again. But Hartford needed to talk. She needed help.

"Jacob," Hartford called. "Take this one." She pointed at the seat next to Sutton.

As I made my way over, I could see Hartford trying to arrange the table so she and I could sit together. At least that way, I'd not be sitting next to Sutton. But by the time I got to the table, somehow, the only free space left was directly between the two women.

My gut seized like I had just been presented with a bad case of advanced leprosy.

I needed to get a grip. I was going to be sitting next to a foundation doctor for twenty minutes. If I could swim in the middle of Hyde Park at five thirty this morning, taking a seat next to a beautiful woman wouldn't defeat me.

I pulled my mouth into a smile and headed to the empty seat.

I set down my tray and pulled out my chair. It was like I was playing the board game Operation, except I was the tweezers. Trying to hold my nerve, I lowered myself into my chair, desperate not to make any contact with Sutton that might set off the buzzer.

Sutton shuffled her chair to give me more room, but all I could think about was touching her, and not touching her.

"You okay there?" Hartford asked, her eyebrows pulled together.

"Yeah, just trying to squeeze in." I sat, pulled my chair in, and quite by accident, knocked my leg against Sutton's.

Electricity sparked between us and she jumped away.

I'd never been much good at Operation.

I shifted, turning so I had my back slightly to Sutton, without making it too obvious.

"So tell me what's going on," I asked Hartford, desperate to pull her focus and mine to our conversation rather than the fact that I'd turned into an awkward, lanky thirteen-year-old boy who thought he'd go up in flames if he touched a girl.

"I don't know," she said. "I'm really behind in my paperwork and I'm working on my research project and studying. I feel like instead of spinning plates, I'm constantly dropping them. I'm thinking of asking for a sabbatical."

"Wow," I replied just as Sutton pushed her chair out. "How long have you been thinking about that?"

"I have to return a call," Sutton said to the person she sat next to. Who was she calling? A lover? A friend? More likely, she was trying to put some distance between us. It was like a cloud had passed in front of the sun—it was both a relief from the heat and a disappointment at the lack of warmth.

I was totally fucked. So totally fucked.

"Oh, just a couple of weeks or so," Hartford said. "I probably won't, but it feels good to fantasize about it sometimes."

I chuckled as I felt Sutton move away from the table. My mind began to focus on the conversation I was having with Hartford. "You want me to look through some of your paperwork with you to see if there's a way we can speed up what you're doing?"

"That would be great if you don't mind?"

"Of course not."

"I know you've got a lot on with the foundation doctors. When do they start on the wards?"

"Week after next." By then, things should have settled between Sutton and me. I would have gotten perspective and become accustomed to seeing her around. Time would have passed from the last time she and I were alone together, and feelings would have faded. Things would look very different in a week.

"When do you find out who's in peds?"

That would be the only fly in the ointment—if Sutton had her first rotation in my department. Four months with us running into each other most days would be hell. Four, eight, twelve, sixteen months from now, she could have her rotation in peds and it would be fine. Whatever was between us would have fizzled out and we could be professional. But if she was assigned to peds as her first rotation, I was going to have to incorporate more than swimming in the lido every day before work to survive.

"Not sure." As soon as we were finished at lunch, I was going to track down Wanda and ask to see the list of doctors assigned to each department. If it turned out that Sutton was meant to be in peds, I'd have to make up some kind of excuse. Or I'd have to hack into the computer and change it. Or something. But it wasn't going to happen. I was sure of it.

ELEVEN

Sutton

After lunch, all the new foundation doctors were gathered in the lobby of the lecture theatres, coffees in hand, as we waited for the doors to open.

"I can't believe he sat next to you," Gilly said. "What does he smell like?"

I grimaced. "I wasn't sniffing him." But I knew he smelled of musk and ginger and everything good.

"I would have sniffed him," Veronica said. "I might even have surreptitiously grazed my leg against his."

I was pretty sure Jacob's graze of my leg with his had been accidental. Sitting next to me hadn't been his idea and to me, he'd clearly been uncomfortable. The woman he was sitting with at lunch was pretty. Beautiful in fact. I'd had a pang of jealousy until I'd clocked the engagement ring on her left hand. A huge chunk of diamond I was definitely jealous of.

Being jealous of Jacob speaking to another woman was ridiculous. If Jacob started seeing someone else, that would be a best-case scenario for me. It would mean no one would be looking too hard at us if we ever encountered each other in the hospital. The door would stay very firmly shut between us. Maybe I could suggest that to him?

"Don't you think he's gorgeous?" Gilly asked me. "Or is he still strictly Dr. Off Limits for you?"

If only she knew.

I shrugged, hoping divine intervention would save me from this conversation. My prayers were answered when someone came and opened the lecture theatre door.

"What's that?" Veronica said, nodding toward the desk on the floor of the lecture theatre.

"It looks like a top hat," Gilly said. "Are we having magic lessons this afternoon?"

My stomach swooped as I remembered my conversation with Jacob about the importance of believing in magic. "We can only hope."

Wanda filed in, along with representatives from each department where we'd be assigned rotations. Which of course included Jacob.

Gilly was right. He was absolutely gorgeous. A man with an almost-shaved head shouldn't by rights be as attractive as Jacob but somehow, he pulled it off. He could probably dress in a clown suit and pull it off. He exuded sexy confidence that had nothing to do with his appearance— though that didn't hurt, either.

"This afternoon, you're going to find out your first rotation," Wanda announced. My heart began to thunder like someone playing the kettle drums in my chest. I was excited. This was what we were here for. All that hard work over the last seven years had been to get to this moment.

So long as I didn't get pediatrics.

Nothing could take the shine off starting my clinical

career other than having to deal with the man who made me feel like I was walking a tightrope between doctor and giddy teenager anytime he was in a five-meter radius.

"Every year we get complaints about allocations," Wanda said. "Every year I have a queue of foundation doctors lining up outside my office asking to swap rotations. It eats away at my time and my patience. And my patients." She let out a small laugh.

"This year, I've printed out all your names." She held up a handful of ribboned paper. "I'm going to put them in this hat and then the heads of each specialty will take turns to pick out names one by one."

Several hands shot up in the air and Wanda shook her head. "I will not be making any exceptions to this process. I don't care what you did your research papers in. I don't care that your dad's next door neighbor's cat told you that you would be able to choose your first rotation. I especially don't care if you think you would be doing me a favor by starting in a different rotation. This is how the process is going to go."

Wow, she was taking absolutely no shit.

I crossed my legs, crossed my fingers, and then crossed my arms.

Anything but peds.

"What are you hoping for?" Veronica asked me, nodding at my crossed fingers.

"Accident and Emergency," I lied. I didn't care what I got. Only what I didn't get.

"Me too!" she said.

Wanda's top hat got passed around among the specialty leads and names got read out, causing a frisson of excitement to flutter across the new doctors. Jacob's turn was last of the five and he took his time.

"Come on," Wanda said. "Anyone would think you're trying to game the system. You don't know how terrible any of them are yet." Wanda laughed and Jacob gave a forced smile before pushing his hand into the hat and pulling out a name. His shoulders dropped and his expression evened out. I knew we were both safe. "Gillian Peters," he read out.

"Dr. No Limits, baby. I'm all yours."

"It's Off Limits," I whispered to her.

She laughed beside me. "Not to me."

I bristled at her response.

The hat went round again and I kept saying my name over and over, desperate to get picked before it ended up in Jacob's hand again. No such luck. Jacob had his turn again. This time he went really quickly, clearly wanting to avoid any questions from Wanda. He pulled out the name and announced, "Robert French." He scanned the people sitting around me, trying to find his newest recruit. Our eyes locked. I looked down at my pad, scribbling my name on the paper in front of me. *Please let the next name pulled out be mine.*

But no, Veronica was next. She got A&E. Lucky her. Before I knew it, the hat was back in Jacob's hand. He grinned and pulled out another strip of paper.

The look of sheer terror in his eyes gave it away. I knew. I knew it was my name on that paper he was holding. I knew I faced four months of total torture. Holy Madonna Louise Ciccone.

"Sutton Scott," he said, holding up the paper.

My heart corkscrewed into my stomach. How was it possible for me to be so intent on staying away from a person only to have the universe flip me *and* my intention off so violently at every turn?

"We're going to be together," Gilly said. "So fun."

"*Sooo* fun," I said, trying to sound as genuine as I possibly could.

The rest of the names were picked and Wanda held up her notepad. "As you've all been picked, I've made a note of who got what specialty. Do not under any circumstances—not even if you think your life depends on it because, believe me, it won't—come and try to change where you are going to spend the next four months. If you do, I will put you on a special laundry rotation I've devised for my favorite foundation doctors.

"Now you know where you'll be heading, you're going to hear from each doctor about what to expect, and what not to expect, during your rotation."

I sat forward on my bench and started taking copious, detailed notes. I wasn't going to remember anything about this lecture and I'd need to have a full record of what was said. If I didn't focus, I knew all I would be able to think about was the next four months working in the same department as Jacob, seeing him every day, having to brief him on patients and ask him questions about medicines. All the while hoping no one noticed how much I was desperate for him to touch me.

The next four months were going to be hell.

TWELVE

Jacob

Thankfully I was due at Nathan's tonight. If I hadn't been, I would have probably driven up to Norfolk. I desperately yearned for something to ground me, something to take away this ache inside me every time I laid eyes on Sutton. I wasn't sure how I was going to get through the next four months without descending into madness.

"You look terrible," Nathan said as he opened the door.

"Thanks, mate," I said, pushing past him. At least I had the day off tomorrow so I could have a couple of glasses of his ridiculously overpriced red wine. "I need a drink."

He followed me into the kitchen and pulled out a bottle from his wine fridge. "I've been saving this for a special occasion, but seeing as it's you . . ."

Nathan stayed quiet as he opened the bottle of wine, like he was a priest preparing for the sacrament.

He pulled the cork from the bottle. "So, how's it going positioning yourself for the head of foundation program?" he asked.

It was exactly the wrong question. I groaned. "I don't want to talk about it. Can we stick to business?" For some reason, Nathan liked to bounce ideas off me. I didn't know anything about business. Yes, I'd had a lucky break at university that made me a lot of money but it was just that—luck. I wasn't a businessman. I was a doctor.

"We can, but it's not like you to avoid—"

"I know. I just need a break from everything tonight. Let's not . . ."

"Hey," Madison said, as she swept into the kitchen. "How are you?" Nathan's fiancée greeted me with a kiss on both my cheeks and put her hands on her hips. "Where's my glass?"

Nathan moved to pour her one and she hopped up onto the stool next to me. "How's your love life?" she asked. I groaned for a second time.

"Yeah, Beau told me he set you up on a date."

If Beau was here now I'd strangle him. "Beau didn't set me up. Beau got me to stand in for him on a blind date. Worst decision of the last twelve months."

"Wow, it can't have been that bad," Nathan said. "Wasn't she your type? Oh that's right, your type is a mash-up between Marie Curie, Florence Nightingale, and Kate Beckinsdale."

"Is it?" I asked, genuinely weirded out by what he'd said, particularly as Sutton definitely had a Kate Beckinsdale look about her.

"Yeah," Nathan said. "They've got to be kind and selfless and off the charts clever—"

"I've never said any of that," I said, a little affronted.

"I don't think you've said those actual words," Madison said. "But the reasons you haven't liked women in the past are because they're not those things. Look at Audrey. What excuse did you use for not making a go of it with her?"

"There wasn't an excuse. She was married, her husband turned out to be a lying thief, and had just been sent to prison. She said she wasn't ready for a relationship."

"Bad example," Madison mumbled.

"We have to make compromises," Nathan said. "That's Madison's point. Look how I put up with a woman deluded enough to think I believe her when she says she never farts."

"I don't fart," Madison said. "And anyway, not farting isn't a compromise, it's a benefit. A compromise would be the way I put up with your obsession with obscenely expensive wine."

Nathan rolled his eyes and turned his attentions back to me. "I'm kidding. You don't have to compromise. Madison is perfect for me. But that's just it—I don't even think you'd be happy if Marie Curie came back from the dead. You'd find something wrong with her. No one's perfect."

"I don't need a therapy session from my younger brother who, frankly, I can't believe tricked a nice woman like you, Madison, into marrying him."

"Just so I know," Madison continued as if I hadn't spoken at all. "What was wrong with the woman Beau set you up with?"

"I told you, he didn't set me up."

"Whatever," she said. "Tell me what was wrong with her and I'll diagnose you. Then I'll leave you to change the world or whatever it is you two are doing tonight."

"Just tell her, mate, or we'll never hear the end of it," Nathan said.

"Nothing was wrong with her," I said. That was the whole bloody problem.

"Nothing?" Madison asked.

"Well, I didn't get her to fill out a questionnaire and have her under interrogation by MI5 but there was nothing —it doesn't matter."

"So you've asked her on a second date?" Madison asked.

"No. She works at the same hospital as me," I replied. "Not that I knew that at the time or I would never have gone on the date in the first place."

"Ahhh," Nathan said. "Could be messy."

"Why would it be messy?" Madison asked. "Surely that makes life a lot easier. You all work so freaking hard."

Nathan was shaking his head. "Dad has always been clear. You keep your private life private. 'Medicine's a very small world,'" he said, lowering his voice and doing his best Dad impression.

"But other than that, you liked her?" Madison asked.

I shrugged then took a seat on the stool next to her. I'd lost my strength to stand and my energy to avoid spilling my feelings. I took a breath. "I really liked her."

I ignored the look that passed between Madison and my brother.

"I *still* like her, and now she's been assigned to pediatrics as her first rotation. I'm not sure what to do. We have this connection or chemistry or something. It's like my biochemistry changes when she's around. I can feel her when she's close." I shook my head. "It's weird." I sighed, exhausted from thinking about it. "I'm sure it will pass. It's just been a long week."

"It's a shit she's in the same hospital. You think she'll move when she passes foundation?" Nathan asked.

"I don't know," I replied. "She only started this week. She's got a minimum of two years left." I just needed to get through the next four months.

"You could kill two birds with one stone and hand in your resignation and come into business with me," Nathan said. "Can I tempt you away from medicine and over to the dark side?"

I let out a half-hearted laugh. "As if."

"Then I don't know what to suggest other than cold showers. And try to fixate on something that irritates you about her. Like maybe she always interrupts you before you finish a sentence. Or maybe she wears too much makeup or —there's got to be something?"

I couldn't think of anything that wasn't completely sexy about Sutton.

"Or maybe don't do that and date her," Madison said. "Call me old fashioned, but just because your dad advised you against something doesn't mean it's the law. I mean, unless the hospital has a policy or something?"

Nathan snorted. "Hospitals are basically huge dating pools. There's no way any hospital could introduce a policy because everyone would just ignore it."

"I think there is a policy, but everyone ignores it," I said.

"So other than your dad disapproving—and he never has to know—I'm not getting why you just don't ask her out." Madison looked at me, just like an investigative journalist interviewing a source.

"Because my dad isn't wrong. I'm trying to position myself to head up the program for foundation doctors. I can't do that if I'm fucking one of them."

Madison pushed her lips together. "Hmmm." She folded her arms. "Unless no one finds out."

"Someone always finds out," I said.

"I guess you just have to figure out whether she's worth the risk," Madison said.

"Can we talk about something else now?" I asked. I

didn't want to think about the possibility of being with Sutton because it *wasn't* possible. I didn't want to start down the path of a dead-end street. I needed to put her out of my head.

"Oh, before we do, I've had an idea about the foundation program," Nathan said. "An idea that will raise your profile among the candidates to take over from Wanda."

He'd caught my attention. I hoped this wasn't a joke. "Go on," I said.

"You need an offsite," he said. "It boosts morale. It helps teambuilding. You can do some hard-skills training in there. I even thought you might do a survey of the staff and ask if they could change one thing in the hospital, what would it be. Then you take that to the offsite and workshop the thing staff mention most."

"That's not really a doctor issue, though. More of an admin thing to figure out."

"Maybe you invite admin staff along to workshop it with you."

"Maybe," I said. "But maybe a medical issue is raised and even if it's not—if the doctors are united in wanting things changed, I'm sure we could make it happen."

"Right," Nathan said.

"Sounds good. Except the cost. Funding is always a problem for these kinds of things. But we could put on a coach and do something in Hertfordshire."

"Or even go into central London."

I nodded. It was a really good idea. "People could stay if they were prepared to foot the bill themselves. Or they could head home." Ideas started spinning in my head. This could be the exact thing I was looking for to position me to run the program and actually do something good to help the hospital run more efficiently. "Taking all the foundation doctors away would show I was ready for the job."

For once, one of my brothers had actually come up with a good idea.

The only problem was, one of doctors on the offsite would be Sutton.

THIRTEEN

Sutton

Gilly and I turned up just before nine at ward six, ready for rounds as we'd been instructed to do. We'd been warned that things would start off very similarly to med school—we'd have a tight leash at first, despite our change of status to doctor.

"Is it just the two of us?" she asked.

I nodded. "I believe so." I knew so. I'd checked the rota carefully to see who would be working. Jacob wasn't on there at all. None of the consultants were.

"Robert and Jean are on nights." Each group of year one foundation doctors had been split between night and day shift. I'd finally caught a break and got days.

"Urgh, I'm not looking forward to the night shifts," Gilly said. "Apparently it's really quiet most of the time and impossible to stay awake."

The second week of orientation had passed by in a blur. I'd only seen Jacob twice and then it was from a distance. I was conscious that he could turn up at any minute and I avoided the doctor's dining room like it was a tropical disease, but I survived. Just like I always did. Now I was ready to start on the wards. Hopefully Jacob had been able to influence my shifts so we weren't on together.

"You think Dr. McDreamy will be the consultant in charge today?" Gilly asked.

I shook my head. "There's no Dr. McDreamy. It's either McDreamy without the Doctor part or it's Dr. Off Limits."

She looked at me as if I'd lost my mind and I shook my head. "Sorry, it's just I was a big Grey's fan. Back in the day. I like to get things right." I was more than a little on edge. I was hoping against hope that Jacob and I could maneuver around this department without having too much to do with each other.

"Me too," she said. "Although I never did understand what he saw in Meredith."

"Dr. Scott and Dr. Peters," Jacob called from behind us. "Follow me." My stomach dove to the floor and kept falling through the linoleum heading straight to the center of the earth.

He wasn't supposed to be here today.

He rushed past us and we had to scurry to keep up. "Let's recap, make sure you haven't forgotten anything from med school. Tell me what acronym we use when handing over patients."

"SBAR," I said from behind him and then immediately wished I hadn't. My plan had been to stay under the radar—to coast along out of sight. Maybe it was instinct or maybe I just wanted Jacob to know I was capable, but the words just kept coming out. I might be older than all the other foundation doctors. I might be able to cut hair on the side, but I had studied hard and I knew what I was talking about. "Situation—a concise statement of the problem. Background—

pertinent and brief information related to the situation. Assessment—analysis and consideration of options."

We stopped and Jacob breezed into a small room just behind the nurses' station. Two people sat around the small table.

"Continue, Dr. Scott," Jacob said. I took a seat so I didn't fall down at him addressing me as doctor.

"Then finally Recommendation—action requested or recommended."

"Dr. Patel and Dr. Musa are a year ahead of you in the foundation program. They're going to be providing handover today. Who's first?"

Jacob was so in charge of this handover it was almost dizzying. He was blunt and to the point without being rude and best of all, he was *teaching*. Testing. Making us better. If I hadn't already slept with him, I'd be imagining what it would be like right around now. His manner was intoxicating.

The two foundation doctors in their second year started to give us a rundown of the patients and any changes overnight. I tried to focus by making copious notes.

We would be seeing four patients during the course of the shift when various test and scan results came in.

"Sounds like you had a good night. Thank you for your work. Go and get some rest," Jacob said. The weary doctors filed out like they were half asleep already.

Jacob's pager started to bleep. "Accident and Emergency need a consult. Let's let things get settled on the wards while we go down to A&E."

Moving at the speed of light, he swept through the door, forcing us to scramble after him again like chicks following their mother.

"How often do we get called down to A&E?" Gilly asked Jacob as we caught up to him at the lifts.

"It depends how often they need a peds consult," Jacob answered and frowned as if he just couldn't bear such an inane question.

The lift doors opened to reveal at least six people already in the lift. They shifted over to make space, but it was tight. Gilly dipped into a space on the left, leaving a slightly bigger space for Jacob and me. He stepped about halfway in and I slotted in in front of him, careful to stand as far forward as possible so there was no danger of us touching.

The lift doors closed and it was like something in the air shifted; all I could think about was the fact that Jacob was right behind me. I could feel his body heat, the sounds of his breathing filling my ears. I just wanted to spin around and push him against the wall and kiss him.

I was losing it.

I needed to focus. I took a deep breath in and tried to recall some acronyms.

We only travelled one floor down and the lift stopped. This lift was completely full now, there was no way there was room for anyone else.

The doors opened to reveal an elderly lady using a frame, alongside six or seven other people. Everyone in the lift shuffled backward to make room for her. Someone slipped in front of me, causing me to stumble backward— right into Jacob's chest.

He emitted a growl that vibrated between my legs.

"Sorry," I said as he took hold of my shoulders and set me back on my feet. His hands were larger than I remembered. They were warm and firm and I wanted to sink back and have them roam all over my body so I could memorize their feel.

The lift started moving again. We made it another two floors before the doors opened again. This time the lift was so full that the people waiting just tutted and eye rolled and let the doors slide shut again.

Jacob sighed and his breath reached the back of my neck. Instinctively, I tilted my head to the side, like my body wanted more and was positioning itself to bask in the slightest whisper of his sighs, like a flower shifting to face the sun.

Finally we made it to the bottom floor. When we got out of the lift, Jacob charged ahead. I'd walked all these corridors, trying to memorize the layout of the place, but each floor was set out differently. My spatial awareness was on a scale of bad to horrendous. I couldn't find my way out of a paper bag without Google maps.

We arrived at the nurses' station and got pointed in the direction of Bay 3.

The curtains were open and a very young woman sat in an orange plastic chair. Next to her was a baby dressed in a baby grow, kicking his legs and smiling. He looked happy enough, except his head was turned to the side. "I'm Jacob, one of the pediatric doctors here at the hospital," he said, introducing himself to the woman. "Can you tell me your name?"

"I'm Amy. And this is John," she said, nodding at her baby.

Jacob stepped over to the baby. "Good morning, John. I'm Jacob." When Dr. Off Limits was being sweet, I could melt all over the floor like ice cream in a heatwave.

Jacob stepped back and addressed Amy. "As we're a

teaching hospital, I have two new doctors with me today. Is that okay?"

Amy nodded.

"If at any time you feel uncomfortable, let me know and Dr. Peters and Dr. Scott will step out."

Amy nodded again.

Jacob smiled and turned back to Gilly and me. He looked between us. "Dr. Peters, what would you do first."

Gilly looked like a deer caught in the headlights. She clearly hadn't been expected to be put on the spot. "I . . . I'd . . . I'd order a scan," she said.

Jacob looked back to me. "Dr. Scott?"

I should mumble that I didn't know, but I didn't want this beautiful, clever, impressive man to think I was an idiot.

"John's blood pressure and temperature is normal. He's nine weeks old and the chart tells me he's in the fiftieth percentile for weight. He seems well to look at him." I turned to Amy. "Is he well in himself?"

She nodded.

"His head is turned significantly to his left." I turned to Amy. "Tell me why you came in today?"

"It's just his head. He doesn't move it. It's like it's fixed to the side." Her voice started to break.

"It's okay," I said. "You've done the right thing by bringing him here. When did you first notice that John's head was bending to the left?"

"It's hard to say," Amy said and she took a deep breath. "He likes to lie on the sofa and watch television. I noticed that if I turn him around, he just stares at the back of the sofa. He doesn't turn his head to the telly."

"Has that been since birth?" I asked.

"Maybe. I mean, I think so," she replied. "Not as bad as this. He used to look forward."

I nodded. "Was everything okay at his six-week check?"

She shrugged. "We've had to rearrange that a couple of times. I'm due to take him next week."

I nodded, trying to give her space to explain why she hadn't taken her baby to see a doctor for his six-week check. "And have you mentioned the issue to the health visitor?"

She shook her head, clasping and unclasping her hands. "She's not been for a few weeks. When she came before, he wasn't so bad."

"So it's become worse recently? Is that why you brought him in today?"

"He's been turned like that for a few weeks now. My mum saw him today and went mental. She said I had to bring him here."

I nodded. The poor girl. She couldn't have been much past eighteen herself. I had a suspicion that she hadn't seen a health visitor for more than a few weeks. They would have picked up on an issue like this before it had gotten so serious.

"Dr. Scott, what would your next steps be?" Jacob asked.

"I'd do a brief exam."

"Go ahead," he said.

I paused, expecting him to say that he was joking and that he'd take over. Then I nodded, set my iPad down on the spare chair, and pulled out some fresh gloves from my pocket. "Is it okay if I examine him?" I asked Amy.

She nodded, her eyes a little glassy. "Should I have brought him in sooner?"

"You're in the right place now. I'm just going to have a look at him. I won't hurt him," I reassured her.

I glanced up at Jacob and he gave me a nod. I needed to remember who I was. John was my first patient as a fully qualified doctor, and one I would remember forever. I stepped toward the cot. "Hi, John," I said. "I'm Sutton. I'm just going to have a little feel, if that's okay." John gurgled back at me and I took it to mean he didn't mind at all.

"Do you like tummy time?" I asked him.

"He hates it," Amy said. "He's much happier just lying on his back. We like to watch telly together."

I gave him a quick examination and found no unusual lumps or unevenness in his body or skeleton.

"You're a very happy little boy," I said. He was adorable with big, edible cheeks and a huge smile.

"He seems happy all the time," Amy said. "He doesn't seem bothered by his neck at all."

I finished my exam and stood back and glanced at Jacob.

"My next step would be to get physiotherapy down here," I said.

"Likely diagnosis?" Jacob asked.

"Congenital torticollis." Our eyes locked for a second. We'd talked about it during our dinner and how much Jacob enjoyed reassuring patients that their babies were going to be okay.

"What's that?" Amy asked, her voice breaking again. "Is he going to be okay?"

Jacob gave me a nod, and it was like he'd turned up outside my bedroom window with a boombox over his head.

"Yes," I said, trying to hide my relief at being able to tell her everything would be okay, and my pride at being the doctor who'd diagnosed John's issue. "It just means that in the womb, he got a bit too comfy in one position. And since he was born, he's still preferred that same position. We'll send the physio down and they'll give John and you some exercises to do. You'll have to make sure you do them just as the physio says and come back here for progress checks, but this condition resolves itself fairly easily in most cases."

Amy sucked in a breath and nodded. "Thank you so much."

This is why I'd worked so hard for so many years. So I could help people like Amy and John. It was clear Amy had been thinking the worst when with just a few physio sessions, John would be much better.

"Will you do me a favor, Amy?" I asked. She shook her head enthusiastically. "Tummy time can really help issues like this. It's ever so good for babies. I know he might not like it, but just keep trying. Try a few seconds every hour and build up. I'm going to have a health visitor pop in and visit you." I was pretty sure I'd covered everything. I glanced at Jacob.

"Do you have any questions?" Jacob asked. I'd forgotten that bit.

Amy shook her head. "Just . . . thank you."

"Okay, so we'll call the physio but there might be a bit of a wait," I said. "The nurses will keep you updated."

Jacob swept out and Gilly and I followed.

"Good job, Dr. Scott," he said as we headed back to the lifts.

"I see what you mean about it feeling good," I said without thinking.

He shot me a smile and then pressed the lift.

"What felt good?" Gilly said.

Shit, why couldn't I just have kept my mouth shut? "Just being able to reassure patients that it's nothing serious. You remember Wanda talked about it on our second day?"

"Did she? I don't remember," Gilly said.

"Dr. Peters, you need to take a breath before you launch into something," Jacob said. "Rely on your training and go through things logically. No need to skip ahead or you'll miss something."

"Yeah, first day nerves, I guess," she replied.

"You'll do better next time," Jacob said.

The lift doors opened and the three of us stepped into the empty lift. No need to worry about falling into Jacob Cove's hard, hot body.

Damn.

FOURTEEN

Sutton

Parker had gone above and beyond when it came to best friend duties over the last couple of months. Today was proof.

Hyde Park was my favorite park in London. There were just so many nooks and crannies to explore.

"It's like you planned this weather," I said as we found a spot overlooking the Serpentine.

"It's glorious," she said. We took either end of our picnic blanket and spread it out on the grass. "And yes, I got exactly what I ordered."

We sat and she put her Fortnum's canvas bag between her knees. "I've got all sorts of treats in here. I hope you don't mind, but Tristan might join us later. He's meeting someone for coffee but if he finishes up early, he's going to head over."

"Sounds good." Tristan was a great third wheel with Parker and me. He could pretend he was watching Bravo when he was really on his phone like a champ. He was also really good at pouring wine and getting us chocolate out of their huge pantry.

"But first . . ." Parker pulled out a bottle of champagne.

"Are we celebrating?" I asked.

"Of course! Your first week as a proper doctor. I feel like I haven't seen you in months. It's only been three weeks. We need to catch up. I want to hear everything. You seemed a bit disappointed in your messages during the first week. Is it better now that you've been out on the wards?"

This week had been good. Great even. I had survived being in close proximity to Jacob. Not that my attraction to him had dimmed at all. I couldn't see a time when it would. Hopefully it would get easier and he'd become like the old Leonardo Di Caprio poster I'd had on my bedroom wall as a teenager—gorgeous but out of reach. If I could make it through life without Leo, I could do the same with Jacob, surely?

"The first week wasn't bad. Just . . . lots of admin and the stress of being assigned to which doctor."

"Any hot docs?" she asked.

I groaned and fell back onto the blanket. I hadn't told Parker about Jacob. I'd been too busy focusing on *not* focusing on him, being angry because he wasn't Beau, then being terrified I'd be assigned to pediatrics. It had all been a bit of a blur.

"Yeah, actually. But he's strictly off-limits."

"You've got to stop denying yourself hotness. It's good to let loose a little. Tell me about Dr. Hot."

"It's a long story."

"It is?" Her eyes widened and she swiveled to face me.

"You know the date with Beau."

"Yeah. The one who was off to Africa. Or is in Africa by

now. You never told me how that went other than a quick, 'It was fine.'"

"It was a little more than fine," I confessed. "It was like . . . the best date ever." I closed my eyes and put my hands over my face. It was good to confess to someone—I felt like I'd been purged.

"Holy shit. How typical. And now he's in Africa."

If only.

"Turns out he's not in Africa." I said. "He's my boss."

Parker's jaw hit the floor repeatedly as I told her the entire story. About Jacob filling in for Beau, about the incredible sex and the almost-stroke I had when it turned out we worked at the same hospital.

"So it's not just you who thinks it's a bad idea to continue things between you?" Parker asked as I caught her up to speed on the last three weeks.

"No, thank goodness. We're both agreed that it absolutely can't happen."

"But if no one was to know?"

"Hospitals are gossip machines. And despite being made up of eight million people, London is a small place. Someone is bound to find out and neither of us is willing to take that risk. Except . . . it's difficult. He's—God, Parker, he's so sexy." Sexy was an easy label to attach to Jacob, but it was like saying Nadal was *okay* at tennis.

"I don't think it would be so bad if I didn't know he was such a great guy and . . . he . . . I mean . . . He knows what he's doing in bed." I was downplaying it. Jacob didn't just know what he was doing—he was the best sex I'd ever had. Dominant without being overbearing. Attentive without being weak. Dirty without being vulgar. I never thought sex could be quite so . . . connecting. An intimacy had developed between us in just a few short hours that shouldn't have felt possible if we'd been together years. It was equal parts exciting and terrifying.

"But this could be the love of your life," Parker said. "Another Jacob might not come around again."

I put my hands over my face. I couldn't think like that. I wasn't the girl who met the love of her life. Things didn't work out like that for people like me. I wasn't the only one who thought Jacob and I were a bad idea. Jacob agreed. He had his reasons too. It wasn't like if I changed my mind, I could run into his open arms. His arms were firmly crossed over his chest.

"It's not going to work out. I've just got to find a way of working alongside him without turning weak at the knees when he asks me a question or gives me a well done." I sat up and grabbed the bottle of champagne. "Let's have a drink and forget about it."

Parker held the champagne glasses and I poured. Out of the corner of my eye, I watched people in pedalos and rowing boats on the Serpentine, splashing and laughing and knocking into each other. Did Jacob ever come down here and lie in the boats to de-stress? Maybe I should suggest it to him.

Maybe not.

"I don't think we should forget about it," Parker said. "I know you want to be focused on work for the next couple of years, but there's never going to be a period of time when you go, 'Okay, the next ten years are looking rather empty, I'm off to find the love of my life.' It just doesn't work like that."

"I know, but medicine is important to me. I've worked hard to get here and I don't want to mess it up over a guy."

"There's always an excuse. Sometimes you have to close

your eyes and jump and trust that you'll land somewhere soft."

I loved Parker—like in the way sisters love each other in films. She was the only person in my life I trusted. The only one who hadn't let me down. But her advice made no sense. I didn't need to jump with my eyes closed to know I wasn't landing anywhere soft. Every time I so much as took a step, I hit hard concrete. That's how life had always been, and I'd long accepted it.

I knew the next few years would be tough. Anything that looked like an easy way out or a soft landing set alarms sounding in my head.

Jacob was the stuff of sirens blaring. I needed to keep away from him.

FIFTEEN

Jacob

Things were finally slotting into place for me. I just had to catch the head of pediatrics, Gerry, and get his sign-off before I started putting details of the offsite together.

I knocked on Gerry's door and squeezed into his windowless office.

"Jacob, have a seat, young man." Looking at Gerry, no one would ever think he was one of the most accomplished doctors in the hospital. His combined clinical and research experience alongside his connections in medicine made him one of those people that everyone in the hospital turned to for advice, no matter the specialty. If he didn't know—he knew someone who did.

"Thanks." I sat opposite him as he continued to scribble on various bits of paper in front of me. At least one of them would be for me. Gerry was constantly looking at ways in which we could all be working better. He looked, he listened, he commented, and things changed. He wasn't showy about it. He just quietly and constantly encouraged small changes that added up to big changes.

"I wanted to talk to you about something," I said.

"Good, good. Talk away."

"I have an idea for an offsite for all FY1 doctors."

He stopped his scribbling, sat back in his chair, and turned to face me. He made a humming sound, his trade-mark alert that he was thinking. It always reminded me of Yoda.

"I want to take all twenty-five of the FY1 doctors offsite for two days. We'll divide the program into three. First is 'If I knew then what I know now.' Deeply practical advice for young doctors from the people who have been there. Recently. So, I would want to involve some FY2s. What did you keep track of, how did you balance your life with study-ing? How did you cope with the lack of sleep, or if you were put in a morally difficult position? Chatham House rules would apply—whatever is shared in those sessions stays confidential."

Gerry stayed silent. If he'd hated the idea, he would have told me by now. I continued.

"The next section would be dealing with each other as colleagues. A lot of effort is now put into bedside manner, but we don't talk about how we get on with our colleagues. Year after year we get complaints from nursing and admin staff about the new doctors. We need to rub the edges off their aversion to anyone who isn't a fellow doctor.

"And then the third and final section, the tables turn a little bit. The idea is to run the offsite when they've been in the job about six weeks. They'll have gotten to grips with how the hospital works—and doesn't work. We survey them about one change they'd like to make. And then we give it back to them—how could they fix the problem and implement a change."

"Management consultancy for free?" Gerry asked. He nodded slowly. "I like it."

"All of it?"

"Most of it. I think we need to refine part two. We can't just roll in and say, 'Foundation doctors are renowned to be arrogant, knock it off.'"

I laughed. "No, but I'd like to."

"Maybe we do it in the context of improving their communication skills," Gerry said. "You could come up with some tasks for them to complete in a team."

"We could do that," I replied.

"How are the new lot shaping up?" he asked.

I thought back to the last week I'd spent on the wards with Sutton. She was by far the strongest of the four I'd worked with. But maybe I was biased. "I've only worked with the four in peds and so far it's a mixed bag."

"I've heard good things about Scott. Do you agree?" Nothing passed by Gerry. He identified the stars of every year and lured many of them into a pediatric specialty without much effort.

I nodded. "Seems very capable."

"Good. Good. And this offsite, you know I'm going to ask you about funding it all. I don't have the budget."

"No, but I found a hotel in Hertfordshire that would discount their rates for the NHS, and I've managed to fundraise the rest of it."

Gerry chuckled. "You mean, you're willing to write a cheque?"

I shrugged. "Maybe." I didn't like to talk about the money I'd made during university. It had been a fluke, and I didn't want it to define me.

"You really are after my job, aren't you?"

I laughed. "Absolutely not . . . until you're ready to retire."

"You're a good doctor, Jacob. A good man. I just hope you don't sacrifice everything for the job."

"I'm fine," I said. Gerry was always too invested in making sure all the doctors in pediatrics were settled in relationships.

"You're not getting any younger. You want children of your own, don't you?"

This was getting weird. "Is that a yes to the offsite if I can get it organized?"

"It's a yes so long as you approve the content with me first. And it's also a *get-yourself-a-love-life*."

I stood. "I'll make sure I work on both."

If only he knew that his rising star of FY1 was the only woman I'd been interested in for a very long time.

SIXTEEN

Sutton

I tugged on the handle of my overnight case, pulling the unwilling wheels over the uneven surface of the hospital road. I'd never heard of foundation doctors going on an offsite before. When we'd been emailed about it, Jacob had sent the message; the sight of his name in my inbox had felt like butterflies in my vagina.

But obviously the email had been *work* related. I certainly hadn't been hoping it was anything else. Absolutely not.

But an offsite? Some of those butterflies had taken up residence. They were interlopers. Squatters. They needed to be on their way. I just couldn't shift them.

"You want me to take your case for you?" Andy, one of the FY1s who had been assigned A&E, came up behind me as I headed up the steep hill toward the car park where we'd been told to meet the coach.

I nearly laughed but I saw he wasn't joking. "I'm good,

thanks. We're only going for one night. I've not brought anything too heavy."

"It's exciting, right?" he asked.

"Sort of," I said. Honestly, if they hadn't needed us in the hospital, I would have been happier to spend the day in bed. I wouldn't even need Netflix. As a hairdresser, I'd been used to being on my feet all day, but studying had turned the soles of my feet into wimps. I just wanted an extended period of time lying down.

"It's good to get out of the hospital," he said. "And the weather's great. Did you fill out your survey about the thing we'd most like to change?"

"I did."

"Are they going to pick the one most people talk about, do you think? And what are they going to do? Tell us they're going to fix it to improve morale?"

"Your guess is as good as mine," I said. The tail end of the coach came into view and I wondered if I was going to get stuck with Andy the whole ride to the hotel.

"I've put it into Google," he said. "The drive is less that forty-five minutes. Even in a coach."

"Good to know." Fact was, I'd Googled it too. I needed to know what I was walking into. I still wasn't sure. All I knew was that the hotel had a pool, so I packed my costume and tried not to think about Jacob being assigned a bedroom next door to mine.

As we climbed the hill, the rest of the coach came into view and I saw Jacob standing by the open door. Kill me now. He looked even more gorgeous than he usually did, wearing a bright white polo shirt and dark blue jeans, the casual attire topped with wayfarers. Why couldn't I have had sex with a really ugly, short, greasy man? Why did the guy I was set up on a blind date with have to be . . . Jacob?

"Andrew," he said, glancing from me to Andy and back again. "Sutton."

"Excited to be here," Andy said.

"We're here," a woman called from behind me. Gilly and Veronica came rushing toward the coach.

"What are you wearing tonight?" Gilly asked me the moment she was close enough to talk without yelling.

I looked down at what I was currently wearing and wondered whether or not I'd missed something in Jacob's email about a fancy dinner or something.

"There will be no need to change," Jacob said. "We're just having a barbeque in the gardens."

Thank goodness for that.

"But I have this beautiful one-shouldered top I bought especially," Gilly said.

Jacob's gaze flitted to mine. What was he thinking? Was he remembering that I'd worn a one-shouldered top on our date? Or how he'd almost ripped it off me before taking my breast in his mouth and—

I needed to stop thoughts like that immediately or I wasn't going to be able to make it through two days of being so close to Jacob outside the hospital.

Gilly gazed up at Jacob, practically stroking him. "I wouldn't want to waste it."

"On the coach," Jacob said. "There's plenty of room to spread out. You don't need to share seats."

I smiled as I climbed the coach steps, fantasizing to myself that Jacob had made the point that we could spread out because he didn't want me sitting next to Andy. But it wasn't like he was jealous. He could have any woman he wanted.

Anyone who didn't work at the Royal Free.

I bagged a seat on my own about halfway down the bus,

behind Veronica and Gilly. Within a few minutes, the coach had pulled off on our way to the hotel.

Veronica and Gilly chattered away, eventually giving up on including me in their comparison of the last few weeks when I didn't really offer much. They talked about what they did and didn't like and what they were hoping to get as their next rotation. Neither of them wanted pediatrics long-term. Truth be told, I wasn't sure whether or not I could see myself in pediatrics. I loved it, but it was rough seeing sick kids all day every day. But maybe it was always rough, no matter the age of the patient.

It was nice to sit down for a bit, catch up on emails and pay some bills. I'd taken an extra shift this week so I'd fallen behind with my life admin.

I glanced down the aisle of the coach and saw the top of Jacob's blond head at the front. His long, denim-covered leg stretched out into the space between the seats.

Was he as aware of me as I was of him?

It was like I had Jacob Cove radar on high alert all the time. I recognized his footsteps on the linoleum of the hospital floor. I knew his handwriting and his preferred way of shortening "attention" to "atten," and the way when he signed his name, the sweeping 'J' reminded me of the curve of his lips.

Our shifts didn't always coincide but when they did, it wasn't fear that spread through me anymore. It was relief. I loved working alongside him. He was a terrific teacher. I'd heard from some of the doctors on different rotations that plenty of consultants found FY1s irritating. Jacob seemed to really want the foundation doctors to learn, and he seemed to enjoy teaching them. I was a better student around him because I wanted to impress him. I found myself more engaged and less nervous because he was so committed.

The more time I spent around him, the more I wanted to be around him.

The more I wished we weren't working in the same hospital.

I was pretty sure I wasn't the only foundation doctor with a borderline obsession with Dr. Cove, but I might be the only one that had also seen him naked.

Maybe if we hadn't had that one night together, I wouldn't be so conscious of him. Perhaps I wouldn't think he was one of the most magnetic people I'd ever been around. But we had had that night together and now, despite those first few days of panic and regret, I was grateful I had.

Jacob shifted, leaned over the arm of his seat, and looked back down the coach. We locked eyes and I don't know what was the matter with me, but I couldn't look away.

And he didn't either.

It was as if time had frozen, and it was just him and me on that coach, trying to communicate how we wished things were different.

Things weren't different.

I offered him a small, sorrowful smile and he gave a long blink and nodded slowly.

The coach turning sharply brought us back into the moment. Jacob rose to his feet.

"Get your things together. This is the hotel."

I glanced out of the window to see a red-bricked, stately home sweep into view. I couldn't quite believe my eyes. I'd expected to be at an Ibis or Travelodge. Maybe it would be horrible when we got inside. Either side of the coach, swathes of carefully manicured green lawn stretched out as far as the eye could see.

"Before you ask, there will be no time for golf," Jacob bellowed from the front.

Wow, this was really nice. It was the kind of hotel more suited for a romantic break than an NHS offsite meeting. But I wasn't going to complain.

"Are we paying for this?" Gilly asked as Jacob stood up.

"Nope," he answered, without further explanation.

Our bags and cases were taken by hotel staff and we were guided straight into a conference room.

There were five round tables in the room, each with four or five chairs around them.

"Please take a seat at the table with the sign for your rotation," Jacob said.

I took a seat with Gilly and pulled out a notebook, ready for a day of listening and watching Jacob.

I wasn't sure if it would be heaven or hell.

SEVENTEEN

Jacob

The morning had gone well, but I was looking forward to getting out into the sunshine. I strode across the lawn toward the haystack maze, leading twenty-five foundation doctors like I was the pied piper. The morning had focused on learning from our mistakes and the most common issues for new foundation doctors. Most of it boiled down to communication, so this afternoon I had devised games that encouraged the doctors to understand the difficulty of communicating in a stressed environment and how it was important to do it anyway. I'd revised the program a little since I'd first spoken to Gerry, and as usual, him pushing me had made things better.

This morning, my gaze had wandered to Sutton more than it should have. It was completely subconscious. I was just drawn to her. She was quietly so determined and confident; it was palpable. She was one of the quieter members of the group. There were doctors like Gilly, David, and Thomas who made their presence felt. I'd learned a long time ago, they were rarely the best doctors. Sutton was the graceful swan in a pond full of over-excited minnows. She wasn't trying to stand out or get my attention—quite the opposite. But she had my attention anyway.

When I got to the haystacks, everyone fanned out in front of me. I slid on my sunglasses. Yes, the sun was out, but my shades were there to cover my subconscious pull toward Sutton. "I'm going to split you into teams of five. Each team will take one of the five activities. Each activity should take around three quarters of an hour to complete. There's a volunteer at each station to show you what to do. I'll be going between groups to observe."

The doctors stood in front of me, most of them nudging each other and swapping in-jokes.

"This activity is a haystack maze. You're going to have to find your way through to collect the prize at the center, then find your way out the other side. You'll be teamed up in pairs. One of you will be in the maze, blindfolded, with your hands tied together, and the other one will be standing on the tower, directing their partner." I nodded toward a platform overlooking the waist-high maze. Each of you will have a chance to direct *and* be blindfolded. It will be a time trial. Fastest couple wins."

Some people laughed and some people groaned. Sutton just stood there, also wearing her sunglasses, hands on her hips, as if ready for battle. She and I could have done something like this on our first date. It would have been fun. Although I wouldn't want to be pitted against her. I'd much prefer to have her on my team.

I picked the teams and they all went to their first stations. Sutton's first activity was the maze. I wanted to stick around and see how this went.

She turned to Andy and asked him to be her partner. I

knew Sutton had said she wasn't interested in a relationship because she wanted to focus on work, but I wondered if things had changed for her. Or whether they would. And would Andy be the guy by her side when they did? I couldn't think about it.

"You can be blindfolded," Sutton said. "I'll be your guide."

Andy shrugged and pulled out the blindfold while Sutton grabbed a map.

"Before you put the blindfold on, let's agree that you're only to take very small steps. Just half a foot in front of the other. That way we can avoid having to go backward."

"But it will be quicker if I use bigger strides."

"Not if you overshoot," Sutton said. "Then you'll have to go backward. Everything will go to shit. Just trust me on this." She was right. I wasn't sure Andy was the guy to listen, though. After a little more to-ing and fro-ing, she slipped the blindfold over Andy's eyes. Sutton positioned him at the entrance to the maze. She gave a little laugh, glanced at me, and then headed to the tower. I wasn't the only one watching her. Her colleagues were, too. This wasn't the time to have a moment.

Sutton refocused and began giving out instructions as Andy shuffled ahead, followed by a volunteer and then me.

She started strong, was confident in her delivery and successfully guided Andy around two corners.

"Stay still," she said. "I want you to turn to your right ninety degrees. Shuffle around."

"Now move forward?" Andy asked.

"Yes, it's about half the distance that you went before. Take it slow."

"Stop," she said. "Now stay on the stop and shuffle

right." Andy turned left. "No, wrong direction, the other way."

"Are you sure?" Andy asked.

"I'm sure," Sutton said.

"But we just turned that way," Andy argued. What was he doing? Why wouldn't he just listen to what Sutton said. She was the eyes in this partnership.

"You need to trust me to be able to see where you're going. You need to turn one hundred and eighty degrees clockwise."

"Really?" He sighed and pivoted right as instructed. Finally.

"Now move forward," Sutton said. "Keep going."

Andy shuffled forward.

"Stop," Sutton instructed. "Now ninety degrees anti-clockwise."

"Surely we're back where we started."

Sutton started to laugh the most delightful laugh, and I had to fight back a smile at the way her face lit up and her ponytail swished behind her as she tipped her head back. I wasn't sure if she was laughing with him or at him. "Now reach forward with both hands." In front of Andy, on a pedestal, was a tennis ball. I moved onto another group in case I could be accused of fixating on Dr. Sutton. Which I seemed to be.

Only another few months and she'd be moving on to a different specialty. Lucky them. It was only a few weeks in, but I was pretty sure she would be the star of her year just like I'd been the star of mine.

I moved onto the second activity, which was a game where everyone sat in a line about a meter apart. The first person in the line was given step-by-step written instructions on how to make a simple Lego house. The last person

in the line was given the Lego bricks. The written instructions couldn't be passed through the line. Instead, the
instructions had to be communicated down the line of five
people and finally given to the person responsible for
building the house. They were about halfway through the
build. It at least looked a little like a house, but the colors
were wrong and they were missing important elements.

I glanced back at the haystacks activity and as I did,
Sutton looked over her shoulder and right in my direction.
She had her sunglasses on so I couldn't be sure she was
looking at me, but something told me this undeniable pull I
felt wasn't a one-way street. I didn't know if that was a good
thing or a bad thing. To some extent, it was comforting to
know it wasn't just an unrequited feeling, but on the other
hand, believing she felt the same made it all the more difficult to resist her.

But I had to resist. My next career move couldn't
happen if I was dating an FY1. Even if I thought it was a
good idea to pursue things between us, she'd pushed me
away when we'd last kissed. She didn't want things to go
any further either.

So here we were, stuck in our respective purgatories.

After forty-five minutes, everyone changed stations and
I went on to an activity which was all about body language
and empathy. One by one each participant had a private
consultation with a "patient" with an easily identifiable
disease. After the consultation was over, the doctor would
be asked what they thought the disease was and why. And
then they were asked how the patient was feeling. Identi-
fying the emotion of the patient, rather than the disease,
was the point of the exercise. They had to remember that
communication wasn't just about words.

This was going to stump many of the doctors. Medicine

attracted bright, focused people, which was a double-edged sword. Many of those who possessed those skills were exactly the wrong people to be doctors. Empathy was a key component in medicine and often one that went particularly overlooked in a hospital setting.

There was also a river-crossing game, with a time critical element that tried to foster good communication while under pressure. Lastly there was a treasure hunt that involved all the teams.

Just before the treasure hunt, I headed to the loo. I'd spent most of the afternoon observing the groups that didn't include Sutton so when I looked up to find her coming toward me, I was a little caught off guard. Over the course of the afternoon, I'd gotten used to not seeing her and now, as she approached, it was like being struck around the head with a frying pan. Her perfect hourglass shape, emphasized by her t-shirt tucked into her jeans, set off electrical impulses in my fingertips. My body buzzed with the need to touch her. As she came closer, my heart began to constrict and seemed to lift. I tried to suck in a breath, to calm down the physiological response I had to Sutton so I didn't end up passing out before we came face-to-face.

As she neared, she gave me a small smile and headed back to the others without even uttering a word.

Just the sight of her had me dissolving into a physical mess.

What was this woman doing to me?

EIGHTEEN

Sutton

I hadn't been swimming since I started med school, but I wasn't going to pass up an opportunity to take twenty minutes for myself to do a couple of laps in a posh hotel pool. As a child I'd found a way to creep into the local leisure center for free. There was a back entrance where the staff took cigarette breaks and if I timed it correctly, usually around eleven in the morning, the door would be propped open but there'd be no one around. Sometimes I'd have to wait for up to an hour to find a lull in the nicotine-addicted staff's schedule, but over the six-week summer holidays where I had nothing to do other than get out from under my mother and her new boyfriend's feet, it didn't matter what I did, as long as I wasn't at home. Usually I'd leave the house before she was awake and come back late in the evening, just to avoid the arguments.

As a hairdresser, I'd still swum but when I'd taken up studying, anything extracurricular was sacrificed. It felt good to put my costume back on. It was a perfect place to reintroduce myself to some breast stroke.

The ladies' changing room was the nicest place I'd ever been other than the hotel bedroom I'd been allocated. When they'd given me the key and I'd made my way through the maze of corridors on the first floor, I thought there'd been some sort of mistake. But the key fit and I was in a huge room, with views of the golf course, a roll-top bath, and a bed the size of a tennis court.

We didn't have long until dinner. Most people were meeting in the bar right away, but Jacob might be there too and I didn't want to spend any more time in his presence than I had to. Swimming seemed a better distraction.

The changing rooms went straight out into the pool area. Thankfully, there was just one swimmer in the far lane, making laps of the pool like it was his job. The pool was long but only two lanes wide. I'd slip into the nearest lane and do some old-lady swimming.

The water was freezing cold and I sank up to my neck and started to swim without putting my head under. I warmed up quickly and leisurely made it to the other end of the pool and turned around. I figured the Olympic swimmer in the lane next to me was doing about three laps for every one of mine. On my third lap, I got to the end at the same time as the other swimmer. As soon as I turned to face him, the short, blond hair gave him away.

Jacob.

I was almost naked a meter away from the very man I was trying to stay distracted from.

He pushed his goggles up onto his head and stood, the defined muscles of his chest covered in droplets of water not helping my heartrate. "Hey. I didn't realize it was you."

I stopped swimming but kept crouched so I was still neck-deep in water. "Hey. I didn't realize you'd be here."

"Yeah." He pushed his hand over his head and his goggles fell off. I caught them and tossed them back at him. "Thanks."

"I thought you preferred outdoor swimming?"

He grinned, a smile I'd only ever seen outside the hospital. "I like the Heath, but the temperature here is much better."

"I haven't swum for the longest time. Before I started studying."

"Before?" He looked at me as if I'd misspoken. "Did you ever stop?" Because we'd sworn off medicine as a topic of conversation at dinner, he wouldn't have known, unless he'd looked carefully at my CV, that I'd come up an unconventional route. It gave me some comfort that the rest of the consultants at the Royal Free might not have checked my CV either. Maybe I really would be able to stay under the radar.

"Yeah, I left school at sixteen. Went into hairdressing before I decided to change route."

He nodded. "That actually explains a lot."

My heart sank at his cruel comment but I gave a one-shouldered shrug, trying to act like it didn't cut bone deep. I looked away and down the length of the pool, wondering whether it would be rude to swim off before he could see how upset I was.

"I mean you were really impressive out there," he said, then he glanced away too. "I shouldn't have said that. It's just you stood out head and shoulders above the rest, and I couldn't figure out whether it was just because of . . . you know, us. But it makes sense that you didn't come straight through. You have a wisdom, a practicality, an empathy that these other FY1s don't have."

Now I had to fight to cover my blush. "Would you like a blow dry with your appendectomy?"

Jacob didn't smile at my joke. "Don't do that. Don't give people ammunition because you don't want them to use it first."

"Why not?" I was resigned to the inevitable jokes and sneers I'd get from my peers once they found out, but it wouldn't break me. I'd survived a lot worse from my mother. "It is what it is."

He stepped closer. "The way you handle yourself in the hospital is impressive. The way you logically think through every situation shows maturity. It shows life experience. You're a good doctor."

"Thank you," I said. "I think after four months being taught by you, I'm definitely going to be a better one." I couldn't think of anyone I'd rather learn from. Jacob was patient but firm, clever and kind and respected by all his colleagues. Was there a better teacher?

"It's my job," he said. "But thank you."

I skimmed my arms across the surface of the water in a circle around me.

"You want to race?" he asked, grinning.

"With you?" I frowned. "Are you kidding? I've seen your body, remember."

He laughed. "How could I forget?" We locked eyes and it felt like I'd taken a seat in a chair that had been made for me. His gaze was comfortable, easy and just right, even though it was oh-so-wrong.

"I try and avoid you," I blurted, like he'd pressed an honesty button on the side of the pool.

"I try and avoid you too," he replied. "It's not working so well, is it?"

"First rotation, first shift and now this? I mean . . ." I looked up to the ceiling. "Whoever's up there took the month off."

"Or maybe not," he said. His lips curved in a deliciously sexy way. I tried to remember if I'd noticed that about him at the restaurant, or whether I'd been in sensory overload being seated next to him. There was so much else to notice.

"You think God just doesn't like me?" I asked.

Jacob groaned. "No, it's not that. We just . . . keep getting thrown together. I wasn't even supposed to be your date that night and now we work together and we're here together and we're almost naked in the water together. That's a lot of coincidences."

"Oh, you think God has a plan," I said.

"I have a plan," he mumbled.

"What?"

He shook his head. "I just don't know how strong my self-control is. You might have to be strong for both of us soon."

"Oh no," I said. "You can't rely on me. I'm here, trying to avoid you in case anyone can see how much I—" I stopped myself before I could say too much. I sank back up to my neck in water again.

"How much you . . .?"

I took a deep breath. "You don't want me to answer that. This is a dangerous conversation."

"That's the problem. I really, really want you to answer that question."

The line between us was fading fast. As much as I wanted to erase what was left, there was too much at stake. I took a step back. "Jacob. We both have our reasons for why we think this isn't a good idea."

"Fuck," he spat. "I know. I need to cool off. Or something."

"You stay here while I get out. I'm just old-lady swimming. You look like . . . like a professional."

He glanced down at me in the water and I couldn't have felt more naked. I wanted to take a step and reach out to smooth my hands around his neck, link my legs around his waist. I wanted to lick his wet skin and press my body against his. I wanted to push my hand into the front of his shorts and circle my fingers around his cock so it grew hard in my hand. I figured he could have my costume off in less than half a second, his mouth on me in less than a second, be inside me in less than ten.

"Shit, I can tell what you're thinking just by looking at you."

I covered my face with my hands. "I've got to get out of here." I backed away.

"Go," he said, putting his goggles back on. "I can't go anywhere right now." Despite his size, he gracefully dipped under the water and headed back down to the other end of the pool. I watched for one then two seconds, then headed back to the changing rooms. Swimming was supposed to distract me from Jacob, but it had done nothing but fuel embers now sparking into flames inside of me.

NINETEEN

Sutton

If it hadn't been for Gilly pounding on my door, I would have spent the evening in a beautiful hotel room in front of Netflix. I told her I wasn't feeling well but it didn't work. She wasn't taking any excuses.

"We get to spend time with McDreamy. You can't just spend the evening in your room. I'm not taking no for an answer."

After my swim, I'd showered and blow-dried my hair, but I was in a robe when Gilly arrived.

"I've got no makeup on."

"You have perfect skin. Put some mascara on. It's all you need."

"I'm not even dressed."

She didn't comment. She just put a hand on her hip. I sighed and pulled out some jeans and a t-shirt.

Gilly was dressed up in a short skirt, a skin-tight polo, and heels. I hadn't even thought to bring anything dressy. I pulled on my jeans and a Madonna t-shirt I'd had since the salon.

"You think Jacob likes heels?"

"I have no idea," I said, slipping my feet into ballet flats.

"He's single, right?"

"How would I know?" I countered.

"Not for long," she said and gave me a wink, before I grabbed the plastic key card and my phone from the dressing table and shooed her out the door.

Dinner was a buffet. Jacob and I managed to stay at opposite ends of the room with our backs to each other for at least an hour. It was all I could hope for.

"I'm going to bed," I said.

Gilly fixed me with a stare. "No, you're not. I simply won't allow it. Will you, Veronica? We get no time off to do anything nice together. We're going to have a couple of cocktails and mingle with our colleagues."

"Cocktails sound good," Veronica said.

"Mine's a sex on the beach with Dr. Cove," Sara, another one of the FY1s, said.

"I'll fight you for him," Gilly said.

"Who are you fighting over?" Andy came over to our table and leaned on the back of mine and Gilly's chairs. "Because there's plenty of me to share around."

"I'm going to the bar," I announced, standing. All this talk of Jacob as if he were a prize to be won had changed my mind. Maybe I wanted to see how he interacted with the likes of Gilly and Sara. Maybe he'd have to hold himself back with them like he'd had to hold himself back today at the pool. Maybe I wasn't special and Jacob Cove was a walking hormone.

When I turned around, Jacob had already left his table. Maybe he wouldn't even go to the bar. Why would he want to hang out with a bunch of twentysomethings he had to work with? He was probably tucked up in bed with Netflix, the way I wished I could be.

One cocktail, and then I'd be heading to bed as well.

We wandered into the bar and found Jacob sitting talking with one of the FY1s I hadn't spoken to before—a short, Asian girl called Lucy. She was pretty. Even though I knew I couldn't have him, and even though it was me who had sworn off all relationships, a wave of jealousy swept through me. He wasn't going to start dating Lucy—I was confident about that much. But he would start dating someone. Eventually.

Someone who wasn't me.

Gilly came over, asked me to order her a cosmo, and then left me at the bar as she went over to join Jacob and Lucy. There might just well be a fight over that blond beauty tonight. But neither one of them would win.

Andy let me cut in front of him.

"Can I get a cosmo and a glass of red wine, please. Andy? What would you like?"

"I'm fine. I'll sort myself out."

"Coming right up," the barman said.

"Did you enjoy today?" Andy asked as we stood next to each other at the bar.

Enjoy wasn't a word I'd use. Being so close to Jacob all day was conflicting. I had to spend every minute of the day fighting my instincts to be near him, touch him, kiss him. And now knowing he was fighting it too? It was worse. The knowledge was like slow burn acid, corroding my logical thoughts. I knew it was ridiculous to think about giving into our desires. Doing so had the power to hurt us both . . . but the desire and need in me was rising with every passing moment.

"It certainly wasn't what I was expecting when I got my acceptance paperwork," I replied noncommittally. I glanced over at Jacob, who was talking to both Lucy and Gilly now. Gilly had broken out her best hair flip.

"You're a great communicator," he said. "And a really good listener."

I smiled. I didn't know whether or not to confess my first chosen profession. I'd had plenty of practice listening to people tell me the most intimate details of their lives, from cheating on their husbands to secretly hating their children. And in between there was a lot of talk about holidays and work drama. My clients didn't need anything from me but a haircut and a friendly nod of the head. Medicine was completely different in most ways, but there were a few similarities.

"Did you enjoy it?" I asked.

Andy told me what he'd enjoyed about the day, which was most things, as fit his enthusiastic nature. The barman presented our drinks then took Andy's order.

"Sounds like you got a lot out of the day." I nodded at my drinks. "I better get Gilly's cocktail to her."

"See you over there."

I avoided looking at Jacob as I took Gilly's drink over.

"Thanks," she said, taking the cocktail from me. "Sit down."

Gilly and Lucy were sitting in the two seats opposite Jacob. The only seat left was on the small sofa next to him.

Gilly clocked my hesitation. "Don't even think about slipping off to your room." She turned to Jacob. "Can you believe I found this one about to head to bed? She wasn't even going to come down for dinner." She shook her head like I was the stupidest person she'd ever met. I took a seat as far away from Jacob as possible without sitting on the arm of the sofa. As soon as I sat, he crossed one ankle over his knee, the movement shifting the air. I took in his musky, clean scent that had embedded itself into my sheets after our date. Shit. I should have given Gilly her drink and told her I was in the middle of a conversation. But here I was, sitting right next to the very man I was trying to avoid.

"We were just saying what an amazing day it's been. I've learned so much."

"Sooo much," Lucy added. "I just know it's going to really help my soft skills with patients and make me think about how I'm communicating during handovers. You know what I mean?"

I nodded. Wow, they were really sucking up.

"What about you, Sutton?" Jacob asked, a twinkle in his eye that told me he was up to no good. "Did you learn anything?"

"Absolutely," I said. "Lots of things."

"Like what?" Lucy asked.

I sighed. "You can't tell what people are thinking unless you communicate properly."

"Yes, no one teaches mind-reading at med school." Gilly laughed like she was having the best time in the world.

"What else?" Jacob asked. He was pushing this, and I couldn't tell whether he was trying to be provocative— trying to get me to confess something—or whether he was genuinely interested in getting feedback.

I shrugged. "I'm a really bad swimmer?"

"Did you check out the pool?" Lucy asked excitedly. "I brought my swimsuit so I'm really hoping I can squeeze in a dip before sessions start tomorrow."

"Oh, I didn't realize there was a pool," Gilly said. "How did you find out about that?" she asked. She and Lucy began to talk about the website and swimming. I could feel

Jacob's gaze on me but I couldn't bring myself to meet it. My self-control was hanging by a thread as it was; one wrong move and it would snap and smash into pieces on the floor.

"You're not a bad swimmer," he mumbled under his breath.

The heat of my blush crept up my neck and over my cheeks. It was barely a compliment. I just didn't want to think about swimming. About Jacob almost-naked in the pool just a few feet from me. About all the things I was missing out on because of Jacob and our stupid rules.

"Don't you think, Jacob?" Gilly asked.

"About what?" Jacob asked.

"We should do this kind of offsite every year."

Jacob chuckled. "Nice thought. I had to sell two fingers to get the hospital to agree to this one."

Gilly gasped and grabbed Jacob's hand. Something primal in me stirred. She better get her hands off of him.

Jacob took it in his stride and pulled his hand away and held up both, wiggling his fingers. "A figure of speech. It's the least impactful on the hospital to have FY1s out this early in their program. There's no way we could repeat this."

"Is this the first time there's been an offsite for FY1s?" I asked. I was forced to look at Jacob.

He met my gaze and nodded. "Yup. If it's successful, I hope it will be an annual thing."

"How are you measuring success?" I asked.

A small grin tugged at the corners of Jacob's mouth.

I couldn't stop myself from asking him about it. "What's funny?"

"Nothing. It's just a very typical question from you."

"Typical?" Gilly and I chorused.

He shrugged. "Insightful. Probing. But to answer your question, we're measuring success a couple of ways." His voice shifted slightly into that authoritative timbre he had that told everyone around him he was in charge. I squeezed my legs together. "Firstly, the results of the participant survey. Second, whether we can successfully workshop an issue for the medical staff that will make life better and make the hospital run more effectively and efficiently. And then thirdly, if the consultants responsible for the foundation doctors notice a shift in the approach of the doctors coming out of these couple of days."

"I'm definitely shifting my approach," Gilly said.

"Time will tell," Jacob said.

"So all this was your idea? The offsite I mean?" I asked.

"Yeah. This year is sort of a trial run."

I nodded. Doctors weren't famous for enjoying soft-skills training. It must have taken a lot of effort to convince the hospital to put this on, not to mention taking twenty-five doctors off the rotas. He must feel passionately about the benefits of taking us offsite like this.

"Don't worry," Gilly said. "We'll give you a really high score."

There was no doubt Jacob Cove scored highly. On every measure.

"Okay, I'm going for more drinks," Lucy said. "What can I get everyone?"

"I'll have another cosmo," Gilly said.

I caught Jacob's eye. Was he sticking around? If I couldn't have him, I didn't want anyone flirting with him. It was completely irrational and immature, but I wanted him to go up to his room. I didn't want Gilly having any piece of him.

"Another red wine?" Lucy asked me.

"I'm okay for now, thanks."

"Jacob?" Lucy asked.

He shook his head. "I'm going to head up in a minute."

"Oh, stay," Gilly said. "We want to hear all the hospital gossip."

Jacob uncrossed his legs and leaned forward, sliding his beer bottle onto the table. "I'm the last person to come to for gossip. I never hear any." He stood. "Have a good night. Make sure you're fresh for an 8am start."

I was part relieved and part disappointed. It was good that he was going, but at the same time, I wanted him to stay.

A couple of minutes later, the scent of musk and fresh linen crept up on me and I turned to find Jacob leaning over the sofa.

"I left my phone," he said. Our faces were just centimeters apart. "Can you get it for me?"

Gilly grabbed it before I had a chance.

"When I leave, check your phone," Jacob whispered under his breath so quietly I barely heard him. Gilly wobbled around the table to hand the phone to Jacob.

"Thanks, Gilly." He glanced at me once and then headed back out.

Check my phone?

Had I imagined that he'd just said that?

"He's so hot," Gilly said. "And he has the biggest hands."

I pulled my mobile out from my jeans pocket and saw a new message. Jacob and I hadn't texted since the day I started at the hospital. But now there was no mistaking a brand-new text from him.

Room 124

My stomach somersaulted, dived, crashed and somersaulted again.

His intention was clear. He wanted me to come to his room. His self-control had finally disintegrated. I just needed to figure out if I had enough left for both of us.

TWENTY

Jacob

I pulled off my t-shirt and tossed it onto the bed. I couldn't decide whether I should jump in the shower and try to cool off or wait to see if Sutton acted on my message.

I'd had enough of denying myself. I wanted her. Yes, it was wrong. Yes, if anyone found out, it could be catastrophic to my plans of taking over the foundation program, but I couldn't bring myself to care enough. Sutton was clever and insightful and patient and funny. And she was sexy as hell. I couldn't pretend I didn't want her anymore.

I didn't know if she'd come to my room. If she did, I didn't know when she'd arrive, but I hoped it was soon.

I switched on the TV and flipped through the channels before grabbing a bottle of water from beside the bed. Then I clicked off the TV in case I didn't hear her knock.

Fuck! What had happened to me? This woman I'd spent one night with was driving me to make decisions that could affect the rest of my career. I knew that. It was a terrible idea if she turned up at my door, but it didn't stop me wanting her.

My phone told me it was ten minutes since I'd gotten to my room. Twelve minutes since I sent her the message.

How long did I give it before I gave up on her coming after me? An hour? Two? Never?

A knock at the door interrupted my thoughts and my knees weakened at the thought of who was waiting behind it.

I took a breath, strode across the room, and swung the door open.

She glanced sideways and then met my gaze. There was a warmth in her eyes I only saw when she was looking at me. I pulled her inside and she backed up against the closed door.

Finally.

She was here.

Far from feel wrong—it felt exactly right. Being near her was like finding a solution to an impossible puzzle, like finally seeing in focus after being surrounded by a blur of colors.

"What are we doing?" she asked.

"It's one night," I said.

She took a breath and shook her head. "You know that's not true. We've *had* one night. A night of too little sleep and too much great sex isn't going to change anything. It's not like we got it out of our systems the first time."

She was right. I'd not thought beyond having her to myself again in a private space where there weren't a hundred pairs of eyes on us.

"I want you," I said, like some kind of sex-crazed neanderthal. It was the only thing I could think to say.

"I want you too," she said. "But there's so much at stake."

"I know," I said, shoving my hands into my jeans pocket.

"And did you have to open the door shirtless?"

She wrinkled her nose in a way that said she was trying very hard to be turned off by my naked chest but it wasn't working.

"No one will know," I said, not even caring if that was true. "It's one night."

She stepped toward me and hooked her fingers into the waistband of my jeans. A shudder passed down my spine at her touch. "It's not though," she said.

I swept my thumb over her bottom lip and she closed her eyes. I cupped her neck with my hand. "Look at me." She did what I asked and I recognized the expression of someone who'd given in.

Her rules and reasons why we shouldn't had been overridden.

For tonight at least.

"Honestly," I said. "It doesn't feel like one night is going to . . ."

"Cure you?"

The corners of my lips twitched. "Maybe there is no cure. Maybe all we can do is try and relieve the symptoms."

"What do you prescribe, Dr. Cove?"

"Kissing," I replied. I bent down and pressed a kiss to the corner of her lips, groaning at the wave of relief that crashed over me at finally getting to kiss her again. I reached around her waist, down over her arse, and lifted her. Spinning her around, I threw her on the bed and crawled over her. "Lots of kissing." I dipped to place kisses on her collarbone, up to her neck, then licked over the seam of her lips.

"This isn't helping," she said.

I pressed my tongue into her mouth, dipping and exploring, wanting to make the kissing part last as long as possible. I desperately wanted it to dull the ache I'd carried since I'd been with her the first time.

I pulled out her t-shirt from her jeans, my hands enjoying the smooth skin of her stomach. "This was my favorite Madonna era," I said, working my way down to her stomach, placing kisses like breadcrumbs as I went.

"Me too," she said. "Borderline is her best work." She groaned as I unzipped her jeans and pulled them off. "Is nakedness part of the cure?"

"Absolutely. It's vital for me to perform a thorough examination so I can provide the best treatment."

I stripped off her underwear and pressed my thumb over her clit and circled. She propped herself up on her elbows and shook her head.

"No?" I asked.

"I'm just so wound up, I think I'll . . ."

I groaned at the thought of her desperate for me for all these weeks. I stroked down her folds, finding her as wet as rain. "Fuck, Sutton."

"I know," she said, shaking her head as if disappointed in herself.

I stood and stripped off my jeans while she pulled Madonna over her head.

"This was going to happen," I said, trying to make her feel better. "I don't fucking believe in fate, but inevitability came at us like a freight train."

"It feels that way," she said, reaching for me. "And now?"

"And now I commence a full body exam."

She laughed, the sound so sweet and pure I wanted to

cheer that I finally got to drink it in, bathe in it. I finally got to enjoy being with her.

I pressed a kiss between her breasts, kneading a nipple between my thumb and forefinger. She arched against me and I soothed the pinched nipple with my tongue as I took the other between my fingers.

"Jacob," she whispered, her voice breathless though I'd barely begun.

I stroked down her body, wanting to know it all. So many times over the last couple of weeks, I'd tried to remember exactly the curve of her hip or the dip above her collarbones. How exactly had she tasted, smelled, sounded as she came? I wanted to commit it all to memory. I knew I wouldn't be satiated tonight and I was resigned to the fact that as soon as the sun rose, I'd want her again, tomorrow and the next day and the day after that. But if she decided tonight was the last time we'd be together, I wanted to memorize every square centimeter of her. I needed to know her body, mind, and soul, but if I was forced to choose tonight, I was going to focus on her body.

Her mind and soul, she could keep.

For now.

I licked and sucked, kissed and stroked my way down her body, avoiding her clit to ensure she didn't boil over too soon.

"I'm not sure I'll survive tonight," she said.

"I'll look after you."

"Such a good doctor," she said on a sigh.

I crawled over her and then she gave my shoulder a gentle push so I rolled to my back. She kneeled up and took my cock in her hand from where it lay rigid on my stomach.

"You've shown me how," she said. "Now it's my turn to examine you."

She pushed her beautiful, glossy brown hair over her shoulder and at right angles to me, leaned forward, taking my crown in her mouth.

Fuck. I'd waited too long for this. Too long to feel her silky skin against mine, far too many days to see the way her body moved with such grace. It didn't matter if it was yesterday, I'd been deprived of feeling how wet she was for me.

She circled my crown with her tongue before taking me deep in her mouth. So deep, I felt the back of her throat and the delicious sensation when she swallowed. If I was in heaven, I was happy to die right there.

Panic took over as my orgasm began to stir. Fuck, I wasn't ready. Not nearly ready.

I stroked my hand along her back and over her arse. It was meant to interrupt her but she moaned, and the feeling around my dick lit a fire inside me. I didn't want her to stop. I wanted to come and then fuck her again.

And again.

And again.

I smoothed my hand down her back again and this time, I pushed my hand over her bottom and between her legs, coating myself in her wetness. I tried to think of something else. Gilly's stupid cocktail. Andy appearing at Sutton's side like a lap dog. I just needed to hold off for just a few seconds until I could bring her with me. She seemed more turned on than before and I shifted slightly so I could push my fingers through her folds and reach her clit. The nerve endings had been fed by her blood supply and it had grown plump. I pushed my thumb into her and she froze as I circled my middle finger over and around, down and up her clit.

Her breathing was quick and short. "I'm not going to . . ."

"Me neither," I replied.

"I want you to come in my mouth," she said.

I groaned. She was killing me.

She wasted no time making it happen. She licked up my shaft in one big stroke as I moved my hand in and out, up and down, unsure if it was her whimpering with my cock in her mouth or the feel of her all over my hand that had my orgasm sprinting toward the finish line.

She reached her hand across my chest and I grabbed it; we grasped each other like our lives were on the line.

I couldn't hold back a second more and pushed my hips up, up, up, emptying myself into her. She shuddered on my hand, her back arching as her orgasm tore through her at almost the exact same time.

She sagged beside me, boneless and defeated.

We'd tried to keep away from each other. We'd failed.

After a few moments she sighed. "Are we cured?"

"Not even close."

"We need to have a clear head for tomorrow," she said. "This offsite is important to you."

My heart squeezed at her thoughtful, caring mind. "It is."

"The bar closes at eleven. I'll stay until twelve thirty and then leave. You need to sleep."

I groaned. "What time is it now?"

"Half nine."

"Three more hours?" I asked. "I want you to stay all night."

"We don't want to fuck this up for ourselves. We're going to need to think about the long game." She sighed. "Though if we were really thinking long-term, we wouldn't be here—"

"Don't say that," I said. She couldn't regret this. I wouldn't let her.

"I'm here," she said, stroking her hand down my chest. "And I want to be here. But if it's possible, I'd like this to stay between us. It serves neither of us if this gets out."

"Agreed," I said.

"So if we're giving into this, we need to have rules and boundaries and retain some self-control."

"You mean no dry-humping you at the nurses' station?"

She laughed and I shifted above her.

"I love that laugh," I said, pressing a kiss to her neck.

"I love that you love it."

She gazed up at me and I swept the hair from her head, tracing the contours of her face with my fingers. She was so beautiful; it was almost overwhelming.

"Shit," I said, falling backward on the mattress. "I haven't brought any condoms. I was determined not to need them."

"How's that working out for you?"

She pushed herself up and lifted a leg over me so she was straddling me. "I got a load of tests done just before I started—I knew I wouldn't have time once the program got underway. Everything's fine with me and I'm on the pill."

"I've not had sex since my last test results. So . . ."

She lifted herself up and wrapped her fingers around my base, guiding me inside her.

I nearly dissolved at the feel of her around me. "You feel so fucking good." I choked out the words, almost overcome at how amazing she was. She was every one of my teenage fantasies made real and then some. I smoothed my hands over her hips and she pressed her palms onto my stomach.

"I think if I move, I might break," she said, tipping her head back and gasping. "I'm so full."

"Shit, Sutton. If you say stuff like that, I'm going to last as long as a thirteen-year-old boy in a lingerie shop."

"I want to stay like this forever," she said. "It's just so good." She moved. Tiny movements, just enough to hypnotize me with the sway of her breasts as they bounced, round and high on her chest.

I pulled her down firmly, pushing myself as deep into her as I could. She cried out. "So deep."

The room tilted. For a flash, I was grateful I hadn't met Sutton earlier. If I had, all the energy I'd put into my studies over the years would have been channeled into wooing her, seducing her, fucking her, and thinking about fucking her again. There would have been no Dr. Cove. No making consultant early. All my goals and ambitions would have been about her.

She moved again, and I tried not to focus on how her chestnut brown hair hung around her shoulders, her nipples peeking out from underneath it, tempting me. I couldn't resist. I cupped her breasts, kneading them together, flicking her nipples, making her moan and writhe on my dick.

"Jacob," she bent over me, her sharp nipples grazing my chest, the change in angle sending me half crazy. "Like this is so good."

I couldn't take any more. I grabbed her bottom and slid off the bed, carrying her. I sat her on the dressing table, in front of the mirror, so I could see the slit between her arse cheeks as I plowed into her. "We don't have enough time," I said. "I want you against every wall, in every position twice."

Her reflection in the mirror behind meant I got to see her from every angle. All of her all at once. And she was beautiful and sexy in every one. When I got home, I was getting my bedroom mirrored—ceiling, floor, and every wall

—as a matter of priority, and then I was taking a month of sick leave so I could fuck Sutton in there every opportunity I got.

She lifted her feet and rested them on the side.

"It's deeper," I growled.

She whimpered. "It's too much and so good."

Sweat gathered at my brow as I pushed up into her, trying to will away the orgasm threatening all too quickly.

She wrapped her arms around my neck, pulling me close to her as she convulsed under me, her lips pressed against my shoulder.

I let go, pushing up, filling her up, wanting to mark her, claim her, make her mine.

I half fell against her, my head knocking the glass behind her. "Jesus. I think you might have the power to end me." My heart was hammering against my chest like it was on the run and my legs were weak, like they were made from unfired clay.

"I'm exhausted," she said.

"We need water." I glanced over my shoulder to see the half-drunk bottle next to my bed. I wasn't sure I had the energy to get it.

Sutton shifted underneath me, turned her head to face me, and pressed a kiss on my cheek. It was such an intimate, chaste thing to do; it was unexpected and it floored me. What was it with this woman that made me feel like I'd known her my entire life?

"Let me get it." She wriggled out from under me and then guided me to the bed, tucking pillows behind me.

She took the water, unscrewed the lid, snuggled up beside me, and held the bottle to my lips.

"I feel like some kind of Greek god being fed ambrosia and nectar."

"Well, I'm here to tell you, you look like one as well."

I circled my arm around her waist and pulled her closer.

"What are we going to do?" I asked. "This isn't over tonight. You knew that when you walked through that door. I'm even more sure of it now."

She sucked in a deep breath. "It's good sex but it's more, too . . ."

"You're in my head constantly," I said. "Not being with you is driving me so close to the edge that if I carry on so distracted, I'm going to end up losing my career."

She tutted. "As if."

"I'm serious. I can't think with you nearby. I've never experienced this kind of . . . chemistry with someone." I wasn't the guy who went around confessing his feelings to a woman because I got hypnotized by good sex. Our connection had a feeling of inevitability that hit me every time I looked at her. It felt like I'd known her my entire life, and I'd end my time on this earth holding her hand.

"If we're going to move forward, no one can know." She rested her head on my shoulder. "Like we don't even tell our best friends. Our families. No one."

I knew what she was saying made sense, but if no one could know about us, how much time would we really have together? "We both work long hours."

"It will be better when we're in different departments."

I pulled away from her so I could see the expression on her face. Was she trying to press pause?

Instantly, she knew what I was thinking. She shook her head. "I'm not saying no. I'm saying when I move departments, I'll be less conscious of everyone being able to hear every internal thought I'm having about you."

"But we have two months left."

"Maybe it will be easier to fake it if you've just crawled out of my bed that morning."

I grinned to myself at the thought of waking up next to her. "Do you like to sleep naked?"

"Absolutely not," she said. "It's too cold."

"I have a way of keeping you warm." I slid her down from the pillow and away from me so she was on her side and I parted her legs. "It's a good job the physical challenges aren't tomorrow. I'm going to make sure every time you take a step, you feel me between your legs."

My dick hardened between us as she twisted her hips one way and another, and I slid inside her, my hands locked over her hips to keep her in place.

I snaked one arm lower, my fingers finding her clit. She bucked away from my hand, driving herself onto my cock. "Please," she yelled.

I knew why she was begging. She wanted that unquenchable thirst sated just as I did but as soon as it was, a dryer, needier thirst seemed to be left in its wake. The more I had her, the more I wanted her.

She continued to wriggle. I pushed her on to her front and held her in place with my hips. Dipping my hand under her body, I circled and pressed her clit. The feel of her wet under my fingers and around my cock was almost maddening. That I had the power to make this beautiful woman come over and over made me feel like a fucking champion.

We were sworn to secrecy, but the seventeen-year-old boy in me wanted to tell the world I was the lucky bastard who got to fuck Sutton Scott. That I got to get drunk with her on tequila and wake up next to her and see what she slept in and what she ate for breakfast.

I was that guy. Her man.

The next few months were going to present some challenges. I was going to have to subdue the forever-horny adolescent inside *and* the thirty-six-year-old who wanted to hold her hand and kiss her in the doctors' dining room, take her out to dinner and go swimming outdoors with her. But there were few things I'd ever wanted in my life more than to be with Sutton, so I'd make it work.

For both of us.

TWENTY-ONE

Jacob

I'd spent the last twenty minutes sorting out the conference room, ready for twenty-five FY1s to shift from doctors to management consultants.

People filed in and I surreptitiously glanced at Sutton, half hoping she'd catch my eye and half praying she didn't, because I was sure everyone would see the electricity between us. How did she look even more gorgeous today? She wore her ponytail high and Madonna had been replaced with Prince on her t-shirt. Apparently she liked her eighties pop.

"You're glowing, Sutton," Veronica said as they took a seat at the table at the back. "That early night last night did you good."

I couldn't help but smirk as I set the flip chart up by the front. Each table had a flip chart as well as markers, Post-it notes, and an array of stationery.

"Please take your seats. Make sure you're not in the

same groups as yesterday." I pulled my phone out of my pocket and typed.

My place for dinner tonight. 3 Holford Road. I'll be back around eight.

I pressed send and heard Sutton's phone bleep. I hoped no one connected the two. I scanned the room. Everyone was on their phones. No one was paying attention to Sutton and me.

As people took their seats, Sutton typed on her phone.

Your place? Isn't that too risky? Don't people know where you live?

It wasn't like anyone could see through my windows. My place was set back from the road and gated.

It will be fine. Trust me. Come at eight. And then again at eight thirty and nine. And ten . . .

I pressed send, grinned at the thought of the blush my message would elicit, and then turned off my phone. I needed to focus. I had plenty of distraction already today just having Sutton in the room.

I deliberately didn't watch Sutton open my message. Instead, I brought the room to attention.

"As you know, we surveyed you about the one thing you would change at the Royal Free if you had a magic wand." If I was honest, the results had been a little disappointing. Most people talked about hours or staffing levels or pay levels. Nothing about any of that could be sorted by us today in this room.

"Out of the issues raised, I've identified three I thought we could work in our groups to try and come up with some kind of fix for. It might not be a complete fix. Maybe it would just ease the problem, but let's put our heads together and see what we can come up with."

The way I saw it, even if we didn't manage to come up

with any solutions, just the idea that the new doctors saw the problems in the hospital as part of their responsibility would provide a useful mindset shift. It was all too easy to blame those in management or lack of funding—and they were understandable targets—but they didn't help morale. If problems at the hospital were perceived as issues that we all could solve, then it may have several effects. It could stop the "us vs them" culture that existed between management and the medical staff, and it might propel doctors into looking at how they could work more effectively and efficiently in every area. It put the responsibility for working practices back in the doctors' hands.

"The three areas that you came up with are one, readmissions. We all know readmissions are mainly preventable and are a drain on money and time. Second, test results, in particular blood test results taking so long to come back. Third, the constant issue of freeing up beds quickly to admit new patients."

I glanced everywhere around the room but at Sutton. I couldn't risk losing my train of thought.

"The benefit of you all coming in here is that you see things with a fresh perspective. You're not burdened with the history of what has been tried and failed before. Nothing is off the table. I want you to pick one of the three issues I just described. In your groups, spend three quarters of an hour thinking up potential solutions—I don't want anyone censoring their thoughts, crossing things out because they might not work. Just put *everything* down. Use the materials on your tables. When time is up, one person from each table should be ready to report back to the entire group."

Murmurs broke out as the tables discussed which issue they wanted to deal with.

"Remember," I said, over the simmer of voices, "don't focus on why something can't work, or how something will work. We're not focusing on implementation."

The room set to work and I left them to it. I'd check my emails and messages before I made the rounds.

I glanced up from my phone about ten minutes later. Sutton was at her table's flip chart. They'd chosen the issue of freeing up beds. She looked beautiful. Her arse in her jeans looked perfectly cuppable, and the beauty spot on her right cheek perfectly kissable.

I went around the groups, checking they didn't need any input from me. A couple of times I needed to stop people dismissing ideas and encourage them to throw as much up on the flip chart as possible. Doctors could be alarmingly narrow-minded and cynical. This was an exercise in being neither.

"Okay," I bellowed at the room. "Your time is up. Please nominate a speaker from your group and get ready to read out your ideas. After this we're going to vote for which problem we all want to focus on and we're going to work through the ideas to see what could work and what wouldn't."

Many of the answers had to do with fundraising or employing more staff. It was a little demotivating. I really wanted something special to come out of this offsite. I wanted to prove that taking doctors out of their normal environment could really add value in the long run, and show how the training and development of doctors wasn't always about their clinical skill and medical knowledge. That had been true while my mother and father practiced, but it was time to move on. Most of the answers weren't the most creative but every now and then, an idea was read out that might just have legs.

We worked through each table's suggestions. Sutton's group was last. Luckily for me, she hadn't been nominated as spokesperson, so I could try and focus on Veronica, who was speaking. She stood and went through the list of things to help the issue of freeing up beds.

"And then there's the reverse-triage idea that Sutton had, and that's it," she finished off. Triage? That was vague, but it sounded interesting. Or was I only interested because it was Sutton's brainchild? I really wanted to ask for more detail, but would it look odd, like I was singling her out?

Before I could help myself, the words were out of my mouth. "Reverse-triage?"

"Yeah." She glanced at Sutton. "Patients in each ward would be grouped according to the likelihood of them leaving that day. Is that right?"

Sutton nodded. "I've noticed there are usually patients in each ward that just need the doctor to sign a prescription or check bloods that have come back overnight, but usually everyone's aware they're probably going to go home."

"Right," I said, wanting her to go on.

"The idea is that two or three of those people are dealt with at the beginning of rounds so they can be discharged as soon as possible."

People started to groan and shout out reasons why that wouldn't work, but there was something in this idea.

"Shhh," I snapped. "I said this is the time when we're not talking about what won't work. We're just discussing ideas."

I looked back at Sutton and she shrugged.

"We need an express lane with just two or three patients in it each day. That would free up beds for morning admissions. Then it would be business as usual for the rest of rounds. You could even have nurses prioritize patients in

the express lane, since they'll have made overnight obser-
vations."

Bloody hell, she was smart. She was really on to something with her idea. I wanted to flesh things out, ask her
more questions, but I had to be patient. The doctors really
had to own this.

"Thanks for that," I said. "Veronica? Anything else?"

She shook her head.

"Now we've heard everyone's ideas, the next stage is for
us all to focus on one problem and come up with the most
viable solution. Let's vote with a show of hands."

The vote for freeing up beds and readmissions was
even, with only two votes going to the issue with blood
results. I could declare that I had a casting vote, but I didn't
want to demotivate people. I wanted them all to have
ownership of this.

"Okay, so it's between freeing up beds and readmissions. We're going to revote between the two."

Lucky for me, they voted on freeing up beds. Sutton
had a really great idea that might actually work.

"Each group needs to discuss the various ideas they and
the other teams suggested. Think about how it would really
work in practice." Sutton's idea had the added advantage
that it could be trialed in peds, and I was pretty sure Gerry
would agree.

If we could successfully implement this idea, it could
really improve efficiency on the wards and show that the
idea of the offsite had really borne fruit.

And it might all be down to Sutton.

TWENTY-TWO

Sutton

I was dressed for thievery. If anyone from the hospital saw me, hopefully the dark glasses and my Wham! hoodie would mean they wouldn't recognize me.

I pressed the single buzzer on the gate and waited, my hands in my pockets, my face pointed away from the road. I was moments away from being arrested.

The speaker crackled and then the gate opened. I stepped inside and tipped my head back to take in the huge four-story house. These were flats, right? But then there'd only been one buzzer. Was this his parents' place?

The imposing black front door was up four steps and it swung open before I'd started to climb the stairs.

"What is it you think we're doing tonight?" he asked, grinning at me like he just won the lottery. "Kicking off a burglary spree?"

I ignored him, dipping under his arm and into his hallway.

I pulled down my hood. "This is just one house? Where

am I?" I asked, turning three hundred sixty degrees. The place was huge, even bigger than it looked from the outside. "Is this your parents' place?"

"What?" he snapped. "Why would you think that?"

I'd clearly said something to wipe the gorgeous grin from his face. I caught his t-shirt as he moved past me and pulled him toward me. "What?"

"You come to my house and assume I'm at my parents' place?"

"Jacob." I smoothed my hands up his chest, hoping to coax his gaze down from where it was fixed over my head. "I know how much you earn. This place is in Hampstead and it's beautiful. In short, you can't afford it. Are we actually robbing banks tonight? Have I unwittingly dressed perfectly for your plans?"

He looked at me finally and smiled. "Sorry, I guess you're right. I told you I got lucky with an idea I had when I was at uni."

"Oh yes, the untapped business potential."

He bent, cupped the back of my head, and kissed me right out of my shoes, making my legs too shaky to stand on and my brain too frazzled to think. It was like a switch was flipped every time I was around him. When he was out of sight, I convinced myself that what I felt when I was around him was nothing special. That I was exaggerating the biochemical and physiological change in me when he was around. Then each time I saw him, I was right back in the same place—giddy, breathless, lightheaded and desperate for more. I couldn't get enough of him.

He grabbed my hand and pulled me into the kitchen slash living room. "Yup. I got really lucky."

The kitchen was huge, spanning the entire back of the house, with window lights in the roof and a huge comfy couch at one end, a dining table in an alcove at the back. Everything was white and bright but cosy and warm.

"What kind of lucky?"

"You want a glass of wine?" he asked.

"Sure. Do you have red with a side of finally confessing details of your mind-reading invention?"

He placed a kiss on the top of my head and went about opening cupboards, pulling out a corkscrew and glasses.

"I just had an idea for a . . . medical device at university that . . . It turned into something unexpected and it snowballed."

"Sounds vague. What medical device?"

He shrugged. "A useful kind of medical device. I don't want to talk about it. I sold my shares in the company in the end. I've done okay."

I wasn't sure if I was impressed with his apparent humility or slightly upset he wouldn't share more detail with me.

He handed me a glass of wine and then guided me to the dining room table, which was already laid with two spaces opposite each other. "I've made my favorite."

"I'm learning so much about you tonight already. I can't wait to see what you cooked. Can I help with anything?"

"Cooked might be an exaggeration," he replied. "Voila!" He returned carrying two bowls and set them down, then turned back to retrieve a big wood chopping board with a loaf of bread on it. "Heinz tomato soup and sourdough."

I laughed, a little thankful it wasn't something more sophisticated. The house was intimidating enough. Then learning a little idea he had at university had paid for it? Not only had nothing like that ever happened to me, nothing like that had ever happened to anyone I knew. This was a different world I was living in now.

"Nothing beats Heinz tomato soup," I said.

He cut up the loaf and I took a chunk, still warm from the oven. "You didn't make the bread, did you?"

He shook his head. "No, but I put it in the oven to impress you."

Should a confession like that make me want to jump a guy? "Consider me impressed." I wasn't even being sarcastic. I genuinely couldn't think of a nicer meal than this one right in front of me.

"I like your hoodie," he said, grinning. "Tell me about your obsession with eighties pop."

I took a sip of wine. "Actually it wasn't *my* obsession. My boss at the salon was a huge eighties pop fan. Massive. It was all we played at work. We used to have theme weeks."

"Theme weeks?" He took a bite of his bread and I couldn't help but watch. Even the way he chewed was sexy.

"You know, Prince week. Purple Rain week. Madonna week, Like a Prayer week. George Michael solo artist week before he came out, George Michael solo artist after he came out."

"Gotcha." He nodded.

"It was either beat her or join her and I decided, just giving into the synthesizers was easier. Although, if I'm being honest, Kajagoogoo week was a low point for me. They really only had one good song and if I never hear it again, that'll be fine by me."

He laughed and I wanted to run my fingers over the stubble that had grown on his chin in the last few days.

"What made you become a hairdresser?"

I smiled because he didn't say it in a sneering way or condescending way. He just seemed really interested.

"Honestly? Hairdressers were renowned for taking

people on at sixteen, and I needed a job to put a roof over my head."

I popped a chunk of bread into my mouth and chewed, watching him watching me.

"And you needed a roof over your head at sixteen because . . . ?"

"Because . . ." Was I really going to tell him? I didn't even like to think about it, let alone discuss it. The thing about Jacob was whenever I was near him, he made me feel safe. Like he was on my side and looking out for me. He'd asked the question and he deserved the truth. "My parents split when I was twelve. Dad moved to America, started a new life, had a new family. My mum . . . She threw herself into finding a new man and it caused arguments. When I hit sixteen, I walked out after a huge row about her sleazy boyfriend moving in. When I went back, she'd changed the locks."

He let go of the spoon in his bowl and sat back. "She kicked you out?"

"I suppose technically I left."

"Jesus. What did your dad say?"

I shrugged. I hadn't been able to get hold of him for weeks after. Stupidly I'd tricked myself into thinking that when I did speak to him, he was going to tell me to get on a plane and live with him. "He sent me five hundred pounds. Basically told me 'goodbye and good luck.'"

Jacob shook his head. "So you didn't make it up with your mum?"

The question made my stomach curdle. "No. I found out about the apprenticeship from my friend's mum. I think my boss felt sorry for me and let me live above the salon."

"God, I'm sorry. She never came after you? Did she know how to find you?"

"Yeah, I was on social media. Years later I found out the salon owner had gone to see her to assure her I was okay. Apparently my mum just shut the door in her face. It was fine." Objectively, it wasn't fine. Anyone listening to my story who had committed parents, or at least parents who didn't hate them, would think it was less than fine. But for me? It was almost easier to leave a house where I wasn't wanted than to stay. "I got a job. I made good money for my age. I had a roof over my head."

He reached for my hand but I picked up my spoon and took another mouthful of soup. I didn't need his pity. I was fine.

"Sutton," he said, a line forming between his eyebrows I hadn't seen before.

I shook my head. "It's fine."

"It's not fine. Your parents should never have had children."

I laughed. "We can agree on that. Honestly, it's all I ever knew. And it means that I'm tough and resourceful and independent."

"You're like a grown-up Matilda."

I scrunched up my nose. "No superpowers."

He laughed. "I'm not sure about that. You're pretty phenomenal—"

I fixed him with a look that said *Don't you dare make this about sex.*

"I was going to say at your job. But yes, you're great in the bedroom too."

I tossed a piece of bread at him.

"Hey, don't waste the sourdough," he said. "Carbs are important."

I tore off a piece from what was still in my hand and popped it in my mouth.

"So when did you change your mind to medicine?" he asked.

I thought back to staring into the mirror at the salon in my popstar-of-the-week t-shirt, counting the hours until my last client was in the chair. "I was bored," I said. "I knew I was bright and capable of doing . . . more. I liked hairdressing. I liked the independence I had. And it was fun. But when I was at school the teachers assumed I'd stay on after sixteen and do my A-Levels, then go on to university. I thought so too. Anyway, I'd pushed school to the back of my memory until one day, a girl from my school came in for a haircut. She'd been in the year below me and she didn't recognize me. I only knew her because her mum always walked her home from school—long after any other parents were still walking their kids to school, and about a decade after my parents last walked me to school."

I laughed but it was sad. I walked myself to and from school from six years old. They used to pay another little girl a couple of pounds a week to walk with me for the first term but after that, I made my own way there and back. They were too absorbed in their crumbling marriage to give a shit about the kid they brought into the world.

"Anyway, I wasn't cutting her hair. The girl with a chair next to mine was. Ellie had just started as a doctor and I just couldn't believe someone younger than me was a doctor already. Someone from my school, come to that. They were discussing gruesome illnesses and vomit and stuff, and I was completely fascinated with everything Ellie was saying. Then a couple of months later, my boss was booked on a first-aid course. The morning of, she was sick. It was my day off but I offered to go. The training was an entire day. I loved it and got to talking to the person giving the course over lunchtime. They were at med school and doing this on the side for extra cash. I grilled him like he was a serial killer suspect, then I just became obsessed with the idea that maybe one day, I could be a doctor."

"So if you left school at sixteen, you didn't do A-Levels."

I shook my head, ready for the look of disdain that so often followed when someone found out I left school at sixteen. "I did them at night while I worked."

"Jesus, Sutton. You're amazing."

"Not sure Matilda had to go to night school," I said and winked at him.

"I saw your grades at med school. You must have been top ten percent of your year all the way through."

"Five percent," I corrected him. "You looked at my grades?"

"Yup. I look through everyone's grades who are on my team. If I didn't think you were amazing before tonight— which I totally did—I would now."

"I don't deserve special treatment because my parents were arseholes."

"Firstly, yes you do. Secondly, the amount of persever- ance and will power—the amount of discipline and determi- nation you had to have to do what you've done in the way that you've done it—is incredible."

"This might sound silly to you, but I'd rather you didn't tell anyone. I just want to keep my head down and get through the next two years. It's exactly why being here is so . . ."

He reached for my hand across the table and this time I didn't move away. "I'm not going to say a word. But I'm not sure flying under the radar is going to be possible. You're a very talented doctor."

I appreciated the compliment, but it wasn't his job to

make me feel better. I was fine. "We probably shouldn't be discussing work."

He smiled and I felt it in my toes. "I remember we tried that once. Got very drunk." He stood, took my hand, and pulled me up from where I was sitting.

"I feel like I killed the mood a little," I said. He circled his hand around my waist. "I don't talk about this stuff with many people. *Any* people, really. For some reason I have verbal diarrhea around you."

"Definitely the preferred type of diarrhea to have." He placed a kiss on my forehead. "I like listening. I like talking to you. I like being with you."

I sighed, relaxing a little in his arms. "I thought maybe after last night things might have . . . shifted. That it was some kind of pent-up physical need."

He shook his head. "But it's not. Otherwise, I wouldn't have risked last night. Neither would you."

"So I guess we need to wear this one out a bit more."

He frowned. "What? Keep having sex until you're bored or over it or something?" He looked at me half amused, half horrified.

"Isn't that what most relationships are? I mean, if people are honest."

He shook his head and let out a half laugh. "I don't know. But I'm not interested in any other relationships. I'm interested in you and me. And I'm not expecting to get bored. Not with you."

"Ever?" I grinned at him. "Is this a marriage proposal?"

He smiled in a sort-of adoring, deliciously sexy way. "Is marriage something you want?"

I pulled out of his arms. "Absolutely not," I said. "I was kidding. We've known each other five minutes."

He pulled me toward him. "There's no need to freak

out. I'm not about to propose. I'm just interested. Given your parents, I would have thought it might be something you either crave or run away from."

"I'm neutral. I don't think about it." I paused and when he didn't say anything, I added. "Is marriage something you want?"

He laughed. "You look like someone just set off a stink bomb."

"I do not." I play-thumped him on his shoulder and my hand rebounded off hard muscle.

"Honestly I haven't thought about it," he replied. "But when I look at my mum and dad, there's nothing about their relationship that would make me set against it."

"They're in Norfolk?"

He nodded. "We should go. They would love to meet you and it would mean we could go out and take a walk. They have a new puppy. We can take him down to Blakeney point."

"You want me to meet your parents?"

"We can escape Hampstead and London and the danger of being seen by anyone in the hospital. Why not?"

When he put it like that, it sounded perfect.

"That sounds good, but only if you promise not to propose."

"Cross my heart."

TWENTY-THREE

Sutton

After rounds, I'd not seen Jacob at all. He was in clinic with Gilly, seeing patients. I was following up a number of things from rounds, checking results of blood tests and ECGs. I'd worked through my lunch to get things done and everything was going pretty smoothly. I was feeling pretty good about myself.

"Sutton," Gareth called from the other side of the bay.

I turned and stepped toward his bed. "How are you feeling, Gareth?" Gareth was nine and recovering from having a new pacemaker fitted.

"I'm fine. More than fine. Will I go home today?"

"You want me to lie or tell the truth."

"Tell the truth, of course," he said.

"I think you'll have to spend another night here. If you're still okay this time tomorrow, we can let you go home." Gareth had had to have a blood transfusion during his operation and we wanted to keep an eye on him.

"But I'm okay now. Why can't I go home?"

"Because we want you to rest a little while longer. If you go home, you're going to be tempted to go out on your bike and get on the Xbox you keep telling me you're so good at."

Gareth looked despondent. "I promise I'll rest at home. I just want to be with my mum."

My heart squeezed at the way his voice trembled. I pulled up a chair next to his bed and took a seat. "You want to call her?" Gareth's father was in the navy and was on deployment at the moment. He had twin baby sisters at home, which meant his mother couldn't stay over at the hospital as much as some of the other parents did. Sometimes I wondered whether my parents would have stayed if I'd ever been in hospital. Maybe when they'd been together, but after the divorce, my mum wouldn't have wanted to be bothered with visiting me. I would have been viewed as a bother if I was in hospital. Hell, I was viewed as a bother by just existing.

I was sure Gareth's mother didn't feel the same. I'd found her crying at the lifts when she had to leave him to go and take care of her daughters.

He shook his head. "It's the twins' nap time. She tries to sleep too. I don't want to wake her."

I slid my hand over his and squeezed it. "She loves you an awful lot." I glanced at his bedside table and the gold and maroon washbag.

"You a Harry Potter fan?"

He nodded his head. "I've read all of the books. Twice."

"Impressive. What about *How to Train Your Dragon*?" I asked.

He frowned like he didn't know what I was talking about.

"You've not read it? Oh, wow. I have a treat in store for

you. Hang on a sec." I'd seen a worn copy of the first book over by the nurses' station earlier, waiting for the mobile library this afternoon. Gareth would love it.

My pager bleeped and I checked it. A&E. I grabbed the book. "Make a start on that," I said to Gareth. "I'll be back later to see how you like it."

I picked up the phone and dialed A&E. "Hi, it's Sutton," I said.

"We need Jacob down here," Fraser, one of the FY1s, said. "As soon as you can. One of his patients. Looks like it might be a heart attack."

"Okay, I'll get him."

Swiftly, I headed toward Jacob's clinic room and almost ran into him as I was passing through the lift lobby. "You're needed in A&E."

"I know. Come with me."

I nodded as he reached around me and pressed the button. Miraculously, the lift doors opened as if they'd been waiting for us and we stepped into the semi-empty lift.

"They paged you?" I asked.

He nodded. "Yup."

"Gilly is still in clinic?"

"Just finishing up notes. I was about to head to lunch."

We hit the ground floor and I scrambled to keep up with Jacob's long, swift strides.

We headed to the nurses' station, where Fraser was waiting, transferring his weight from foot to foot, which made him look like he was desperate to go to the loo. "Brittni Handle," he said. "Six years old. You've treated her for a ventricular septal defect. She's falling in and out of consciousness." He pushed his iPad toward Jacob, who immediately shared it with me. We saw her vitals. The

EEG didn't look like she was having a heart attack, but in children, things could present so differently.

"Hi, my name is Jacob, I'm one of the doctors. I think we've met before," he said to Brittni's parents.

I kept my gaze fixed on Brittni. Her eyes were open, but her face seemed swollen. Her chest was rising and falling quickly and she looked pale. But the thing that stood out to me was her hair.

It was almost jet black, and clearly dyed.

A six-year-old with dyed hair.

Nothing about it felt right.

"Can you tell me what happened?" Jacob asked.

"Sorry, can I interrupt a second?" I asked. "Have you dyed Brittni's hair?" I asked her parents.

Her mother's eyes grew large and flitted from her daughter to her husband. "I mean, why would you ask me that?"

That was a yes if ever I heard one.

I approached Brittni and pulled on my examination gloves. "My name's Sutton. I'm a doctor. I'm just going to check your head, Brittni," I said. "I'm not going to hurt you."

The child didn't even blink. She was clearly very poorly. I stepped forward and parted Brittni's hair. Yes, clearly recently dyed and the product hadn't been washed off properly. The dye was still on her scalp and around her hairline.

My heart began to bang against my chest, telling me I needed to act.

I turned to Jacob. "She needs adrenaline. She's having an allergic reaction to PPD."

Jacob put on his gloves and I showed him the excess dye. "When did you dye her hair?" he asked Brittni's mother.

"Just this morning. But I used proper hair dye. My friend's a hairdresser and she got me the real stuff. Brittni was desperate to do her hair like mine."

Jacob caught my eye. I knew I needed to get the adrenaline that was always kept in the drugs cabinet.

"And after that Brittni started to get drowsy? Is her face more swollen that usual?" Jacob asked as I flew to the cabinet.

I was back moments later with a syringe, needle, a vial of adrenaline, and a trolley to prepare it all on.

Her father stood. "Yes, her face is swollen now you come to mention it."

"Please prepare the injection," Jacob said.

I took a breath, unwrapped the syringe and needle, attached the two as Jacob talked Brittni's parents through what was happening and what we needed to do about it.

"Where will it be administered?" Jacob asked me as I unwrapped the vial and jabbed the needle through the top of the vial.

"Naught point three milligrams?" I asked, wanting to check the dosage.

Jacob stayed silent. He wanted me to be sure. He wanted me to have confidence in my ability.

I nodded. Yes, it was naught point three. She was six years old. "The anterolateral aspect of the middle third of the thigh."

He nodded once. "Go ahead."

"Brittni," I said. "I'm going to give you an injection." I turned to her parents. "It would be good if you could chat to her, just to keep her mind on other things."

They both stood but stayed silent.

"Brittni, tell me your teacher's name," I said as I uncovered her leg and began to clean the area.

She closed her eyes. I needed to go ahead and inject her. She was deteriorating fast.

I jabbed the needle into her muscle and she barely moved. I pushed the adrenaline and withdrew the needle.

One of the nurses came up with a sharps box and I discarded the needle, then placed the used vial and my gloves into the bin at the bottom of Brittni's bed.

"I'll talk to the nurses about getting her head shaved," I said.

Her mother gasped.

"I thought you just gave her medicine. Won't she be fine now?"

She couldn't be worried about her daughter's hair when her life was at stake, could she? "The medicine has stopped her falling into a coma, but the dye is still on her scalp. It wasn't washed off properly," I said. "It's had a chance to seep into the skin. It needs to be shaved and her scalp thoroughly washed."

"She's going to have to stay overnight," Jacob said. "We're going to have to monitor her."

"Mummy," Brittni said. It was the first word I'd heard her speak. The adrenaline was doing its job. Shame her parents couldn't say the same thing.

Her mother looked at me. "Thank you," she said.

I nodded. I wanted to tell her not to be so ridiculous next time and not dye a six-year-old's hair. Or at least do a patch test and use a home dye kit rather than salon products at home. I didn't. Nothing I said would change her mind if the near-death of her daughter hadn't already.

"I'm going to leave you to write that up," Jacob said as we moved away from the bay.

"Absolutely," I said, my hands shaking as if I'd had the syringe of adrenaline.

"Good work."

"Thanks."

"I mean it. It was a very good catch," he said. "If we'd been waiting for scans and bloods, it might have been much more serious. Your background and life experience are things you can draw on. You have nothing to be ashamed of. Believe in yourself."

He wasn't touching me but it felt like he was wrapping me in his arms and holding me close.

I gave him a small smile of gratitude for his encouragement.

Jacob headed back to the lifts and I grabbed one of the free chairs behind the nurses' station to write up what had just happened.

Suddenly, I was exhausted. It had all happened so fast and it could have so easily gone another way. But whatever way you looked at it, I'd had a hand in saving a child's life today. I wasn't sure the job got much better.

Maybe Jacob was right. Maybe my convoluted journey to medicine was an asset, rather than something to hide from. Not that hairdressing incidents were likely to crop up regularly in A&E, but maybe the way I approached things could help me. Maybe I didn't need to have gone to Oxford to gain an advantage. Maybe my advantage was my street smarts and life experience.

If Jacob Cove believed in me, maybe I needed to start believing in myself.

TWENTY-FOUR

Jacob

Sutton turned off the radio and dipped her head so she could take in my parents' house from where we were parked. We'd spent the entire drive to Norfolk listening to her favorite eighties pop songs, with her telling me stories from the salon—the time she cut someone's neck, the woman who used to come in and insist Sutton massage her feet. We swapped stories of med school, too—late nights, Red Bull, and a lot of anatomy jokes.

Three hours of enforced no touching had been easier than expected. She was just always the best company.

"It's so pretty," she said.

"Not as pretty as you." I cupped her neck and pulled her in for a kiss.

"Did you just compare me to a house?"

"Is that bad?" I grinned against her. It was nice spending so much time, even if the last few hours had been an education in eighties pop.

"Just don't say it to someone you're serious about. They may take offense." She laughed but I didn't.

"Just so you know . . ." I kissed her again on the mouth. "If I wasn't serious about you, I wouldn't have broken my golden rule." I winced. I'd not spoken to my father about Sutton. I'd just told my mum I was bringing up a girlfriend. She'd not had a chance to ask me any questions because the new puppy had peed on the floor and she'd had to go supervise Dad clearing it up. It meant I hadn't had the chance to tell them we worked together.

"What?" she asked.

"I'm not sure my mum and dad will like that we work together."

"I get why I don't like it. And why you don't like it—I think. But why will they be concerned?"

"It will be fine. They just gave me the advice to avoid dating in the workplace when I started as a foundation doctor and it's advice I've always followed . . . until you."

She looked concerned. "So they're not going to approve of me, and you tell me this as we pull up to their house?"

"Sorry, I just thought . . . I wanted to tell you before we went in, in case my dad says anything."

She put her hand on her chest and exhaled in a self-soothing gesture.

"It's going to be fine. It's not *you* they won't approve of—just the fact we work together."

She shook her head. "This is our first fight, by the way. I need more heads-up than this in future when it comes to . . . anything."

"Honestly, it will be fine."

Mum appeared at the door to the house and a blur of red fur raced through her legs and out to greet us.

I leapt out of the car and rounded the engine to Sutton,

who was out of the car before I had the chance to open the door for her.

"Dr. Cove," Sutton said, holding out her hand to my mum. "It's an honor to meet you."

"Call me Carole." My mum shook Sutton's hand then pulled her in for a hug. "John, the bloody dog is out again," she called over her shoulder. "You need to get her."

"I'll get her," Sutton said, and before I could step in and do it myself, Sutton was chasing around the front garden after the dog. "What's its name?"

I joined her. "Dog."

"The dog's name is Dog?" She laughed.

"I know. My mum insisted my father name him."

"Well, it's efficient," she said, then sat down and crossed her legs. "Let's sit down," she said. "We're chasing a dog who wants to be chased. Maybe if we sit down, she'll come to us."

As soon as we stood still, Dog realized we weren't chasing her anymore, turned, and hurtled toward us like a rocket. More accurately, she hurtled toward Sutton and didn't stop when she got to her, sending her backward.

"I knew you'd fit right in," I said, as I grabbed Dog's collar and pulled her off Sutton. "If I didn't know you were into me, I'd be jealous of that make-out session."

Sutton laughed. "Gotta keep you on your toes."

I slid my arm around her as the three of us headed into the house.

"Oh, you got her." Mum looked up as we came into the kitchen from where she was preparing something. "She's a total scoundrel. I keep telling your father she needs to go to puppy school but of course, he's far too soft. I'm going to have to pretend I'm taking her for a walk one day and just send her somewhere residential. It's total chaos at the moment. She's barely housetrained. It's like rolling the clock back thirty years."

"Hey, Mum, I was housetrained by six."

She laughed. "You, but not the others."

"Now, Sutton," Mum said. "Can Jacob get you a cup of tea? Glass of wine? It's six o'clock somewhere and Jacob's father has been driving me to distraction today. You know his latest thing is growing beans, which is a total and complete disaster because he won't spend the bloody money to do it properly. I've told him he needs to protect it all from the foxes. Will he listen?"

"Dad never listens," I said, moving around Mum and washing my hands. Sutton did the same and then I handed her the towel.

"Is this you?" Sutton asked, holding the towel up so she could see clearly my picture printed across it. "Why are you on the towel?" She glanced at my mother's apron, which also had pictures of my face all over it. "And there?"

"He does it to wind his brothers up. Wine, Jacob, please."

I pulled out some wine glasses from the fridge. "Shall I grab some of Dad's malbec?"

Mum laughed and continued to chop her onion. "Don't you dare. You'll get us both shot."

"No one touches Dad's wine," I explained to Sutton.

"There's some white in the fridge," Mum said.

"Is that okay with you?" I'd never seen her drink white wine.

She nodded. "Tell me about your face over everything."

"I like to pretend I'm my mother's favorite. Makes up for the fact that I'm a constant disappointment to Dad."

Mum rolled her eyes and pulled out a frying pan. "Your

father is just in a permanent bad mood. Don't take it personally. Besides, you are my favorite. Don't tell the others."

I leaned over and pressed a kiss to my mother's head before pouring out two glasses of wine.

"Can you fill up the dog bowl, as well?"

"With wine?" I asked, holding up the bottle.

"Yes, Jacob, let's get the dog drunk," she replied. "That's all we need. I swear, Sutton, having to deal with Jacob's retired father and a new puppy is much more demanding and chaotic than any operating theatre."

Sutton smiled and then slapped her forehead. "Oh, I forgot something in the car. I'll just get it." Before I could offer to go for her, she sped out of the kitchen.

"Leave the bags," I called after her. "I'll get them in later."

"She seems lovely, Jacob. Very pretty." Mum transferred the chopped onion to the frying pan and began to stir.

"She's lovely. I really like her."

Mum turned to me, her eyebrows raised as if to say *Are you my first-born son or is this a case of invasion of the body snatchers?* "That sounds promising."

"The only problem is . . . We met at work." I braced myself for my mother's disappointment.

Predictably, she groaned. "Don't tell your father or he'll be on a fifteen-minute rant before you know it."

"Yeah, I've warned Sutton. But Dad just likes to rant at me. If it wasn't this, it would be something else."

"Pass me the olive oil?" I reached up in the cupboard and handed it to her. "Is Sutton the first woman at the hospital you've—"

"Yes, and I know it's not ideal. We met each other before she started. It's a long story but for the first time ever, I've met someone who's worth the risk—of Dad's rants."

"Sounds like I need to get to know her. After Nathan's whirlwind romance, I need to take more notice of the women my boys bring home."

She was a woman to take notice of. A woman I couldn't stay away from, no matter how hard I tried.

"You'll like her, Mum." I could never be sure of my father, but I knew my mum would like Sutton. There was no doubt about it. Sutton had a good, pure heart, worked hard and never took anything for granted. My mum would love her.

She reached up and patted my cheek. "Of course I will."

Sutton came back in from the car, carrying a tin. "It's probably not nearly as nice as anything you could make." She handed it to my mother. "I should have just bought something but I had some free time last night and I fancied baking."

Mum took off the lid. "Cake!" she said, her eyes lighting up.

"It's lemon," Sutton said.

"My favorite," Mum said, which was a lie. Her favorite was coffee cake. "That's so kind of you to bring this. Jacob, why don't you put it all on a plate and we'll have a slice with our wine. John will be delighted. He loves a slice of cake."

"What are you saying about me?" My father burst in, his shirt hanging out of his trousers and his hair standing on end.

"Dad, you look like you've been caught shagging the scullery maid. Where have you been," I said.

"Scullery maid indeed," he said. "I've been gardening."

"This is Sutton," I said.

Sutton spun around and offered up her hand. Dad dumped a trug on the kitchen counter and took Sutton's hand in both of his. "Welcome, welcome. How my boys attract such pretty girls, I have no idea." He dropped Sutton's hand and moved to the sink, shaking his head.

"Sutton's a woman, darling," my mum said. "You can't call women girls."

Dad grizzled as he washed his hands and I guided Sutton to the table. "Have a seat."

"Can't anyone wash their hands in the downstairs loo like normal people?" Mum said. Now I've got mud on the carrots."

"They're used to it, my dear. It won't frighten them off." She flipped him with the tea towel and then he flicked her with water. Mum started laugh-shrieking and I grabbed some plates and moved out of the way.

"Excuse them," I said, nodding at my parents, messing about like teenagers. The way I saw them now, both retired and empty nesters, was totally different to my experience growing up. The eldest of five boys, I may have been the only one aware of how difficult things were at the time. How Dad was never home and Mum fell asleep whenever she sat down. Being with them now was much more enjoyable than being with them as a kid.

"It's wonderful. They're . . . warm and just lovely."

"They'll do as parents. Do you want to do the honors, seeing as you baked?" I handed her a knife. "You really didn't need to. Although it's a sure way of getting my parents on your side."

She shook her head, her gaze sliding to my parents' antics. "You do it."

"John, stop it," Mum said. "Look, Sutton made a cake. Do you want a slice?"

"Cake?" my father bellowed. "Never say no to cake. Anyone fancy a glass of wine?"

"Way ahead of you, Dad. We've cracked open some of your Argentinian malbec, that's okay, isn't it?"

The steam started to shoot out of his ears before he spun round and caught sight of the three glasses of white wine next to the cake. There was never any doubt when my father was pissed off. He wasn't a man who masked his emotions—disappointment, anger, frustration. I'd been painfully aware of everything he felt toward me growing up.

"Very funny. That malbec's not to be joked about. I bought it in Argentina, don't you know."

"We know," Mum and I chorused. I grabbed Dad a glass and poured the last of the bottle.

"We don't need the story again," Mum said. "Right, I'm sitting down. I'm having a glass of wine and a slice of cake and I don't care if the dinner is burnt by the end of it; Zach can go out for fish and chips."

"Zach's coming?" I asked.

"He arrived last night," Dad said. "I'm thinking I might move out. Hand over the keys to my five sons and I'll go off and buy a boat to live on. It would be more peaceful than living here. I was told each time we had another son that once they turned eighteen, I'd never see any of you again. Chance would be a fine thing."

I shook my head, smiling, but I caught Sutton's eye and she looked panicked.

"He's kidding," I said. "He doesn't mean it." I hoped it wasn't triggering for her. For a long time, I took my father's rants to heart. It took about twenty-three years and a title of doctor, but I'd gotten used to it.

"Should we not have come?" she asked.

"Ignore him," Mum said. "He loves having people

around. Have a bit of cake and stop moaning, John. Come and sit down."

The four of us sat around the old pine table while I cut and dished up the cake.

Mum raised her glass. "Here's to new friends," she said, smiling at Sutton.

Sutton raised her glass and I clinked mine against hers and then Mum's. "Dad?"

"What? Oh okay then." He raised his glass. "So, what do you do, Sutton? Are you a doctor?" The way he just assumed I'd bring home a doctor niggled at me. I wasn't sure if it was because he'd guessed correctly or that he thought the only people with value were in medicine. He better not start offering her career advice or berating her about starting late or something.

"Yes," Sutton glanced at me. "I'm just starting my first foundation year."

"Very good. Which hospital?" he asked.

"Do you like the cake, John?" Mum asked. "Better than I could make?"

"Don't be ridiculous," Dad replied. "Your cake is second to none. You won a prize for your cake making."

Dad could be gruff and annoying and impatient. As kids, he'd been critical and demanding of us. But he was always Mum's biggest cheerleader and I loved him for it.

"I was fourteen when I won that prize. I'm not sure it's right to still be taking credit for it all these years later."

"A prize is a prize," Dad mumbled. "But this is delicious, Sutton. Thank you. So which hospital did you say you worked at?"

"Drink some wine, Dad," I said, raising my glass.

"Are you trying to get me drunk? I've got beans to tend to, don't you know? And Dog needs a walk."

"Just trying to help."

"Well, stop it," he snapped. "I'm trying to get to know this lovely young lady you've brought home and you won't let her speak."

This was it. Dad wasn't to be blown off course. There was no getting away from the fact I was going to have to tell him that Sutton and I worked together.

Lucky for me, at that moment, the kitchen door swung open and Zach appeared. "Your favorite son has arrived."

"I didn't know you were going to be here this weekend," I said.

"Wanted to be here when you told Dad that you've been dipping your pen in the hospital ink. Dad? Did you know that Jacob and Sutton work together?"

Why couldn't I have been an only child?

"Zachary, go and take Dog for a walk," Mum said. "We were having a perfectly nice conversation until you came in."

Dad raised his eyebrows and took a mouthful of cake. Thankfully, he didn't say a thing. But I'd be hearing about it.

There was no doubt.

TWENTY-FIVE

Sutton

If I'd thought my introduction to the Coves yesterday had been a baptism of fire, breakfast this morning had proved it was only the start. Another of Jacob's younger brothers, Dax, had turned up late last night and insisted on cooking breakfast for everyone this morning. John was supervising. Zach was doing—I wasn't sure what.

It was chaos.

But fantastic.

Carole was sitting at the table, flicking through a magazine, no doubt trying to zone out the bickering among her husband and her sons. It was all in fun and had an underlying warmth to it that betrayed intimacy.

I binge-watched from my chair like it was my favorite boxset and all I was missing was the popcorn. There was something so compelling about their dynamic—they clearly loved each other, liked each other, and enjoyed each other's company. They shared in-jokes and a history I was completely jealous of.

I couldn't remember the last time I'd seen my parents. When I'd gotten into medical school, I'd called my mum to tell her. It had been awkward because we hadn't spoken since I'd left. I hadn't been accusatory or asked why she changed the locks on her sixteen-year-old daughter. She gave no hint of a desire to reconcile, so I didn't reach out again. I spoke to my dad from time to time but he wasn't interested in me or my life. I'd given up hoping that would change.

Watching the Coves, it was clear how much I'd missed out on.

"Dad, they're tinned tomatoes," Zach said. "We don't need instructions."

John was squinting at the can. "Jacob, can you get my glasses from the office?" John asked Jacob.

"Have you checked the top of your head?" Jacob asked, winking at me from across the pine kitchen table.

"Ha bloody ha," John replied, but reached up and felt his head, just in case.

Jacob tilted his head toward the door. "Come with me. I'll show you the office of the great Doctors Cove."

Jacob took my hand and we headed across the dining hall and down a corridor painted daffodil yellow.

"You okay?" Jacob asked. "I figure if you don't have brothers, three of us can be a bit overwhelming."

"It is overwhelming. But not in a bad way. Growing up in your family must have been . . . wonderful. You all seem so . . . connected." I tried to think back to a time I felt any kind of connection with my parents. There must have been times when my mum and dad soothed me or sang me to sleep or read me a story or laughed with me, but if there were, I couldn't remember.

"We have our fair share of disagreements. My dad and

I fought a lot when I was younger. But we're family." We came to the end of the corridor. "Sorry if that's insensitive."

I shook my head. "It's fine. I'm well aware that family means different things to different people. I've always been okay with that. Being here . . . it's the first time I've ever felt . . . well, jealous, I suppose."

He pressed a kiss onto my forehead. "You're amazingly normal, considering . . . *Matilda*." The door creaked as it opened and revealed a huge office. In the middle stood an old, dark library desk with heavy, antique chairs on either side.

The low ceiling was a crisscross of beams, and the deep, red carpet made it feel almost womblike. The walls were covered bookcases stuffed with texts and papers.

"Wow, I could imagine King Arthur in this place."

Jacob chuckled. "No knights around here. They're pretty much completely retired, but every now and then Dad will give a speech or they'll give Mum some kind of award or name a building after her or something."

I wandered over to the bookshelves and traced my finger over the spines of familiar and not-so-familiar medical texts. On one shelf were a stack of what looked like photo frames, but when I moved closer, it was clear they were framed certificates.

"They're my mum's. She should put them on the wall, but there's no space. Even her OBE is there somewhere, dumped like it's a rock she pulled from the beach."

"Your father got an OBE as well, right?"

"CBE actually. Rumor has it, he's up for a knighthood."

"CBE? What's the difference?"

"One's Commander of the British Empire and one's Order. I think Commander is meant to be more prestigious.

From what they've said, both involve a trip to the palace and a handshake with the Queen."

What a pedigree Jacob had. It was a far cry from my family's medical credentials, which consisted of my dad's infected ingrown toenail and my mother's kidney stone.

"You must be so proud."

"Absolutely," he replied. "But . . ."

How could there be a but?

I slid my hand around his waist, not rushing him to finish his thought.

"But sometimes, I wish they both ran a greengrocer's on the high street, you know?"

I frowned. "I think that would be a terrible idea, what with the way the big supermarkets dominate the field."

He laughed. "I just mean, growing up, there was . . . We have plenty of fun together now. Growing up . . . there was less of that."

I snaked my other arm around his waist and gazed up at him. "I can't imagine growing up in this family was anything but fun."

He shrugged. "I imagine that's how it looks, but now they're both at home. It was a lot to live up to."

I frowned. "Everyone thinks you're an excellent doctor."

He shifted his jaw, clearly uncomfortable. "Not good enough. I'm ambitious. If I progress in the hospital, I never want to be in a position where I can't be promoted because there's conflict of interest." He slid his hands around my back. "It's why being with you is such a risk. I really want to head up running the foundation program within the hospi-tal. If I'm sleeping with one of the foundation doctors, it's going to be hard to give me that job."

Even though I knew he never did relationships at work,

and even though I felt the same way, there was still a sliver of disappointment that buried into my gut at his words. I didn't want to be something he had to feel bad about. Something he had to hide. "Right," I said. "That makes total sense."

"But we're keeping this just between us which makes it . . . you know, better."

I nodded. There was no other way. I needed to get through this year and not sully my reputation because I banged my boss.

"Shall we go for a walk?" he asked. "I want to show you the Norfolk Coast path along Blakeney. It's beautiful."

JACOB and I walked hand in hand along the footpath beside the narrow road toward the start of the path he wanted to show me. On one side, there were buildings built right up to the single lane road and on the other, the water and boats moored on the quayside. We dodged the children and their parents set up on the wall with buckets and nets.

"They're crabbing," he said. "There are loads down here."

The breeze was warm but enthusiastic, and my hair whipped around my face.

"Did you come here as a child?"

He nodded. "We lived in London but Mum comes from the area. They had a holiday house—tiny compared to the place they live now. We used to come for holidays and weekends every now and then. Got the best of both worlds —the opportunities and resources of the city and the peace and freedom of the country."

"And this was one of the walks you'd do to clear your head when you were first starting out in medicine?" I asked.

"Yeah, it's a cliché, but the fresh air and exercise really did help. It's difficult to carve that into your timetable at your stage, but it's important." He nodded to the left. "Down here. We're heading past those boats."

"Out into the sea?"

He chuckled. "It feels that way. I've never been to a place like it where you're surrounded by water. You have to remind yourself you're still on solid ground."

I laughed. "Sounds like life as a foundation doctor."

Another couple came toward us, holding hands in matching blue cagoules. We moved to the side to let them pass us.

We exchanged smiles and I couldn't help but wonder how long they'd been together and whether or not things had started out unconventionally and they'd overcome it. I'd only been seeing Jacob a few weeks, but it felt different to any relationship I'd ever felt before. Our physical connection was beyond anything I'd ever experienced, but we also talked about stuff. Important stuff. I shared things with him I'd never spoken about with anyone. And I got the feeling he didn't go around talking about the burden of having the Coves as parents to too many people either. We connected on so many levels that I couldn't help wondering what our future might hold. Matching cagoules or more hiding and secrecy.

He squeezed my hand. "You're rock solid. We shouldn't talk about this, but you're doing really well."

"No, we shouldn't, but thank you." I wanted to ask him about the award—who was in the running and whether there were any obvious stars—but I stopped myself. I didn't want to put him in a compromising position. He shouldn't tell me anything that would get him into trouble. "It's overwhelming at times."

Following the footpath, we turned left, leaving the road and the village of Blakeney behind us. We headed straight out toward the sea. Once we got past the boats, either side of the path were reeds and marshes and pools of water. "When I think of the coast, I think of the rugged rocks and sandy beaches of Devon and Cornwall. This feels like an entirely different country."

He chuckled. "I know what you mean. But it's beautiful, right?"

"Completely." The wide blue sky stretched in front of us punctuated only by the spikes of the reeds and grasses. It felt deeply peaceful. "I can see why you would come here to de-stress. Will you show me where your boat was?"

"The rowing boat I'd hide in?"

I laughed. "Yes. Your de-stressing chamber."

"Sure, it's along here."

We plodded forward, enjoying the view, enjoying the peace, talking and not talking.

"It was here," he said eventually as we came to a pool on the right of the path, surrounded by reeds. "I don't know if the tides changed and it got trapped somehow. Maybe some kids pulled it over the pathway into this part of the sea."

"There's hardly anyone around."

"People come up from the village for a little look, but unless you're going to follow the trail right around to the next village, people don't usually get this far. So it's only the committed walker that passes by."

"And you'd come out here to walk off the stress of the job and . . . the Cove legacy."

"Look, I know I'm privileged. I'm sure I've had opportunities I wouldn't have had if it hadn't been for my parents. I just . . . sometimes I wish I could have done it on my own merit. Like you."

I laughed. He couldn't be serious. "Let me tell you, studying at night and cutting hair during the day to keep a roof over your head isn't anything to covet. It's hard work and it means sacrificing a lot."

"Sorry, I wasn't trying to downplay it."

I shook my head. "It's fine, I know. I'm just saying, there are pluses and minuses of either route." I grinned. "On balance, I'd rather have the loving family and the legacy that goes with them."

He dipped and pressed a kiss on the top of my head. "Yeah, me too."

The warmth from the kiss spread down my entire body. I pulled at the collar of his coat to kiss me some more. We may have come from opposite sides of the tracks, but we were on this ride together now—come what may.

TWENTY-SIX

Sutton

Norfolk seemed a long time ago, even though we'd only been back a week. Before we'd given into each other, I'd been concerned my feelings for him would be displayed in glaring speech bubbles over my head. Now I was worried our intimacy would be revealed in a misplaced touch or a prideful glance. I was still always on my guard when he was around.

"Are you heading to the cafeteria?" Veronica asked as she came up beside me.

"Yup, you?"

"Yes. We can have lunch together. How often does that happen?"

"I don't think it's happened since those first two weeks, which feels like a lifetime ago," I said.

"Right? Two months has gone by in a flash. How's it going? Got a day off anytime soon?"

"I just had three days off in a row. Not sure how I managed that one."

"Wow, are you banging the person in charge of the rota?"

I laughed, trying to sound as genuine as possible, despite the fact that her question left me a little on edge. I knew Jacob hadn't said anything about the rota—he wouldn't risk it—but her question had cut a little too close to the bone. "I thought we all were."

She cackled, the kind of laugh that came from a place of sheer desperation to laugh. I got it. "Wouldn't it be good if the canteen sold wine?"

We continued down the corridor, moving to the side when a bed was wheeled toward us, then we rounded the corner toward the café.

"Absolutely not," I said. "Too tempting."

"That's true. So how's it going? How's peds? You think that's where you might want to end up?"

We turned into the café and each grabbed a tray. "Way too early to say. How about you? Are you enjoying A&E?"

We joined the queue for the salad bar. And then we'd be in the line for chips. The two were inextricably linked.

"Honestly, I think it's good experience but I don't think I could do it my entire career. You're basically holding people together with sellotape until a specialist can see them." She covered her mouth and looked around, hoping she hadn't offended anyone. "I'm not saying there isn't skill involved—of course there is. It's just, I think I'd rather be more focused."

"That's fair," I said. "And all the lates and the week-ends. That wouldn't ever stop, even when you made consultant."

"Exactly. I'm not sure I can handle it." Veronica ordered an egg salad and I picked the halloumi. Without discussing it, we joined the queue for chips.

"Andy's loving it, though. So are Claudia and Garth. In fact, Claudia seems like the department star. I'm sure she's going to be in the running for foundation award."

For some inexplicable reason, my stomach pinched in irritation. "Really? For the rotation or the big award?"

"Both? You know what it's like with the stars. They show their true colors immediately."

I knew I wanted to fly under the radar. I'd learned from the arguments that prefaced my parents' divorce that big, explosive scenes rarely helped anyone. I didn't want anyone to have a reason to stop and look at me more closely. So why did jealousy snake up my spine when Veronica spoke about Claudia being an *obvious* star? Maybe because had things been different—had my parents not split up and my mother become obsessed with finding and keeping another man— things might have been easier. I might not have had to put myself through university by hairdressing.

I might be an obvious star.

"I hear Gilly's scoring highly with Dr. Off Limits."

I frowned. "Scoring highly?" I asked.

"Apparently, he thinks she's great. Is she getting all the best cases and stuff?"

I thought about it. "Not that I've noticed. Where did you hear that?" Was that the reason Jacob had told me to believe in myself? Was he trying to let me know I needed something extra in order to make a mark?

"She told me so, so of course it could be bullshit."

"Probably. I don't share every shift with her, so maybe she's making a mark and I'm just not seeing it."

"Or maybe she's sleeping with the boss to get ahead. Not that I could blame her. Is he as brilliant as everyone says he is?"

Sleeping with the boss to get ahead? That's what

everyone would think if they found out about me and Jacob. There would be no flying under the radar. My competency as a doctor would likely be questioned.

"Dr. Cove?" Maybe I'd taken it too far. It was clear she was talking about Jacob.

She snort-laughed. "Yes, Dr. Off Limits. Is he as amazing at the job as they say?"

I shrugged and we picked up our chips. I hoped that was the end of our talk about Jacob. "He's great to work with. Focused." I couldn't underplay it because when it came to her turn in peds, she'd know I was covering for something, but if I overplayed it, she might suspect something. The fact was Jacob was brilliant, even taking into account I was sleeping with him. He was laser focused, kind, and clever. Best of all, he was an excellent teacher—pushing and testing and expecting a lot. I loved working with him.

I glanced down the queue to see how long we'd have to wait before Veronica would be interrupted by the cashier. I was sure I had *I'm a liar* scrawled over my forehead.

"Shall we eat outside? At least that way we can gossip without being overheard in the doctors' dining room." Anything to avoid a run-in with Jacob.

"Good idea," I said, grabbing a napkin and fork before swiping my hospital card to pay for my lunch.

As we headed out, Jacob was coming in. We almost smashed into him.

"A&E almost had three more admissions." He smirked and carried on. I didn't dare even catch his eye. I'm sure I was emitting waves of lustful vibes as it was.

As we crossed the corridor to the exit, Veronica let out a small groan. "He even smells good, doesn't he? How can you concentrate with him around? It must be terrible.

Wanna swap?" She laughed and we headed out to sit under the small patch of grass in front of the car park.

"You really think the foundation award has already been decided?" I asked.

Veronica looked at me. "Do I believe Gilly? No. Do I think they get a feel for the candidates during the first rotation? Absolutely."

I took a forkful of halloumi and nodded.

"Do I think you're a candidate? I do."

I let out a small laugh. That wasn't going to happen. I didn't want it to. I just wanted to stay focused and keep my head down. But the more and more time I spent with Jacob, the less likely that was. Jacob was occupying more of my headspace than he should. I was concerned what shift he was on and whether I'd be working with him, and then I was concerned that someone had realized we were sleeping together. My focus was all over the place. And then there was the constant concern that people were going to suspect. The worry hung over me like the sword of Damocles.

Things weren't going to plan. In my life, they rarely did.

TWENTY-SEVEN

Sutton

I lay back on the picnic blanket, staring up at the fluttering bright green leaves overhead.

"Champagne in the park. This is one of the most romantic afternoons ever," I said.

"Agreed," Parker said. "Don't tell Tristan."

I laughed. "I promise."

It had been Parker's idea to picnic on Hampstead Heath, and it was one of her better ones. "I much prefer to be under a tree sipping champagne than hanging off one, holding on for dear life."

"We're not trying to distract you now. I'm trying to relax you."

"You're a good friend." I felt shitty that I'd not told her about Jacob. It had just happened so quickly and work was so frantic, I'd hardly seen Parker since it happened.

"That sounds ominous."

"Does it?" I sat up. "It's not meant to. But I do have something to share with you."

"I hope it's about Jacob."

"How did you know?" I asked.

"I'm so pleased you gave in. Tell me what happened."

I told her what had happened at the offsite and how I would go over to his place after my shift. How I'd gone to Norfolk and met his family. Jacob and I had initially said no friends or family should know, but going to Norfolk had already violated that rule. It seemed only fair that Parker should know. She was as close to family as it got for me. "He's wonderful. Really wonderful."

"Don't let there be a *but*," Parker said.

"Of course there's a but. A big but." I fell back onto the blanket.

"Surely you can let it be complicated. Or choose to let it be simple."

"Life is never easy. For a start, he's my boss. I've worked hard to get where I am. I don't want people to look at me and think I owe any of it to the fact that I was sleeping with my boss. I just want to stay in my lane and get through the next two years unscathed."

"Who cares what they think?"

"Me," I said. I loved Parker but she'd had opportunities in life that meant when something good happened to her, she never questioned it. Our backgrounds were very different. "And not just me, but everyone who gives me a job from now to the end of time will be wondering if I'm less good at my job because of the way I got into med school. So it's important I don't add fuel to the fire. I don't want people thinking I had to sleep with the boss to get by."

Parker groaned. "People are arseholes."

"You know that's what some people will say."

"I get it," Parker said. "But it can't be *career over* if you two get discovered, surely."

I shrugged. "Maybe not career over, but there'd be a question mark over my head. And after all the work I've put in, I don't deserve that. I can't help thinking that when it's all over, I'm going to regret it."

"Maybe it's never over."

I laughed. "What? You think I'm going to marry this guy?"

"Maybe," she said.

I shook my head. Only Parker could say something like that. "Not going to happen. It's all too easy with Jacob. There's bound to be something that will derail us at some point. I just don't know if . . ." Whitney's "Didn't We Almost Have It All" started playing in my head. You could take the girl out of the salon but never the salon music out of the girl. "I don't know if the ride will be worth the fall. But at the same time . . ." Jacob would be at work now. Maybe he'd be in the dining room at this very moment. I'd not seen him out of the hospital for three nights and I missed him. How was that possible? He was going to come round to my place after his shift. Maybe I'd cook for him.

"But at the same time?" Parker interrupted my thought process.

"But at the same time, I don't want to give him up."

Parker rolled to her side and propped her head up on her hand. "Because it's good sex or because it's more?"

"It's definitely good sex. Like . . . I mean, I don't think what I've been doing before can be counted as sex, if I compare."

Parker laughed. "I know that feeling."

"And it feels like more, but maybe it's not. Maybe it's just because we're sneaking around and can't go to Pizza Express on a Saturday night and then to the cinema. Maybe it's more exciting because it's forbidden."

"Only one way to find out. Go public."

I shook my head and sat up, crossed-legged and facing Parker. "No, for all the reasons above. Also, Jacob wants to keep things between us for his own good reasons."

"So what, you just continue as you are until the end of time? You're like forty with two kids and a dog and you still can't be seen out in public together?"

I laughed. "Well of course not." I took a sip of the champagne going warm in the sun. It was still delicious.

"So you're thinking that if it lasts, at some point things have to change. If they can change in the future, why not change them now?"

"And then we break up next week and I compromised my reputation for no reason."

"Okay, so when? What's the line you have to cross before you say, okay, I'm ready for everyone to know this is my man?"

"Maybe the year after next? When I finish the program." Realistically, we would never last that long. There were a thousand things that could break us apart between now and then.

"You're going to wait two years? And everyone in the hospital will think you're a big fat liar and not believe anything you say from then on."

I groaned. There was no easy answer.

"The fact that you're breaking your rules for this guy, the fact that you're telling me it's so great between you and it's so easy—that's not a problem. Unexpected things work out. Look at me and Tristan. No one saw that coming."

I narrowed my eyes at her, incredulous that she could be so naïve. "What are you talking about? Everyone saw that coming! You two had heart eyes every time you were in a mile radius of each other. Your father invited Tristan to that fundraiser because he wanted to introduce the two of you, then he gave you a real honeymoon for your fake marriage so you were forced to spend time together. Come on."

"Okay, maybe you're right. I'm just saying that if you're prepared to break your stupid rules for this guy, he must mean something to you beyond the good sex. And if he does mean something, you can't live like vampires. At some point you're going to have to come out into the sun."

Parker was right. Jacob and I couldn't stay in hiding forever. There was no low-key dating Jacob Cove. He was the hospital heartthrob. I was going to get low-key hated by at least eighty percent of the women on staff and a hefty proportion of the men. There was no easy answer except calling it quits.

TWENTY-EIGHT

Jacob

I was so exhausted that I couldn't contemplate doing anything tonight other than eating dinner and falling into bed. Flu was spreading through the staff and three members of the team had called in sick today.

I knocked on the door to Sutton's flat, bracing myself against the doorframe to stop myself from falling over.

She opened the door and it was like a shot of adrenaline straight to the heart.

"You look beautiful," I said, sweeping my gaze down her Lycra-clad body.

She laughed. "I look sweaty. I just came back from a run." She went up on tiptoes for a kiss, but I grabbed her bottom, hitched her up, kicked the door closed, and pushed her against the wall, pressing my lips against hers.

"How was your day?" she asked.

"Better now I'm here with you."

"Dinner's ready."

"I'm hungry for you," I said. I was always hungry for

her. Even on days when I thought I didn't have the energy, as soon as I saw her, I couldn't get enough.

She pressed a kiss on my cheek and pulled me tightly toward her, like she hadn't seen me in months rather than days. "I've missed you."

My stomach flipped and I realized that was exactly what I needed to hear. I kissed the top of her head. "I've missed you too." It was time to share some food and talk. The sex could wait.

"How was the run?" I asked as I let her go. She led me into her tiny kitchen.

"Honestly, I think I could have walked quicker, but running sounds better, right? I ordered takeaway and it arrived about two minutes before you did. This kitchen is . . . hardly a chef's kitchen."

Her flat was tiny. Her kitchen barely qualified for the title.

"Parker asked me to move in with her and Tristan again the other day when we went for lunch in the park." She laughed. "As if."

"You don't want to?"

"I don't want to share with a couple. And a fairly new couple at that." She pulled out some boxes. "I got Lebanese."

"We should spend more time at mine," I said. "I'll get a key cut so you can come and go as you please."

She turned to me, half smiling, half frowning. "Are we ready for an exchange of keys?"

I shook my head. "No offense, but I don't want a key to this place."

"You mean you don't want to enjoy my basement view of the car park? How dare you." She smiled as she got out two plates and set them down. "A key though? Is that . . . I mean, we've only been dating a few weeks . . ." She was cautious, bordering on suspicious of things between us, or me. I couldn't decide.

"Is there some rulebook you're working with that I'm not aware of? Because if you are, I think I need a copy to see what's meant to happen when. I don't want to miss a milestone."

She prodded my arm. "There's no rulebook."

"My place is a little more spacious. And I have a kitchen we can cook in. It makes sense to spend more time there. And if I give you a key, it means you don't have to leave with me at the same time, and you can come round early. It's not a ring. It's a key."

She handed me a plateful of food and held up a fork. "Okay, if you put it like that, I'll take the key."

"Good," I said.

"Good. I really don't know why you had to make a big deal about it." She grinned at me and I shook my head.

We padded back into the living room-slash-bedroom, where A-ha was playing softly in the background. We sat on the floor, our plates balanced on her small coffee table. "So how was lunch with Parker, apart from her asking you to move in with her?"

"Good." She sighed like it was the opposite of good.

"That doesn't sound good."

She shrugged and ripped off some of the flatbread. "I told her about us."

"And that's bad?"

"Why would you think that's bad?"

"Oh, I don't know, the look on your face?"

She stayed silent for a beat too long as she chewed and swallowed her flatbread. "She just thinks that I'm stupid for not wanting to take our relationship public."

I sighed. Okay, so the best friend was weighing in on the relationship. "And what do you think?"

"I think she doesn't understand the stakes. For either of us."

"Right," I replied. "So, what's with sighing and the expression of doubt?"

"Things are complicated." She shook her head. "And I'm overthinking."

"Not like you," I said sarcastically.

She rolled her eyes. "She just made a joke about how we'd be forty with two kids and we'd still be pretending to everyone in the hospital that we weren't dating."

I laughed. "Forty is only four years away for me. Not so inconceivable."

She wasn't laughing. "I guess she just got my brain whirring. I started to . . . think about stuff."

That didn't sound like a positive thing, certainly if the look on her face was anything to go by. "Maybe we don't need to think about four years from now."

"Exactly," she said, not sounding very convincing. "We're just borrowing trouble, right?"

"Right. Except I'm not sure you're entirely convinced."

"Oh, I completely believe trouble is just around the corner. I don't need any convincing. I just need to . . . relax."

I couldn't imagine what it was like to live ready to fight. It must be exhausting. I wanted to take that away from her. Shield her from everything bad.

"Sutton, tell me what's on your mind. What's really bothering you?"

"I'm not bothered exactly, it's just . . . I like you. And I don't see that there'll ever be a time when it's okay for us to be a public couple."

"I don't think we need to worry. Right now, it's difficult.

I'm trying to position myself for this promotion; you're trying to prove yourself. It doesn't work at the moment but things shift and change. We can't pre-empt anything. We can't see into the future. Things have a way of working themselves out."

"Says you. Things just don't 'work out' for everyone."

"No, you're right. We're surrounded by evidence of that all day long. But in terms of relationships and two people being together—we will make it work. If you remember, we were both determined to stay away from each other. Look how that turned out."

I put down my fork, shifted to outstretch my legs and then pulled her onto my lap so she faced me. I got the feeling this was about more than us—that she was braced for bad things to happen. It was understandable, and it broke my heart a little.

I tucked a loose strand of hair around her ear. "At the moment, I think we're both doing what's best for right now. Do I think if we're together down the road, we'll still be sneaking into each other's houses? No, I don't. I think we need to cross that bridge when we come to it unless you're unhappy right now. Are you?"

She shook her head. "No. Right now I'm the opposite of unhappy."

I wasn't sure if she was trying to be funny or whether she had an issue with allowing herself to say she was happy. Maybe she was afraid of being happy. Given the way she grew up, it would be completely understandable.

"We should get away," I said. "Norfolk was great. We could relax and not worry too much about who was watching."

"Where were you thinking?"

"How about the Cotswolds? Or Bath?"

"Bath is further away. We're less likely to see someone we know."

"Okay, next time we both have two days off at the same time, we'll go to Bath. How does that sound?"

"I feel a lot better. It's like you can see inside my head sometimes." I felt exactly the same about her.

"That'll be the CAT scan I did in your sleep the other night."

"I'm sorry for freaking out. There's just so much at stake," she said. We both had a lot to lose, but I was beginning to realize Sutton was braced for a fight all the time. It was almost as if she was expecting things to go wrong.

"Don't ever apologize. You've worked hard to get where you are. Of course you want to protect that."

The look of doubt had gone and I had smiley Sutton back in my arms. "I mean it, you always know the exact right thing to say to me."

"It's easy when you tell me what you're thinking."

"You don't want to know what I'm thinking right now," she said, smoothing her hands over my chest. Her tongue darted out to wet her lips.

"You should know you're an open book. Don't take up poker."

She leaned forward, pressing a kiss against my neck. "Shall we take a shower?"

I couldn't help but laugh. "Here?" Her shower was only just big enough for me on a good day. There's no way we'd both fit.

She twisted her hips, grinding herself against my crotch.

"I think right here will do," I growled, before flipping her to her back and crawling over her. I was already hard. My erection pressed against my fly, eager to move things along. "You're so sexy."

"Do you mean sweaty? Even though my run was more of a walk, I'm still pretty gross."

She couldn't be gross if she tried.

I pressed a kiss to her neck then ran my teeth over her skin. I wanted to devour her. I'd never craved someone like I craved Sutton. With her, it was a physical need, but it was also more. I wanted to know every thought she was having, take away every drop of self-doubt, heal every wound.

She wiggled her hips underneath me, impatient.

"I can get you sweatier than a run." I cupped her breasts and smoothed my hand over her stomach. "I can get you panting, desperate to catch your breath." I slid my hand down the inside of her Lycra trousers, wanting to feel her heat, her impatience, the wetness that was just for me. My fingers found her clit and I slid through her slick folds as she gasped. Like it was a shock how good I felt despite the fact we knew it was always good. So good.

"Jacob, more," she cried. I caught the plea in my mouth, kissing her roughly. I wanted to show her that the doubt and anxiety about us was misplaced because we had *this*. This connection that was physical and mental and completely unquenchable.

She began to grind against my hand but I wasn't going to let her come like that. No, not after our conversation tonight. I wanted to be inside her, as close as possible when she came each and every time tonight. I withdrew my hand and stood, pulling her onto her feet and bending her over the bed. Before her hands hit the mattress, I yanked down her leggings to her knees and undid my trousers. I wasn't prepared to wait for us to undress. I was impatient to be inside her. I wanted to make her come, to explain in more than words why we'd overcome any obstacle that came our way.

I rammed into her, pulling her hips back against me, in a movement so sharp and sudden, she lost balance. But I had her. My grip around her was solid, my fingers pressed firm into her flesh. I slammed into her again and she reached around for I don't know what. She needed to understand that I had this for both of us.

I was going to make it so good, so fucking hard and deep and tight that she'd be coming in seconds.

I thrust again and again and again, driving into her relentlessly. "You see, Sutton. It's always good between us. When it's slow and intimate or when it's fast and deep. It doesn't matter. We're us. We're good every way."

She started to shake beneath me. Her thighs, her arse, her entire body dissolved into orgasm and as I watched, my climax broke out of its hiding place and hurtled up my spine and I exploded.

I hadn't got my breath back, but I knew we both needed more.

"Again," I bit out. I knelt and pulled her leggings off the rest of the way, then stripped off my shirt and trousers. She didn't move, still bent over the bed, trying to recover.

I turned her to her back, pulling her legs up my body. She gazed up at me and I made a mental note never to miss another opportunity to watch her expression as I fucked her. She always wore an expression of awe and wonder that made me feel like I was the luckiest man on the planet.

"You're amazing," she said.

"*You're* amazing. Strong. Determined. Sexy." There was nothing the woman beneath me couldn't do. And deep down, she knew it. The problem was she was always braced for disaster. But we weren't a disaster. We were anything but.

TWENTY-NINE

Sutton

I wasn't sure what it was about waking up at Jacob's place, but I just felt more rested than I did at mine. The eight hours sleep probably helped. The Egyptian cotton sheets and perfectly air-conditioned bedroom didn't hurt either. Being at Jacob's place was like sleeping in a luxury hotel.

The only drawback was the lack of room service. I knocked the bedroom door open with my foot and slid the tray of coffee onto the bedside table. I'd gotten showered and changed and packed up all my stuff and was ready to leave. Nothing had stirred Jacob. Maybe the smell of coffee would rouse him. Maybe not.

"Don't leave without a kiss," he said in that gravelly voice he always had when he woke up. The timbre sent vibrations between my legs and I squeezed my thighs together. I was going to have to take a cold shower on my break. I couldn't be late for work.

He reached out for me and pulled me onto the bed and into his arms.

"I have to leave."

"Call in sick," he said.

I pressed kiss after kiss after kiss along his jaw. "As if."

He released me and I leaned over the bed to place a kiss on his forehead like he so often did to me.

"I'd rather stay here with you, but I have to go."

"I'm going to look at the rotas. You haven't had a day off at the weekends for weeks." Jacob was lucky—as a consultant doing mainly elective procedures and weekday clinics, he didn't often work weekends. The rest of us covered.

"Please don't," I said. The last thing we needed was Jacob suggesting a change to my schedule—we might as well hold hands around the children's ward. "I'm going to go."

"You're coming over after?" he asked. "I'll cook."

"Sounds good." I turned to leave and he grabbed my hand and pulled me back to him, cupping my face in his hands and kissing me into next week.

Giddy, I pulled away. "I'm going to be late. I've put coffee by the bed. Have a good day."

I hooked my backpack over my shoulder, scooted downstairs, and unlocked the front door. Outside, the air had shifted. The weather had been so beautiful the last few weeks I hadn't thought to bring a coat last time I was at my place. But this morning, the blue sky had been covered over with a blanket of grey-white clouds threatening rain. There was a real chill in the air.

Hopefully I'd make it to the hospital before the rain started. It was only a few minutes' walk.

At the gate, I punched in the code, which released the lock. On the sideway just outside, I ran straight into Gilly.

I froze, completely unable to move or speak.

Shit. Shit. Shit.

"Hi." I tried to sound breezy as my heart thundered in my chest. I knew *easy* was just the prologue to disastrous.

She stopped and narrowed her eyes. "Hi." She glanced back at the house.

"Are you starting at eight?" I asked, walking in the direction of the hospital.

"You don't live there," she said.

I didn't reply. I was in the middle of a minefield. Wherever I trod, I could get blown to smithereens.

"I'm really hoping I get to work with Hartford," I said. It turned out Hartford was married to one of Tristan's best friends. London could be a small place at times. "She's back from sabbatical today. Did you hear?" I was hoping to distract Gilly from asking me where I'd been.

"Are you sleeping with Jacob Cove?" Her voice had a tinny edge to it I didn't recognize.

My heart sank into my stomach and I wanted to throw up. "Why would you say that?" I asked, very deliberately not answering the question. I don't know how I kept walking, but thankfully my feet carried me forward, toward the hospital.

"Because you just crept out of his house at eight in the morning carrying a backpack."

I kept my gaze forward. I couldn't risk catching her eye, trying to think of something to say. How did she know this was his house?

"You must really want that foundation award."

I frowned. "You think I'm sleeping with Jacob to get an award?"

"Oh, so you admit it? You are sleeping with him."

"I didn't say that. But I can assure you my personal life and my professional life are completely separate. I would never sleep with someone to get ahead."

"That's not what people will think when they find out. You know it's always the women who end up with the short end of the stick in these situations."

"In what situations?" I couldn't outright deny that I was sleeping with Jacob without lying to Gilly. And given she knew where Jacob lived and knew our shifts, it wouldn't be too hard to catch me in my lie.

"You know, sleeping with the boss. Don't worry. I won't say anything. But like it or not, it's bound to come out." She linked her arm through mine. "Stick with me. I'll be there in your corner when the shit hits the fan."

"Gilly, I think you've got the wrong end of the stick, I just—"

"No need to say a word. Your secret's safe with me. In a way, it works better for me. There's no way he can single you out as the most promising foundation doctor on his rotation now, is there?"

My chest grew tight and I wanted to pull my arm from hers so I could breathe. What was she saying? That I'd disqualified myself from the foundation award because of Jacob? Or that if Jacob didn't disqualify me, she'd make sure our secret wouldn't be so secret anymore?

There was a definite subtext to what she was saying. However it translated, it didn't look good for me.

Five minutes ago, I was excited about going to work. Now I was anything but. Now, I wanted to run back to Jacob so he could tell me everything was going to be okay. But it wasn't going to be. Jacob wasn't God. He couldn't perform miracles.

How this situation went was up to me.

I hadn't worked this hard for this long for Gilly to come along and ruin it. I had to take matters into my own hands.

"I'm not sleeping with Jacob," I said. The words came

out without touching the sides of my mouth. I'd been here before—in a situation where I had to sink or swim. I was working on autopilot.

Gilly laughed. "I told you, I won't tell anyone."

"If you did, you'd be a liar. I can't imagine Jacob would take very kindly to an FY1 spreading gossip around the hospital about him." It might not have been true before. But it was now. There was no way things could continue between us.

"Rumors can come from all sorts of places," she said.

"You're the only one who thinks Jacob and I are sleeping together. We're not."

She laughed. "Why else would you be coming out of his house so early?"

"For your information, I dropped off a book he needed and couldn't get hold of. He's doing some research and I had a relevant coursebook from my second year at med school. That's all." The lies were coming thick and fast, but I wasn't sorry. This is what had to happen.

"Come on, Sutton, I wasn't born yesterday. Why wouldn't you give him a book at the hospital?"

"Not that it's any of your business, but he's writing a paper. The deadline is today and he's off. He lives on my way to the hospital. I told him I'd drop it in."

She stayed silent and I mentally crossed my fingers and toes, hoping she was buying my story.

"What book was it?" she asked.

I sighed. She thought she had something over me, but she hadn't met me. No, I didn't want to lie, but I wasn't letting Gilly Peters of all people back me into a corner. I wasn't about to let her bring me down. Gilly had led a privileged life up until now. She'd attended a private school, got into one of the best universities, left without any student debt. Life had been good to her. She'd be punching above her weight if she tried to low-key blackmail me. There weren't people like me in her world, people who had to fight to get where they were, rather than just float down to a gentle landing. From sixteen, I'd had no one to count on but myself. I'd had to make hard decisions about whether to choose between heating and food.

She'd underestimated me.

Something in me had shifted gears. I'd reversed back in time to when I'd eaten nothing but cornflakes for three straight months, to pretending I didn't feel the cold to the girls in the salon to explain why I wasn't wearing a coat in the middle of winter. I'd done what I'd had to do. "He asked me not to mention it to anyone. This paper he's writing is pretty high profile and he's trying to keep it private."

She scrunched up her nose. "So why would he tell you about it if you weren't having some kind of relationship outside of work?"

"Jesus, Gilly, stop being so suspicious of everyone. He'd seen on my CV that I'd taken the course at uni. He wanted to ask me a couple of questions about my tutor. It's no big deal. But if you go around telling people we're having an affair, the only one becoming ineligible for the foundation award will be you."

She shot me a look and I shrugged.

"Believe me or don't. It's up to you. But having a reputation as a gossip won't be a good thing. You know how it is," I said. "People always vilify women much more than they do men."

It was her turn to stare ahead this time. "I'm not a gossip." Her tone had lost its confidence.

"*I* know that, Gilly. I get that it was just a misunderstanding on your part. I'm not sure what Jacob will say. You know how well-connected he is. You don't want things to be over for you before they begin."

She let out a fake laugh. "Of course they won't be. Anyway, like you said. It was just a misunderstanding. I was just *hoping* the two of you were having some kind of illicit affair. Then I could live vicariously."

I pulled my mouth into a smile. "If I were having an affair with Jacob Cove, I'd want to shout it from the rooftops."

"Wouldn't we all? You think he's single?" she asked.

I let out a long, slow breath. "Who knows? Have you asked him?"

"Maybe when we change rotations, I'll suggest a drink."

The idea of Jacob spending any time with Gilly outside of the hospital made me want to vomit, but at least the attention had been focused away from me.

I'd been lucky this time. I wouldn't put myself in a position where I had to rely on a roll of the dice again.

THIRTY

Jacob

Sutton and I had a deal that we didn't text if one of us was on shift—the focus stayed on the job. So getting a text from her when I knew she was at the hospital was out of the ordinary. The tone of her message cemented things. Something was up. Her second and final text asked me to drive halfway around the North Circular to meet her in the Ikea car park in Tottenham. There were only so many people in my life that I'd do something like that for. Sutton was one of them.

As I pulled into the multi-story, I spotted the blue VW she'd told me to look out for. I pulled in next to her like we were about to do a drug deal.

I cut the engine and went to open the door, but she opened the passenger door and slipped inside.

"Hi," I said, leaning over to kiss her.

She didn't exactly flinch, but it was close. Dread settled in my gut.

"What's going on?" I asked.

"Gilly saw me leaving your place this morning. She

tried to suggest my career would be derailed because of a conflict of interest."

I let out a short laugh it was so ridiculous. "Of course it would be Gilly you met. She's poisonous."

She fixed me with a stare. I was being unprofessional.

"I know," I said, taking the admonishment I knew was circling in her brain. I lay my hand face up on her knee. She hesitated but eventually linked her fingers through mine. "Tell me what happened."

"Like I said, Gilly saw me coming through the front gate as I was leaving."

"How did she know it was my house?"

"Really good question," she replied. "Maybe she's researched where you live because she was hoping to accidently-on-purpose bump into you?"

"Research how though? By following me home?"

She pulled in a breath. "I didn't think about it, but I wouldn't put it past her. She was never my favorite of my year, but I didn't think she was quite the bitch it turns out she is."

"So, you see her and then what?"

"First of all, I tried to skirt around the issue by not saying anything. She basically said there would be consequences if we were sleeping together and I figured gloves were off. I told her you were doing a research project on a topic I studied at uni. We'd got talking about it and you were working on it today and needed a book I had."

"Wow," I said, trying to take it in. "That's quite the story."

"I needed a reason to be at your house that early in the morning. It was the first thing that sprang to mind."

"You think she believed you?"

"I think so." She winced. "I might also have suggested

that if she started gossiping and it got back to you, it could ruin her career."

I pushed my hand over my head. This was getting really messy. "What's the research project I'm supposed to be doing?"

"No idea."

"Okay, well, we can think of something. Maybe I'll even do some actual research and write an article about it."

She lifted the corners of her mouth into a small smile. "It was awful. I thought it was game over for both of us."

"Any other person you'd have run into would just assume you were leaving your own house. Or your boyfriend's house. They wouldn't be borderline stalking me and know where I lived. We were just unlucky."

"Right," she agreed. "This time we were lucky. But I think we should take it as a sign." She glanced down at our hands and rubbed her finger over my knuckle.

"What kind of sign?"

"That we're cutting it too close."

Jesus, we were being really careful. We never left the hospital together. We never went out, day or night. The only time we'd acted like a normal couple had been in Norfolk. "Okay, then we'll be more careful."

She shook her head. "How? I can *never* go to your house now. It's impossible. She'll probably lie in wait, just hoping to catch me out. And she'll be looking for other signs, no doubt."

The swirl of dread in my stomach picked up speed and spread into my lungs. "It feels like you want to tell me some-thing else."

"I don't *want* to tell you anything." She shifted in her seat so she faced me. "But . . . there's no way forward for us."

My breath stuck in my throat and I tried to tell myself it

was just anxiety, that my body wasn't starting to shut down. Subconsciously I'd known what Sutton was going to say from the moment I got the text. There'd only be a couple of reasons she would have broken her rules to contact me during a shift. Ending things between us was one of them.

My breath started to seep back into my lungs and I found my voice. "Let's find a way forward," I said. "I don't want to walk away from you."

She bowed her head. "I've thought about nothing else all day, which is another reason why this isn't a good situation to be in. I should have been focused on the job."

This was everything Sutton had been worried about when we'd gotten together.

"Don't be so hard on yourself." The bar Sutton set for herself was several meters higher than most foundation doctors. But I knew my words were wasted before I'd finished my sentence. Sutton couldn't help but be hard on herself. It was how she'd survived what she did. It was how she was sitting next to me. "I'm sure we can make it work," I said.

"Not everything works out for the best." Her tone was worn with experience.

"We just need to let things cool off until . . ."

"Until when? Like Parker said, I'm not going to secretly be pregnant with everyone wondering who the father is. It was inevitable that this is where we would end up. You're always going to be going for the next promotion—it's who you are. And I'm never going to want to be sleeping with the boss. That's who I am. I don't see either of those things changing."

My thoughts were scattered in every direction. I was searching for a solution and coming up empty. She was right, but I didn't want her to be.

"So even though I hate Gilly, she's just made us skip to the end a little quicker than if things had taken their course."

She seemed so matter-of-fact about things. Maybe because she was used to disappointment. She was used to sacrifice. It didn't make it any easier to bear.

"I really like you," I said.

"This has nothing to do with whether you like me. Or whether I . . . Whether I think you're just about the best man I've ever known." Her voice cracked at the end of the sentence and she paused. "It's nothing to do with any of that," she whispered. "It's about doing what we need to do to get where we're headed."

"I'm not sure where I'm headed now." It was a flippant remark. I knew exactly what she meant and she wasn't wrong. Perhaps we should have never given in when we were in Hertfordshire. Maybe my heart wouldn't feel quite so heavy in my chest at this moment if we'd managed to stay away from each other.

"It's for the best," she said, squeezing my hand.

I wished we weren't in the car. I wished I could at least pull her into my arms. Feel her hands on my chest one last time.

"At least we switch rotations in a couple of weeks. There's a chance we can avoid each other."

My stomach churned at the thought of having to avoid her. I didn't want to. But she was right, it would be easier if she wasn't around me all day, demonstrating her good instincts, brilliance, and warmth. "It will take more than just a different department for this to be okay."

She nodded. "I know."

I wanted to get out of the car and run somewhere. I wanted to transport myself to Norfolk and fill my lungs with sea air and walk until my legs wouldn't carry me any further. I wanted to scream at the sea about how unfair this all was.

"Maybe . . ."

She shook her head before I finished my thought, let alone my sentence. "Don't say maybe there's a chance things will change or we'll find a solution. We both know it won't happen. It will be easier if we just accept the way things are."

I hated seeing her so steeled. We could figure this out. "I think you're bright and special and wonderful and—"

She squeezed my hand as if willing me to stop.

"I should go." She stared at our linked hands but didn't try to move.

"Look at me," I said.

Quick as a flash, she withdrew her hands and pressed her palms to my cheeks. "Thank you." She pressed her lips against mine. Almost before I'd registered it, her warmth had left me, the breeze from her opening the car door hitting me in the chest. All I could do was sit as she got back into her car, reversed, and drove away.

I couldn't chase after her—this was what she wanted. This was what I wanted.

Wasn't it?

THIRTY-ONE

Sutton

Chopping onions was therapeutic. That's what I'd told myself when Parker had assigned me the job. She and Tristan were hosting dinner for her and some of Tristan's friends. I'd gotten to meet a number of them over the last few months, but hadn't gotten to chat much with a couple of them. They all seemed lovely. I just could have done with a night in with Parker and a tub of Haagen Dazs. I was dreading telling her about Jacob. I didn't want to bring it all up in my thoughts again. The last few days, I'd managed to push them down and keep myself busy. As soon as I told Parker, I knew we would discuss nothing else for the rest of the evening.

"How many more?" I asked.

"We need five all together," Parker said as she busied herself butchering a chicken.

"Five onions is a lot of onions," I said.

"Tristan has a lot of friends. Well, they're our friends

now," she said, smiling. "Not that anyone will ever replace you."

"Better not."

"Of course not. They're your friends, too."

"Is Tristan my boyfriend too?" I smiled at her.

"You already have one of your own."

I kept my smile in place just long enough to be interrupted by the doorbell.

"That will be Stella. You've met her, right?"

I nodded and glanced at the clock over the door. "She's really early." It was only five and I thought things were kicking off at seven.

"She's having the day off work and said she was bored, so I invited her over for pre-game drinks. I hope that's okay."

I nodded. The idea of a dinner party with a bunch of couples was my own very special brand of hell, but Parker was my friend and I wasn't going to not come just because my heart was broken. A wave of regret rose in my stomach and crashed to my knees. Not regret for making the decision to end things but regret that the decision was unavoidable. Regret that Jacob's boyish optimism hadn't carried us through as I'd let myself hope that it might. Regret that I'd let myself get a little bit too comfortable—I should have known better. Now I was to face an evening with a bunch of couples when I'd broken up from the only man who I'd ever felt was completely in my corner. The only man who made me feel like I wasn't dating up, despite him being clever and kind and brilliant and everything I could ever have dreamed up.

Parker burst back into the kitchen. "Stella's brought champagne. Not that we don't have enough already."

"Sorry, I must stink of onions," I said as I waved.

"Oh, we have to hug, onions or no onions," Stella said, rounding the kitchen island and pulling me into her arms.

Stella was blonde and beautiful and the kind of woman whose appearance made me reassess my wardrobe choices—effortlessly stylish but not overdone.

"You two carry on with what you're doing. I'll get some champs opened and then you can give me a job." She pulled out a bottle of champagne from the tote she was carrying and set it on the side, then headed to the cabinet with the wine glasses in them. She must come here a lot. I felt a pang of jealousy. Did she and Parker have girls' nights I wasn't aware of?

"Oh, I saw the details of the house Dexter sent you," she said. "It's so great. And in Hampstead, which I know you wanted. Even though I want you to move to Mayfair."

Parker shook her head. "We have our hearts set on Hampstead. I'd never see anything of Sutton otherwise. And of course, I love the area."

Stella popped the cork and poured the first glass of champagne.

"We're going to view it on Saturday."

This was news to me. Parker hadn't said anything about a house viewing.

"Beck and I will come with you. That way, Beck can tell you all about what the potential of the place is like. You're never going to find something perfect, but as long as you can adapt it . . ."

The two of them went back and forth about non-negotiables and what was important in a house. Their voices started to fade out and all I could focus on was the ball of jealousy in my heart. I'd never been jealous of Parker before. She'd grown up with a family who loved her and more money that I could even dream about, but I'd never felt envious of her.

Until now, as she was discussing her requirements for the perfect house with her perfect friend in her already perfect kitchen as I helped her prepare the perfect meal for all her other perfect friends. And I hated myself for wanting all that for myself too.

I tried to focus on getting the onion chopped as finely as I could, one slice after another after another and another.

"Sutton?" Parker said.

I snapped my head up from the chopping board and realized I hadn't heard what they were saying for the last few minutes.

"Sorry, in another world. What were you saying?"

She narrowed her eyes. "Are you okay?"

I nodded and continued to slice over and over and over and—

The blade of the knife slipped and caught my finger. "Shit," I said, dropping the knife and pressing my finger over the wound.

"Sutton!" Parker said. "What happened?"

I headed to the sink. The juices of the onion made the cut sting and I bit down on my cheek to stop the tears forming in my eyes.

Parker got to the sink before I did and turned the tap. I pushed my hand under the running water and the blood mixed with the water like the closing credits of a budget horror movie. "It's fine," I said as I caught Parker's eye. "The knife slipped. I'm totally fine. Do you have a plaster?"

I could tell by the way Parker didn't respond that she didn't believe I was *totally fine*.

"Have you been on the booze before I arrived?" Stella asked.

"Remind me to be sick during my surgery rotation," I said, trying to make light of the situation.

I cleaned my wound, stuck a plaster on, and then headed back to the chopping board.

"I don't think so," Parker said. "No more chopping for you. I'll finish that off. You take a seat and sip some champagne. I want to hear about your week."

Parker and I had spoken a little less than usual this week. After I drove off from breaking it off with Jacob, I got the urge to keep driving, but given I'd hired a car and couldn't afford the penalties, I figured I'd drop the car off and go back to life before Jacob. Except my life before Jacob didn't include my job, so it was a completely impossible task.

"What do you want to hear about? I worked. I slept. I ate. And then I worked again," I said.

"Did you see Jacob?" Parker turned to Stella. "Jacob is another doctor at the hospital. Total hottie by all accounts. And they're secretly dating because of hospital politics."

"Actually we're not secretly dating. We're not dating at all. I called things off."

Parker set down her knife and stared at me, her mouth open. "Why didn't you tell me?"

I looked down at my glass. I really didn't want to talk about this. I knew I'd made the right decision and I just wanted to skip to the bit where I felt fine.

"Gosh, I'm sorry. Had you two been dating long?" Stella asked.

"No, just a couple of months," I replied, as my eyes filled with tears. Parker rushed over to me and pulled me in for a hug. "Don't be nice to me."

"I will so be nice to you. There's no way I'm not giving you a hug. What did he do?"

I sucked in a breath, determined not to crumble. "He didn't do anything. That's the worst part."

Stella topped up our champagne glasses as Parker just hugged me tight and I told her what had happened when Gilly spotted me coming out of Jacob's house.

"You were right," I said, my voice faltering. "It was never going to work long term anyway, so I don't know why I'm so upset."

Parker held me by the shoulders. "The ones you really like, really hurt. Look at the mess I was in when Tristan and I hit our road bump."

"Except there'll be no happy ending for me," I said. I had to be realistic.

"If it helps at all," Stella said. "The guy I thought was *the one* for me ended things. The next thing I knew, he was engaged to my best friend and . . . get this, he sent me an invitation to the wedding."

"You're kidding," Parker said.

Stella shook her head. "And I ended up going."

A revelation like that was enough to knock me out of my wallowing. "You went to the wedding of your ex-boyfriend and your best friend?"

"Long story, but yes. I kind of got an offer I couldn't refuse from Beck—who was a total stranger to me at the time."

"Beck wanted to go to the wedding?"

"Yup. I ended up going to the wedding of the man I thought I was going to marry, only to end up finding my true soulmate while I was there. This Jacob guy is just the one before you meet your endgame."

I smiled like I believed her, but as I'd said to Jacob, things didn't always turn out for the best. "Thanks, Stella."

"I know you really liked him," Parker said, knowing that

platitudes weren't going to make me feel any better. "You'd never have bent your rules for just anyone."

Stella meant well, but she didn't understand how difficult giving up Jacob had been. I hadn't expected it to be so wrenching to say those words to him in the car, to pull away from him and leave. It had taken everything I had. I'd comforted myself with the knowledge that the pain would fade. But here I was, days later, with a wound as fresh as it had been.

"I just didn't expect it to hit me so hard," I explained.

Parker and Stella exchanged a look.

"And there's definitely no way, though?" Stella asked.

I shook my head. "We've both tried to think of a solution but we've come up blank."

"It's such a shame," Stella said. "It's not like one of you wants to end it and the other one doesn't. It sounds like you're both in love but the logistics don't work. It's heartbreaking."

In love . . .

I'd suspected. Yes, she was right—I was in love with Jacob. I'd avoided defining my feelings for him—too scared of the implications—but there was no denying it. What I felt for him was different from anything I'd ever felt for anyone. The problem was, love wasn't enough.

Parker caught my eye. She was looking for confirmation that Stella was right, that I was in love with Jacob.

"He sees the best in me and wants the best for me," I said. "And I feel the same about him. It's not just sexual chemistry, it's . . . he's . . ." I shut my eyes, willing it all away. I'd dealt with hurt before and I knew it subsided. The pain would evaporate. It had too. Only, Jacob had left a mark on me I wasn't sure would ever fade.

THIRTY-TWO

Jacob

Norfolk was the only place I could be right now. I needed to be away from the hospital. Away from Hampstead. Away from London. I couldn't be anywhere near Sutton because there was no telling what I'd do if I ran into her.

There was nothing *to* do.

She'd been right—there was no way through for us.

"Shall we have another cup of tea?" Mum said, looking up from her magazine. We were both sitting at the kitchen table, the radio on in the background. Mum was almost always busy, so I knew that sitting opposite me, doing nothing but being with her eldest son, was her way of holding my hand.

"I think I might go for a walk," I said.

"Maybe just hang on a few minutes. In case it rains."

I looked out of the kitchen window at the sky. It was a low blanket of white-grey cloud that was definitely set in for the day, but there wasn't a hint of rain. She was trying to keep me from going out on my own. "I just need to clear my head." I'd explained to her that Sutton and I had split up because it was too difficult trying to keep our relationship private. I'd expected her to be relieved; I knew how she felt about relationships within the hospital.

"I know your father is adamant that you boys shouldn't be seeing women in the hospital, but that's how we met."

I nodded. I'd heard the story a thousand times. "I know, Mum."

"Your father and I gave that advice to you and your brothers when you were all young and . . ." She raised her eyes to the ceiling and shook her head. "Having fun."

"I know, Mum. Like I said, Sutton and I met before either of us knew we were working at the same hospital."

She reached over and peeled my hand from my mug of finished tea, grasping it between her own. "I'm not criticizing you. I'm saying, you're not a boy anymore. You're a thirty-six-year-old, accomplished, caring doctor."

Accomplished? Not compared to her and Dad.

"And you and Sutton seemed like . . . a good match."

I groaned and pulled my hand away. I didn't want to hear about how well-matched Sutton and I were.

"Jacob, I'm saying in your circumstances—where two people are serious about each other—it's different."

"We've been dating a couple of months. Things were good but who knows if we were serious. What I do know is that I'm not going to be promoted to head of the foundation program if I'm sleeping with one of the foundation doctors."

"Well, I have two things to say about that. First, it doesn't take more than a couple of months to understand if someone is right for you. I knew I was going to marry your father the night I met him."

A pressure released from my chest as my mother spoke, like a restrictive dressing had just been cut away, the wound beneath it healed. Sutton felt right for me. I'd known it since that first evening we'd spent drinking tequila and sharing our lives. Sutton had been different from the start.

It was confirmed when I couldn't stay away from her. Yes, we had a physical attraction stronger than my will, but it was more than that. I admired her. Respected her. I wanted to make her happy and make her smile. I wanted to share every part of my day, every thought, every moment with her. "What was the second thing?"

"There will be another promotion. One that doesn't involve the foundation program."

"I've been working toward that promotion for as long as I can remember."

She sighed, pulled her hand away, and stood. "You know your father and I never planned out our careers like this. We did what interested us. Some decisions led us down dead ends, but at least we enjoyed the day-to-day. Other decisions led to fantastic opportunities."

"I get that, Mum, but honestly, things are different now. I'm your son. People's eyes are on me. I can't make mistakes and go down the wrong route. But if I make the right choices . . ." I didn't want to hurt her. It wasn't a bad thing that she and my father had had such distinguished careers. It just meant it was harder for me to establish myself in my own right. "I need to make the right choices."

She pulled out a bowl of cold roast potatoes from the fridge and set them on the table. Not even my favorite thing my mother cooked could encourage me to eat at the moment.

"Have you ever considered why your brothers aren't as . . . careful as you are, despite them also being our sons?"

"What do you mean?"

"You're telling me you have to make the right choice,

that people are watching you because you're a Cove, but none of your brothers feel like that as far as I'm aware."

"They're not at the same stage in their careers."

She pushed her lips together in the way she did when she didn't agree with what you were saying but didn't want to make a thing out of it. "You've always been the same. A total overachiever, but somehow you don't see it." She shook her head and her eyes dropped to her lap. "I feel like I've failed you."

"Mum," I said, shuffling my chair around to hers and putting my arm around her shoulders. "You've done anything but fail me. How you brought the five of us up and had the career you did, I have no idea. Dad wasn't much help."

She laughed. "When you were growing up, your father was . . . He was in a very high-pressure job, as the Chief Medical Officer. It didn't leave much room for family time."

"I don't remember him much back then, if I'm honest." That wasn't quite true. I remember when he was around, he was grumpy and used to bark instructions at me. I remember being pleased he was gone a lot. I remember thinking that no matter what I did, it wasn't good enough. There were no big rows or falling out. Just questions about what I'd gotten wrong when I'd come second in the school in my chemistry exam at sixteen. Remarks about how there was always room to do better when I'd got a biology prize at fourteen. And then of course, the merciless teasing from the entire family when I was at university and I made millions from designing and selling a female urinal that got sold to hospitals and care homes worldwide.

"He felt very guilty at not being there when you were younger. I don't think he handled the conflicting commitments very well, if I'm honest." It was the first time I'd ever heard my mum say that about my father, but she was right. "He was hard on you. I think he thought he should be. He was trying to figure out how to be a dad while working. The way he describes it was that he wanted to make up for not being around a lot and wanted to make a mark when he did. He wanted to guide you and keep you out of trouble. I think he ended up undermining your spirit a little."

"You've talked to him about it?"

"Of course I have. Your father and I talk about everything. That's why we've lasted so long."

I wasn't asking whether they'd had roundabout conversations about parenting—but more specifically, whether they'd talked about me.

"You were our trial run. Our first born. The one we made all the mistakes with. You have to live with that and so do we. It got easier with each of you. We relaxed. Your father stopped trying to shape his children into perfect humans before they could speak. It took years, but eventually he realized that perfection in parenting doesn't exist."

We sat in silence as I let her words permeate.

"You'll see when you have children of your own. It's hard, particularly for your father. He's programmed to be the best at everything and he wanted to be the best dad. It took him a while to realize that being a father was just about being around, listening, laughing with and loving his boys."

"It feels like I can never measure up to you both. That I'm a bit of a letdown."

Mum pushed away from me so she could look me in the eye. "How on earth could you of all people consider yourself a letdown? You're kind and generous and a brilliant medic."

"But I'm never going to be Government CMO, am I?"

"Jacob Cove, you were a self-made multi-millionaire at

twenty. Not many people could say that about themselves. Certainly not me or your father."

"I got lucky. And made myself a laughingstock of the entire family at the same time. An added bonus for Dad and my brothers."

"A laughingstock?"

"This isn't news to you, Mum. Even now no one can talk about going to the loo without making some joke."

"Come on, Jacob—it's funny. A female urinal? You have four brothers. You can't expect them not to find your weakest spot and exploit it. Especially when you're the older brother who gets to try everything first—and not just try it, but be excellent at everything he turns his hand to."

I shrugged. My brothers' jabs didn't bother me. I gave as good as I got. But Dad's barking criticisms? They were easier to internalize. "It's better with Dad now. He doesn't land the low blows."

"Your father adores you." She took her hand in mine. I couldn't remember the last time she had. As a small child, I must have held it all the time, but there must have been a last time—when my desire for independence meant I no longer wanted the comfort her soft fingers provided. I squeezed and made a mental note to hold her hand more often. "He got it wrong when you were younger," she continued. "There's no doubt about that. He was too focused on his work. Too hard on you because he was worried he was going to fail you. He's so proud of you, Jacob. We both are. Not because you're following in our footsteps, but because you're plowing your own path. Honestly, I know we joke about it, but when you invented the urinal, we were both—"

The kitchen door flew open and Dad appeared, his hair sticking on end as usual.

"Those bloody foxes," he said. "I might get myself a gun." He headed over to the sink and began to wash his hands.

My mother shot me a look and shook her head.

"What are you two talking about? You look very comfy."

"Just about Jacob's invention at university."

He grabbed a towel from the Aga and leaned against the sink while he dried his hands.

"I was saying how proud we were of him."

"Of course. Not many twenty-year-old men would be thinking about the gap in the market for something like that. Too busy drinking beer and messing about with corpses or women." He began to chuckle. "Or both."

"John, I'm being serious. What Jacob did was amazing. And the money he made? It was incredible."

"Of course it was," my dad said. "Very typical of him. Thoughtful. But what I thought was more impressive was not the idea—although he fulfilled a serious need—but the fact that he went off and got the legal protections, the protype, put it into production, and then sold it." He raised his hands in surrender. "There are plenty of doctors who would moan about not having this or needing the other thing—like me. I'm an excellent complainer. You, on the other hand, are a doer. You have ideas and you follow through. No one can underestimate the power of that."

Mum squeezed my hand and an unfamiliar swirl of pride circled in my stomach.

"If I'd had a mind like that," Dad continued, "there's no telling what I would have been able to achieve."

"Dad!" I said. "You've had one of the most distinguished careers of anyone in medicine. You're about to be knighted, for goodness' sake."

"I'm not half as capable as you."

"Don't put pressure on him, John."

"Sorry," he said. "I've been guilty of that your whole life, haven't I?" He chucked the towel back on the Aga and came to sit down. "I'm always pushing. Always looking for better. For me, for you, for everyone. It's a curse."

"We're talking about Sutton," Mum said.

I groaned and reached for a cold roast potato. Now I was going to get the long-awaited lecture about keeping my private life private.

"Seemed like a nice girl. Bright. Pretty. You marrying her?"

"Jacob and Sutton have split up," Mum announced.

"Well, you need to make it right, Jacob. I wouldn't be as successful as I am if I hadn't had your mother. Having someone in your corner, someone to lean on and cheer you on, is invaluable."

"I get it," I said. "I just haven't found that person yet."

"Are you sure?" he said.

"I thought you didn't approve of having relationships in hospital," I said.

He shrugged. "These things happen. If it's the right person, it's the right person."

How could he be so blasé? He'd been adamant for so many years.

The sound of car tires on gravel caught my attention. I glanced out the window to see Zach's car pulling into the drive.

So that's why Mum hadn't wanted me to go out for a walk. She'd called the cavalry.

Shame it was a wasted journey.

"Oh, I wasn't expecting to see Zach," she said.

"You're a terrible liar," I said and stood to greet him.

He was the other side of the door when I opened it.

"What's going on?" he said. "Mum said you were upset and it was an emergency."

"Zach!" Mum said.

"What?" Zach asked. "You did. And I've driven up here just like you asked."

"Come on," I said, resigned to the fact that I was going to have a companion on the walk I'd hoped would be solitary. "Let's go for a walk."

"Let me change my shoes," Zach said as he toed off his shoes and grabbed his walking shoes from where all ours were dumped in the corner of the porch.

"Aren't these supposed to be in the boot room?" I asked.

"Dog now owns the boot room," Mum said. "I'll make some bread while you're out."

We shut the door as we left and it felt like I was leaving behind a lot of baggage that had been weighing me down for a long time. Things weren't as I'd thought they were and it was going to take time for me to assimilate the unburdened me. The one whose father not just admired him but thought him more capable in some ways. It had just been a conversation over cold roast potatoes, but one that had shifted the ground I walked on.

―――

THE ROAD down to the quayside was only wide enough for a single car and had no footpath. The village had been established a thousand years ago and wasn't built for two SUVs coming in opposite directions. It was all part of the charm that kept the place feeling a world away from London. Being here was exactly what I needed.

"You know I'm not good at the whole talking thing," Zach said, "but I'm not the worst listener."

"Said who?" I asked. "I'm pretty sure you'd score pretty low as a listener if we surveyed the family."

Zach half smiled, which was the equivalent of a roaring laugh from him. "Maybe."

Despite wanting to be on my own, and despite me not wanting to talk about Sutton, I relayed what had happened between us. I started from Beau's initial favor, to the pact to keep away from each other, to breaking that pact, to breaking up in an Ikea carpark.

"Why Ikea?" he asked.

"I don't know. Maybe because it's easy to find?"

"I'm not sure it matters," he said.

"I'm sure it *doesn't* matter."

When we arrived at the quayside, we turned left onto the coastal path, the opposite of the direction Sutton and I had gone. This way we were quicker to lose the people around us. Soon we were alone as far as the eye could see.

"So, now you're just miserable," Zach said.

"Thanks for reminding me."

"Well if you'd forgotten already, I'm not sure why I've driven up from London."

"Did you just make a joke, Zachary?" Zach was the most reserved of all of us. The most careful. The most considered. Perfect. He was uber-focused—the kid who just sat there taking everything in. Like the sober friend at a stag party who could relay all your worst decisions the morning after. He was infuriating but useful.

He didn't respond. "So what's the solution? You get back together and—"

"No, we can't get back together. I've told you why not. It's impossible."

"Okay, so you spend the rest of your life miserable. You'll get used to it."

I groaned. "Thanks."

"Maybe you'll look back on your life and say to yourself that you had a shot with the woman you were meant to be with forever and you messed up. I suppose at least you had a couple of months, right?"

"You're being annoying."

"Well, is she the woman you're supposed to be with?"

"It doesn't matter," I said.

"It very definitely matters," he replied. "We're not talking about an Ikea carpark. If she's the woman you're meant to be with for the rest of your life, you don't want to fuck it up."

"How am I fucking things up? Even if I said I don't care about the promotion, I don't care about tainting the Cove legacy by sleeping around, I don't care about establishing myself as a doctor in my own right rather than just my parents' son, she doesn't want to go public with me either."

Zach stopped and shoved his hands in his pockets and shook his head. "You really are an idiot."

I stopped and patted him on the shoulder. "Great talk, mate. We should do this more often."

I started walking again and he joined me.

"I can guarantee Beau doesn't concern himself with the Cove name and legacy when he makes choices. He's certainly not going to give a shit about establishing his own legacy."

"So you're saying our brother is going to destroy the Cove name whatever we do, so we might as well give up?" For the first time in days, I cracked a smile.

"What if you let go?"

"Let go?"

"Of the idea that you're living in our parents' shadow.

That you have to make the right choice all the time. Of the promotion."

"Even if that were possible, which it's not, I'm not the only one with skin in the game. Sutton ended things between us, if you remember. She's ambitious and wants to make a name for herself."

"I liked her."

Pride I had no right to bloomed in my gut. She wasn't mine to be proud of anymore, but Zach rarely liked anyone and never so much as noticed most people.

"She's a great person, a good doctor and . . . it hurts."

"You know the stuff with the pee bottle at uni—"

"Yes, Zach, I was there. I remember."

"Sometimes I wonder why you didn't join the company and start doing other inventions. You made so much money."

"Because I wanted to practice hospital medicine."

"Like Mum and Dad."

I nodded. "Exactly."

"You had a plan and you stuck to it."

"Mum and Dad are two of the most successful doctors in the country. It worked for them."

"But they didn't plan it out."

"So Mum just said. I'm not planning things out so I can have exactly the same career as them. I've learned how to navigate things as a result of their career."

"Really? I'm not sure that's true. I think you have a plan in your head that two and two equals three. If you do this, this, and this, then you'll have maintained the Cove legacy, but distinguished yourself and everything will be fine."

"So what?" He was saying it like it was a bad thing.

"So you might gain those things you think you will— though there's no guarantee. But have you ever thought about what you'll lose along the way? I'm not saying you shouldn't plan, but I don't think you should be so narrow-minded that you lose out on things that could be bigger and better than you and your plan could ever have imagined."

This didn't sound like Zach. "Who is inhabiting my ultra-sensible brother's body right at this moment?"

"I mean it. I'm not saying I don't have a plan. I do, but if a bigger and better opportunity came along, I'm not going to say no because it wasn't on my list."

"Okay. But I'm not saying no to some huge opportunity."

"I guess it depends on what your ultimate goal is and how you see Sutton."

He paused and I let his words sink in. I'd been clear about my ultimate goal—I wanted to be successful. And I wanted to not shit all over what my parents had done.

"I can see you thinking," he said. "Your ultimate goal should be a good and happy life that you enjoy. If you think that's what you're going to achieve with this promotion, that's great. But if you think being with Sutton will help you live a good and happy life, then maybe she usurps the promotion. The goal remains the same but the paths change. It's no different than going through the foundation program and changing your mind about what you want to specialize in. The goal is still to be a doctor."

I sucked in a breath, taking in the clean, cool sea air. "I get it."

"You've always been so focused, Jacob. But with that focus comes a lack of flexibility. I know you want this promotion, but what happens if you didn't get it? Say they chose to give it to someone else."

I raised my eyebrows. "I don't want to blow my own trumpet, but it's unlikely."

"Of course," Zach replied, unsuccessfully covering his sarcasm. "But just say some overseas specialist came in—or maybe they got rid of the role entirely. Then what?"

"Then I'd figure out another way to . . . Oh, so you're saying if it's possible to find another way if it's forced on me, then . . ."

"Then if Sutton's worth it, you can figure out another way of getting what you want. But more than that, maybe Sutton is part of your ultimate goal and you just haven't let yourself see it yet."

We continued walking as I thought about the reality of taking myself out of the running to head up the foundation program. I wouldn't know what direction I was headed if I did that, but maybe Zach was right and I was missing other opportunities because I was so set in one direction.

"Say for argument's sake that I dropped the idea of the promotion. And maybe Sutton is part of my ultimate goal . . ." I paused. There was no doubt being with her made me happy. I could see us together, whacking each other with tea towels like Mum and Dad did, laughing about nothing, sticking by each other. I could see that future and it made me happy. "I think being with Sutton would make me happy. But none of that matters because Sutton has her own reasons why she can't be with me."

Zach sighed. "Maybe she's questioning those reasons too."

Sutton was at the very start of her career. She had almost two years of the foundation program left. I knew how important it was for her to prove herself during those two years. She wasn't going to give that up—not for me, and not for anything. "I doubt it."

"Maybe she just needs to understand how you feel."

She knew how I felt. She knew I didn't want to end

things, even though we were forced to. "I don't want to put any pressure on her."

"You know her best," he said.

I knew her better than Zach did. But I wanted to know more. And I wanted to know her forever.

THIRTY-THREE

Sutton

I hadn't been in the lecture theatre since our first two weeks in the hospital, which seemed like a lifetime ago. But in just two weeks we were on to our next rotations, and Wanda was about to announce who was going where.

I couldn't help be pulled back to the moment I'd seen Jacob standing in front of me, realizing he wasn't in Africa. I couldn't regret what had happened between us—I just wish it hadn't been doomed from the start.

We filed in and took our spots. The only difference was I wasn't sitting near Gilly this time. I'd steered clear of her since our conversation outside Jacob's house. There'd been no leaked rumors about me and Jacob so I knew she hadn't said anything. Either she believed what I'd said about dropping off a book or she understood that she shouldn't cross me. I didn't care which one it was.

"Feels like old times," Veronica said.

It did and it didn't. I was less enthusiastic than I had been a little over three months ago. Since then, I'd fallen in love and had to give him up. For this job. The decision had robbed me of my enthusiasm. Hopefully it would come back.

"Do you know what rotation you want next?" I asked.

"I don't mind," she said. "I'm going to see where the wind blows."

What a privilege it was to just let things take their course. This was probably the first time since I'd left my mum's house at sixteen that I'd had such a luxury.

"I heard they're going to be announcing the top six FYıs today—one for each rotation," Veronica said.

Everyone was so worked up about the award, but I knew a job in this hospital was the real prize.

"We're only two weeks away. I heard if you don't win recognition along the way, it doesn't exclude you from the final prize." She shrugged.

"Who did you hear this from?"

"A couple of people."

Wanda came in waving a clipboard in her hand. "Let's get to it. None of us have time to mess about. Just to reiterate—nothing has changed. When I announce which rotations you're in next, there is no discussion, no swapping, no special cases. You will take the next rotation you are given without complaint or comment. Is that understood?" She looked up from where she was running her finger down a page.

A murmur of agreement rippled through the now-weary twenty-five of us.

"Let's start with general surgery," she said.

I was the second name she read off the list. Veronica the third.

"Eeek," Veronica whispered from beside me. "We're together."

"And fewer nights," I said. I didn't think I'd end up a surgeon, but I was prepared to keep an open mind and give it my all.

After all the rotations were announced and we got answers to questions about various administrative issues, Wanda said, "If there's nothing else, we can get back to it."

Gilly's hand shot straight up into the air.

Wanda nodded.

"When are the interim announcements for the foundation award?"

Wanda narrowed her eyes. "The foundation award being . . . the award that's given to the most promising foundation doctor at the end of the program?" Her smile widened and she shook her head.

"Yes," Gilly said. "I heard there was going to be an interim announcement."

"There's no interim announcement. I can't believe that rumor is still in circulation. I'm here to tell you that not only are there no interim announcements, there is no award at the end of the two years. We're not in competition with each other. The only person you need to be competing with is yourself. You will all have some skills that are more developed than others. Some of you will naturally gravitate to certain specialisms and some of you will be good at most things. There is no one-size-fits-all doctor and there is no one-size-fits-no-one prize. Hospital medicine is all about working in teams—teams of doctors, nurses, radiographers, porters, admin staff—you name it. And it's also about working between our disciplines. There's no award because it makes no sense to single people out. Will there be stars of the year? For some, probably. Will there be late developers? Yes, indeed. Will there be oddballs and misfits and thinkers and doers? Yes, yes, yes, and yes. We welcome you all. A hospital needs lots of different brains and abilities to be able to function.

"I don't want to hear about competition anymore. I want to hear about cooperation. About learning. About development. I want you all to push yourselves to be the very best doctors you can be. That, as far as I'm concerned, is the best award you'll ever receive."

I couldn't help but laugh. All these people had been focused on a reward that didn't even exist.

It didn't change anything for me. And it didn't change anything between Jacob and me. I didn't want my professional success questioned because I happened to be in a relationship with such a high-profile consultant.

Foundation award or not, Jacob and I simply weren't meant to be.

THIRTY-FOUR

Sutton

Wearing woolen mittens in summer was just plain wrong. So was ice-skating. But here Parker, Tristan, and I were, doing both.

"I haven't skated since I was a kid. And it shows." It had been the Christmas before the divorce—the last time I felt like I had a family. After the split I remember watching other families having fun and thinking how I wished I could turn the clock back.

But going back wasn't possible. Not ever. I just had to make the best of what I had and plow forward.

"Can we get a hotdog?" Tristan asked as he came up behind us, clinging onto the three-foot-high penguin meant to help the smaller kids stay upright. "This is the worst idea ever."

"Hey," Parker said. "This was my idea."

"It wasn't your best," I said.

"You hated the ropes course at first and you loved it by the end."

"No, I was grateful to be alive at the end. There's a very distinct difference."

Parker groaned and led us all off the rink, towards the queue for hot dogs.

"But at least it took your mind off things for a bit," Parker said.

"That's true. My mind was fully occupied with the idea that my future career options could be narrowed with a broken wrist or severed spinal cord."

Tristan ordered our food and we found a bench facing the rink. "I don't think ice-skating is my kind of sport."

"I don't think it counts as a sport if you use the penguin," I said, taking a seat one side of Parker. Tristan was on the other.

"Next time you break up with someone," Tristan said. "I suggest we get a villa in Spain or something. Or maybe go wine tasting in the Loire." He bit into his hotdog.

"Good to know you're planning the aftermath of my next relationship," I said. "But I opt for wine in France, if I get a say."

"It's a deal." He held out his hand and I shook it.

"Don't I get a say?" Parker asked.

"No," Tristan and I chorused.

We watched the skaters as they made their way around the rink. Some were clearly more expert than others. The kids were the fastest—unaware of the danger they were facing with every move they made.

"It's been worth it though," Parker said. "Bet you haven't thought about Jacob once since you've strapped your skates on."

I gave her a small smile. Jacob was all I thought about. I managed to corral my attention at work, but as soon as I stepped through the sliding doors into the outside world, all my thoughts rushed to him.

"Can I add my two pennies?" Tristan asked, leaning forward in his seat so he could look at me.

"On my needing Parker's trademarked distraction techniques?" I asked.

"More on you and Jacob. I know I've never met him and it's not like you and I have been friends for decades. It's just that if breaking up with a guy you've been dating can make you this sad for this long, it strikes me that you shouldn't have broken up."

"Tristan," Parker said in a warning tone. "She didn't want to break up with him."

"Right, and I understand why you did. But why don't you just say fuck the lot of them? Who cares if some people think you've done well because of who you're sleeping with? You'll know the truth. Everyone who works with you will know the truth."

I got what Tristan was saying, but he wasn't in my shoes. "It's complicated," I replied. "Life isn't that easy."

"Isn't it?" Tristan said. "Does life always have to be a struggle? You've worked hard to be a doctor. You've proved how committed you are, how resourceful. It shows how dedicated you are. But at some point you have to enjoy the fruits of your labor. At some point, life is allowed to be easy and fun. Why don't you let yourself be with Jacob? Fuck the haters."

"It's easy to say when you're not the outsider."

Tristan shook his head. "I think if you label yourself an outsider, that's what you're going to be."

"I didn't label myself an outsider. I *am* an outsider. You think people are just going to—"

"I think people are going to do all sorts of things. I imagine most of the more senior people in the hospital won't give a shit because most of them met their wives and husbands and partners at work as well. They'll have seen doctors who come through from the fancy schools with top grades and do badly. They'll have seen the opposite and everything in between. If you got the position at the Royal Free, you deserve it. They know that, and they're the people you want to impress. Who cares about the gossip from the people at your level? They'll come around. Or they won't and they're arseholes."

I glanced at Parker to see her expression. Did she agree with Tristan? Did she think it was that easy?

She took my woolen-covered hand in hers. "I totally get why you don't want people to judge you. But I don't think the people who matter will. And I think Tristan's right—it's not a fluke that you got accepted at this hospital. It wasn't some administrative error. You worked hard. You deserve it."

I deserved it? I'd never thought about it like that.

"You've spent most of your life fighting for scraps, so when someone offers you a meal, you think it must be a mistake. It's not. I'm not going to lecture you on letting go and just being happy—I know I've not had the same life experience as you. But I know you deserve to be happy."

I leaned my head on Parker's shoulder and squeezed her hand, a silent thank-you for her words.

All my anxiety about dating Jacob publicly had been because I didn't think I deserved my job.

It was clear to me now.

"I worked really hard," I said.

"Harder than really hard," Parker said.

"I still work really hard."

"Super hard," Parker said. "But not only that, you're just as capable and just as deserving as everyone in your year."

I nodded. "Yeah."

She pulled me into a hug and then Tristan wrapped his long arms around both of us.

"Thanks, you two."

"That's it," Tristan said. "I'm taking these skates off. They're killing me and I feel like my work here is done."

Parker laughed. "You earned a reprieve."

"Are you going to call him now?" Tristan asked.

"Jacob? No. Even if I'm okay dating Jacob publicly, the feeling isn't mutual. If I was to call him and say let's dry hump in A&E—"

"For the record, I didn't advocate for dry-humping at work," Tristan said. "But I didn't *not* advocate for it either. On balance I'm probably pro as a general rule, but I think you might want to hold off, given your job is to save the lives of people around you and everything."

I smiled. "What I'm saying is even if I was okay with dating Jacob, he's not okay with dating me. His reasons are bigger than mine. There's no way he'd risk his career trajectory. I have to just accept it's over."

We knew from the outset that it wasn't going to last between us. I just didn't expect it to hurt so much. I didn't expect to lie in bed at night, unable to fall asleep because all I kept thinking about was how it would feel if Jacob were next to me.

"If Jacob feels for you what you obviously feel for him, he needs to figure out a way through," Tristan said.

Easier said than done. I knew it was never going to

happen. Tristan had been trying to help, but in the end, I was pretty sure he'd made it worse. Maybe life didn't always have to be such a struggle, but as far as I knew, I didn't have a magic wand either. There would always be insurmountable obstacles between Jacob and me.

I had to make peace with that.

THIRTY-FIVE

Jacob

I could almost pretend I was in Norfolk if I blocked out the distant sounds of the traffic, laughter, chatter, and occasional shouting from the bank of the Serpentine. Lying in a rowing boat in Hyde Park didn't exactly recreate the anti-stress chamber of the old, abandoned rowing boat I'd discovered in the marshes just off the north Norfolk coastal path, but it was as good as I was going to get in central London.

I was trying to figure out my next steps. What did I want out of life, my career, my legacy? Where did I see myself?

The only image I could see was Sutton. I wanted her. I didn't want to just date her. I wanted to spend the rest of my life with her. The more I thought about it, the more it became clear.

I just wasn't sure how I could make it happen.

After I solved that mystery, I needed to figure out what I wanted in my career. I knew in my gut that I loved teaching med students and foundation doctors, but I could do that and not head up the foundation program. I did it at the moment and it was the best part of my job. Heading up the foundation program would just mean a bunch of additional administration I wouldn't enjoy. Like my mum had said, I needed to focus on enjoying what I did and staying open to possibilities and opportunities.

I tucked my hands behind my head, enjoying the sensation of floating without a tether or destination. I loved my job. And I enjoyed the conversations I had with Nathan about business. Just like Mum said, maybe there were other opportunities I'd been blind to because I had such a fixed goal in my mind.

Maybe I didn't need a plan.

I stared up at the sky and tried to not think about anything, but Sutton's face kept coming into focus.

There was officially nothing stopping me from dating Sutton anymore. I didn't know if that was better or worse given we still couldn't be together because of her desire not to be sleeping with her boss. One problem down, one to go.

MAYBE IF I stayed in this boat long enough, I'd figure out how to create a future with Sutton by my side. All I knew was I was going to lie in rowing boats as many times as it took to find a way forward.

THIRTY-SIX

Sutton

It was Sunday, which meant libraries were shut and art galleries were overrun with tourists. But I needed a place to think—somewhere to calm my rising anxiety over my next steps with work and with Jacob. I wasn't sure there was a next step with Jacob, but I needed to clear my head to be sure.

I was on a mission to find myself a rowing boat to lie in.

The conversation with Parker and Tristan had helped me realize I needed to understand that my background didn't make me a worse doctor. And that I shouldn't care what people thought. I wasn't fully on board that ship, but I was staring at the gangplank—it was a start. The thought that Jacob might be waiting for me on the other side was enough for me to want to commit to believing in myself more. I'd get there. I always did.

I just couldn't see Jacob giving up what he needed *for me*.

I needed to figure out a way through for him. Maybe the rowing boat would help.

The forecast had said it was going to rain all day, but the blue sky and bright sun proved the weathermen wrong. I'd slipped on my favorite summer dress—blue and white striped with blue puffy sleeves—and taken the bus to Hyde Park. It was the only place I could remember seeing rowing boats in London—on the Serpentine.

People were probably going to think I'd lost it when I wanted to take out a boat by myself. The emergency services were probably going to get called when I pulled in the oars and lay down, but I didn't care. The people around would all be strangers. They wouldn't dictate my day. It would be good training for me.

As I came down the knoll by the boat hire station, I couldn't help but smile at the smattering of pedalos and rowing boats across the water. People enjoying the weather with their lovers and friends and children. Everyone was having so much fun and didn't seem to be thinking too much about anything at all.

I took a seat on the grass and enjoyed the view. There was a couple drinking champagne in one boat. What were they celebrating? An engagement? A first date? Three girlfriends were in another boat, organized like an Olympic team.

The pedalos seemed to be less cause for shrieks and laughter. The peddlers were far more sedate, without the need to coordinate the oars and the direction of their boats. The entire scene reminded me a little of Norfolk and the Cove family—noisy and all over the place, but full of fun.

One boat had obviously come untied from the side and had drifted, captainless, toward the bank nearest me. Someone needed to rescue that boat.

Just as I was wondering whether I should report it, a man sat up in the boat. He'd been there all along, lying down out of sight.

My heart began to clatter in my ribcage and my breath caught in my throat. I knew that short, blonde hair and tanned skin.

It couldn't be, could it?

I stood, as if height was going to give me a better look, when the man in the boat turned his head and looked straight at me.

No mistaking those blue eyes or the gaze that told me he knew me better than I knew myself.

We locked eyes and I waved.

How was he here?

Why was he here?

Without thinking, I started walking toward him like I was a magnet and he was my north.

He stood, but the boat wobbled and he sat again, picked up the oars and began rowing toward the boat drop-off point. I followed the outline of the bank to meet him.

THIRTY-SEVEN

Sutton

My pulse was thundering in my ears as if my heart were trying to climb out of my throat. I had to hold myself back from running up the jetty to meet Jacob. Instead, I stayed on the bank, transferring my weight from foot to foot while Jacob climbed out of the boat.

When he saw me, it was as if the rest of the world fell away. It didn't matter that we were in Central London surrounded by thousands of people. Only the two of us mattered.

"Hi," he said as he approached me.

"Hi," I replied. I'd always found Jacob more attractive than any man I'd ever laid eyes on, but now, his sexy swagger and the coy smile twitching at the corners of his lips, those hands pulling the sunglasses off the top of his head and shoving them in his pocket—it was almost overwhelming.

"I wasn't expecting to see you here," he said.

I shook my head. "Same. I came to . . . lie in a rowing

boat."

He laughed. "Me too. But you already knew that."

"It's a nice day for it." I glanced skyward then back at Jacob. What was I doing? Making small talk. What else was there to do? Lying in the boat was supposed to give me the answer to what I was going to say to him.

"I've missed you," he said. My knees weakened and I stumbled. He wrapped his hands around my shoulders to steady me. The heat of him was hypnotizing.

"Shall we sit?" he asked.

I nodded and he guided me away from the path, onto a patch of grass.

We sat opposite each other—me with crossed legs, him with his legs outstretched to the side of me, his arms propping him up behind him.

He glanced up at the sky and then back to look me in the eye. "It's been hard being apart from you."

It was as if my heart was trying to squeeze between my ribs to get free. "It's been really hard. I've missed you . . . so much." I'd spent so much of my life being independent that missing someone was a new experience for me.

He glanced over to the lake. "I came here to try and find a way through for us."

I frowned. "You did? So did I."

"That's why you were here today?"

"Yeah. I had a long talk with Parker and Tristan about everything. I realized a lot of things."

He nodded but stayed silent, letting me formulate my thoughts.

"I think I've been too focused on proving I'm worthy of my position at the hospital—like I'm spending every day interviewing for a job I already have. Parker said I act like it was an administrative error that I got the position, rather than because I deserve to be there."

He raised his eyebrows but didn't say he told me so. He knew I knew.

"It won't be an overnight thing, but I'm going to do my best to focus on the job, rather than proving to everyone I deserve the job. If I didn't, I wouldn't have got it."

"I think that's amazing," he said. "I think *you're* amazing."

I closed my eyes, trying to soak in his words, wanting to capture the feeling of warmth and comfort they gave me.

"I decided I don't want Wanda's job," he said. "Too much admin."

As he spoke, I opened my eyes. "I thought if you wanted to replace Wanda, you needed to—"

"I've changed my mind."

He said it in such a relaxed way that I thought for a second I must have misunderstood him.

"But I thought that you wanted to—"

"I've not decided what I want to do. I'm going to take a while to reassess things. I wanted to replace Wanda so I could have my pick of positions at the hospital, but I think I need to enjoy what I'm doing at the moment. And that's teaching other doctors and med students. I don't want to jump too far forward."

"Right," I said. "Did you just decide this?"

"Over the last few weeks. Losing you made me look at my life and my career and question what I was aiming for."

"Tell me you didn't do this for me. I would hate you to give up something you love and have you resent me for it later."

He frowned as if I'd disappointed him by asking the

question. "Not directly. This is the right move for me, whatever happens between us."

I tried to take in what he was saying. Wasn't his ambition to head up the foundation program the reason why he couldn't be with me? "So . . ."

"So . . . it seems there's not much keeping us apart now."

"There must be something," I said. It couldn't be that easy, could it?

He laughed. "You really don't believe in happy endings, do you?"

I shrugged, unable to stop a smile spreading across my face.

He lifted my hand and threaded his fingers through mine.

"What about you wanting to make a name for yourself outside your mother and father's legacy?"

"I still want to do that," he said. "Or maybe I don't. I've realized I can decide what my future is no matter my last name. Planning everything out and forcing myself to take jobs I don't want isn't the way forward. My parents are quite the force to be reckoned with, but I know that doesn't matter as much to me as creating a future with you."

I exhaled in relief at his words. I didn't need to find a solution for Jacob and he didn't need to find one for me. We'd both come to our own conclusions that had led us back to each other.

"You know, I might just start believing in happy endings after all," I said.

He pulled me onto his lap. "Good. Do they include a proposal?"

I pulled back to get a better look at him. "A marriage proposal?"

He shrugged. "Yeah. I want to marry you. The last few

weeks have been miserable without you. I don't want it to happen again."

"Marry you?" I repeated, not quite believing what I was hearing.

"Yeah," he let out a half laugh. "You sound like I'm asking you to run away to the circus."

I laughed and wrapped my arms around him. Just being close to him felt as if all my pieces were back together again, like I hadn't been fully me without him and now I was with him, everything was as it should be.

"I'd run away to the circus with you," I answered. Marriage was a different question and . . . difficult.

Instead of getting upset and defensive, Jacob, as usual, set his ego aside. "Tell me what you're thinking."

"I'm thinking that I want to be with you but I'm not sure how to be your wife. What you're used to with your parents' marriage isn't my experience. We grew up very differently and I'm not sure I can give you what they have."

He pressed a kiss to my forehead. "I don't want my parents' marriage. I want marriage with you, whatever that looks like."

My heart swooped in my chest. How did he know exactly the right thing to say? I placed my palm on his cheek. "I love you."

"I love you too. I probably should have said that before I proposed. I haven't planned this out."

"Either way works for me. I just like hearing it. I think you're a special man and I want to be with you forever. But I come with battle scars." His family was perfect and mine was broken. I wasn't sure how to operate if I wasn't pulling myself out of disaster. Could I be a good enough partner to this man who was everything?

"I love you for your scars, not in spite of them. It doesn't matter where or who you came from—you're a good person. There's no reason to doubt yourself. There's no reason to doubt us."

I shook my head, incredulous that he was so easily able to see what I was thinking and extinguish all my uncertainty.

"I love you and I want to marry you," I said.

His smile unfurled across his face. "To think, I was just lying there in the rowing boat, trying to find a way back to you."

"And now here we are."

"Engaged."

He cupped my face and pressed his lips to mine in a way that was so reverent it felt like an exchange of vows right there and then on the bank of the Serpentine, over-looking the rowing boats.

"I told you things had a way of working themselves out," he said.

"So this is what a happily ever after feels like."

I'd never thought this kind of happiness was meant for someone like me. I knew Jacob would spend the rest of time making my life better than I ever thought it could be. We'd be in each other's corners, as each other's champions, cheering the other on until we were too weary to do anything other than hold each other.

Forever started now.

EPILOGUE

A few days later

Jacob

I might not have known how my dad was going to react to me dating someone at the hospital, but I knew Gerry would be delighted that I was engaged.

Sutton wasn't convinced and was sitting in the hospital cafeteria, waiting for a debrief.

I put my head around Gerry's half-opened door.

"Dr. Cove, how good to see you. Come and take a seat." He patted the worn leatherette visitor chair he'd cleared of its usual papers. "Margo was asking about you the other day. You must come to dinner."

I took a seat. "That would be lovely, Gerry. Thank you."

He smiled and nodded at me and I waited for the bit where he'd tell me to bring someone to dinner with him and his wife. Instead of telling him I wasn't dating anyone, I would drop my news. But for once, he didn't mention my dating life. Something must have been up.

"So what can I do for you?" he asked eventually.

"I wanted to talk to you about a potentially tricky situation."

Before I'd finished my sentence, he was shaking his head. "Don't believe in tricky situations," he said. "Just clever, creative solutions, and that's what you're great at. So what is it?"

That hadn't been the reply I'd been expecting.

"I'm engaged to Sutton Scott, the FY1 doctor."

Gerry beamed back at me. "An engagement. How wonderful." He didn't seem even the slightest bit surprised. "Well, where is she? I want you both in here so I can finally see you together."

He was acting like he already knew, but that was impossible. No one knew. "She's actually waiting in the cafeteria. She's not on today. Shall I call her?"

"Absolutely."

I typed out a text asking her to come to Gerry's office and letting her know there was nothing to worry about. Sutton always expected the worst and I was going to have to make sure her expectations never bore fruit.

While I was typing, Gerry made a call. I only heard him with half an ear, but just as he hung up, it became clear he was asking someone to join our meeting.

Before I got a chance to ask him, there was a knock at the door and Wanda stepped into the cupboard-slash-office.

"As she's Sutton's direct line manager, I thought she should join the celebration."

"The more the merrier," I replied, wondering whether Sutton would outright faint when she saw the three of us in here together.

Sutton's knock was assertive. Maybe she was ready for a fight.

Gerry leaned forward and opened his office door. "Sutton. So wonderful of you to join us."

I made sure the door shut after her so no one could overhear us. We might have an oxygen shortage if the four of us were in here for too long.

"Let me be the first to offer you my sincere congratulations." Gerry kissed a completely stunned Sutton on the cheek.

She managed a tight smile and glanced at me. "Thank you."

"Wanda?" Gerry asked.

She nodded. "I have them here," she said, pulling out two pieces of paper from her armful of files. "The hospital waiver for intra-hospital relationships."

"Tsh tsh, I didn't mean that, Wanda. I meant my twenty pounds." Gerry pulled some lowball tumblers down from his book-stuffed shelf and hauled a bottle from an old shopping bag. "We're here to celebrate."

Gerry began to pour whatever was in his bottle into the four glasses while Wanda muttered under her breath and pulled apart her hospital pass.

She found and unfolded a twenty-pound note.

"Here," she said, throwing the money on Gerry's desk. "Congratulations."

I got the impression her good wishes weren't directed at us.

"Thank you, Wanda," Gerry said, passing Sutton and Wanda a glass of the fizzy brown liquid he'd poured. "I told her I can read all the doctors I've ever had under my supervision like a book. I could tell the first time I mentioned Sutton to you that we'd end up here today."

"Standing in a cupboard drinking warm ginger beer?" Wanda asked.

Gerry ignored her and raised his glass. "To a wonderful union. May you both have a marriage that lasts as long as this hospital stands."

I slipped my free hand into Sutton's as we sipped on our drinks. The look on her face told me she hadn't figured out what was going on.

"Thank you," Sutton said. "We thought we'd been discreet."

"You were," Wanda said. "I never heard the slightest word—apart from this one." She nodded at Gerry. "But you know how he's always matchmaking." Wanda turned to Sutton. "Yes, he's a Cove, but that doesn't mean your career has to take a back seat to his. You're clever and capable. All you lack is a little confidence."

Sutton squeezed my hand as if to say *Can you believe she's saying this stuff to me?* "Thanks, Wanda."

Wanda took a mouthful of ginger beer and winced. "That's disgusting, Gerry. And if you don't mind, I'm going to excuse myself. It's the end of my shift and I'm going home to have dinner with my husband."

"Husband?" Gerry exclaimed. "I didn't know you were married."

Wanda winked at Gerry. "You might know a lot of things, my friend. But you don't know everything." She excused herself and left, leaving behind a stumped-looking Gerry.

"I must have them over for dinner," he mumbled to himself.

"We should leave you to arrange that," I said.

"Yes, and don't think I've forgotten about you two,

either. Margo's been dying to meet you, Sutton, since I told her about you and Jacob."

"Thank you for understanding," Sutton said.

"Understanding? I'm delighted. Now off with you two. I'm going to fill Margo in."

I ushered us out of the office and shut the door behind us.

"Well that didn't go as I expected," Sutton said.

I chuckled. "You probably expected Gerry to morph into a fire-breathing dragon, so no wonder it wasn't as bad."

"Just got to find Veronica and tell her, and then I'm going home. Parker is coming over and we're going to day drink."

"Good to know," I said. "I'll look forward to seeing you both sprawled on the sofa later."

She grinned and I wanted to pull her toward me and kiss her, but we'd agreed to keep things strictly professional at the hospital.

"What are you doing here?" Veronica appeared from out of nowhere and glanced between Sutton and me.

"Actually, I was looking for you," Sutton said. "Free for a coffee?"

"Yeah, I'm just heading to lunch and—what's that on your left hand?" She glanced at Sutton's ring finger.

"See you at home," I said to Sutton. Veronica started to squeal.

"You have to tell me *everything*," I heard Veronica whisper as I peeled off and headed back to my office. It was clear that telling Veronica wasn't going to lead to any awkward or difficult conversations for my fiancée. Sooner or later, she'd learn that our life together could be smooth sailing.

The next day

Sutton

I lifted the suitcase out of the boot of Jacob's car and it landed with a slam on his driveway. I glanced at my left hand, just to check my ring. I'd only been wearing it for twenty-four hours and I was scared stiff the enormous stone would fall out of its setting or the entire thing would just slip off.

But there it was, glistening in the London sunshine, firmly fixed to my left ring finger.

"Sutton?" a woman called from across the road. "Is that you?"

I looked up to see Gilly coming toward me, a salacious grin spread wide across her face. Somehow news about Jacob and me hadn't spread through the hospital as fast as I thought it would. Maybe people didn't care as much as I had expected them to. Gerry and Wanda certainly hadn't. Or maybe Gilly just hadn't found out yet. I should have closed the gates to the drive. We were going back to my place for the rest of my stuff as soon as we unloaded, so it hadn't seemed worth it. I sighed at the inevitable conversation we would now be forced to have.

"You can't tell me you're dropping off another book for Jacob?" She glanced down at my suitcase.

"Nope," I said, hauling the suitcase upright.

"Hi, Gilly," Jacob said, coming back from the house to collect some more stuff. "What are you doing here?"

"Oh, just passing," she said.

"Do you live around here?" Jacob asked.

Gilly blushed and shook her head. "No, just like to take a walk on the Heath in the mornings sometimes."

Jacob and I exchanged a glance. She'd either been hoping to catch me here again or she'd been hoping to run into Jacob for her own reasons.

"Let me take that," Jacob said, taking the suitcase from me. "You don't want to catch your ring."

I shook my head. I wasn't sure who liked the ring more —me or Jacob. Dexter, a friend of Tristan's, was a jeweler, and we'd got to go to his Knightsbridge store after hours to pick it out. The place was like a diamond cave—the most expensive jewelry I'd ever laid eyes on everywhere I looked.

I'd spotted my ring as soon as they set the tray on the counter. It was a large, round, brilliant diamond.

It was the first one Jacob pulled out and slipped on my finger, and we didn't bother with any others. It was just perfect. When something was meant to be, you didn't walk away from it. We'd learned our lesson.

Gilly glanced at my hand, which had no doubt been part of Jacob's intention when he mentioned my ring.

"You're engaged?" she asked, glancing between me and Jacob.

"Yes," I said and I held up my hand, my palm facing inward. I wiggled my fingers, letting the stone catch the sunlight.

I figured I didn't owe Gilly a bigger explanation than that.

"To Jacob?" she asked as if I'd been unclear.

"Yes," I said as I peered into the back of the car.

"But you said that you were dropping off books. Does this mean you're going to resign? You can't blame me if I go and tell Wanda. You told me yourself. There's no way you should be working in the same—"

"Excuse me, I'm going to take this inside." I didn't need to listen to Gilly's response to my relationship. It really was nothing to do with her. She could tell who she liked. I didn't care. I pulled out my framed degree certificate, an umbrella, and the lamp I'd bought from Ikea because the one in my rented flat smelled of fish whenever I turned it on. I closed the boot of the car and headed inside, leaving an open-mouthed Gilly on the pavement.

All I cared about was getting to spend the rest of the day, all night, and every night after that with my soon-to-be husband.

As I got to the top of the steps to the front door, a beep of a horn nearly made me drop everything.

"What the hell—is that Zach?" Jacob asked. "What's he doing driving a van?"

Gilly had disappeared, luckily and now Jacob was going to get a nicer surprise.

I couldn't stop the grin spreading across my face. "He's helping me with something." I'd been added to the Cove family WhatsApp group and had been instantly treated like a sister by all the Cove brothers. It was a new experience for me having all these people invested in my life, wanting the best for me. I loved it.

"Helping you? Zach is far too perfect to drive a van. It's not his vibe at all."

Apparently, Zach never put a foot wrong and ribbed mercilessly for it. "He's so perfect, he agreed to drive a van for me," I said.

"Someone's going to have to help me in with this," Zach called out.

"I'll do it." I handed the lamp, certificate, and other things I was holding to Jacob and ran down the steps toward Zach.

Zach unlocked the back double doors of the van to reveal the gift I'd bought for Jacob. It was perfect.

"What's all this about?" Jacob said as he approached us.

"It's a present. For you." I beckoned him forward. "Come and see."

A grin unfurled on his face. He slid his arm around my waist as he looked into the van.

"A rowing boat," he said, and pressed a kiss on the top of my head.

"I thought we could put it in the back garden. Then you don't have to go to Hyde Park to think. I bought it in Norfolk. I know it's not exactly the same boat you laid in all those years ago, but I hope this will do."

"It will more than do, Sutton. I love you. It's wonderful." He chuckled.

"Why are you laughing?"

He reached around to his back pocket and pulled out a folded sheet of paper. "Because I've been working on this." He handed the paper to me and I opened it out.

It was a sort of architect's drawing of something but I couldn't quite work it out. "It's a library. For you. I thought we could convert the attic. I've had the plans drawn up."

I pressed my palm against my chest. "You are the most thoughtful man. I love you so much."

Zach coughed, interrupting the moment, but I couldn't help but laugh. "Are we nauseatingly in love?" I asked.

"A little," he replied.

"Zach's a psychopath. He doesn't do feelings," Jacob explained. "Let's get this boat round the back and then I can show you the samples I've got for the attic."

Is this what my life would be like from now on? A husband who was always trying to think of ways to make me smile. Brothers-in-law that were rooting for me and each other. A mother and father-in-law that already meant more to me than my own parents. Life was so good. So easy. So entirely full of love and laughter that I knew that a part of me was going to have to keep reminding myself that it was all real.

Another week later

Jacob

As we pulled into the gravel drive of my parents' house, and squeezed in between Nathan and Zach's car, I could tell something was up.

"I thought it was just going to be your parents here," Sutton said.

We'd driven up as soon as we both had days off at the same time. We'd FaceTimed Mum the night we got engaged —there was no point in trying to get my dad involved. He didn't even like talking on the phone. She'd been excited and wanted to celebrate with us, so we'd come up with a bottle of champagne. I was hoping that if I asked her nicely, she might cook a roast dinner tomorrow.

"Dad's right—there's always more than one of us around. They genuinely never get any time by themselves."

I opened the car door as my mother backed out of the house. It looked like she was carrying something. As she backed out farther, I realized she was unfurling a banner that said *Congratulations*. Zach was holding the other end, his expression more funeral than congratulatory.

Dad, Dog, Nathan, and Madison followed Zach out to greet us. Mum dropped the banner and rushed toward us, pulling us both in for a hug.

"I knew the moment I met you that you were the one for Jacob. I even told him so, didn't I?"

"You did, Mum. Always right, as usual."

"Welcome to the family," Dad said, enveloping Sutton into a hug. "Why anyone would want to marry this trouble-maker, I have no idea." He turned to me and winked, then pulled me in for a hug. "I'm kidding. You're my least troublesome son. Always been the one I've not had to worry about, but don't tell Zach or Nathan."

"We can hear you, Dad," Nathan said.

"I said what I said," Dad said, pulling out of our hug and patting me on the shoulder.

Sutton started to laugh like she couldn't believe what she'd signed up to.

"You've said yes," I said. "There's no going back."

"She's not changing her mind," Mum said. "I see the way she looks at you. I have another daughter and I'm not letting her go." She turned to Sutton. "You're family, now and forever."

I could tell Sutton was trying to swallow her tears. She was a Cove now, whether or not she chose to take our name.

"Come in, come in," Mum said. "Nathan, get their bags. Zachary, open some wine, we've got some celebrating to do."

Madison finished rolling up the banner that had been abandoned in the driveway. I slung my arm around Sutton and we headed in.

"I've made apple pie and a roast dinner in celebration of our newly engaged couple," Mum said.

"I made the apple pie," Dad said. "Even the bloody pastry."

"That's true. He did. Under strict supervision, mind you."

"Carole, I threw a few apples in some pastry. I didn't need supervision."

Mum rolled her eyes but was happy to let him think he'd made the apple pie on his own. "Who's in charge of drinks?" she asked.

"Me," Zach said. "Give me a chance. It's like catering for a wedding every time we open wine for the family."

"It will be," Carole said. "Speaking of weddings, have you thought where you might have it and when?"

I glanced at Sutton. We hadn't discussed it at all. We'd only just got engaged, and neither of us seemed in a rush.

"When do you want to get married?" I asked Sutton.

"Don't mind," she replied. "When do you want to get married?"

"What about a winter wedding?" Zach suggested, handing Sutton a glass of champagne.

"Maybe winter," I said.

"I think I prefer summer," Sutton said.

"Summer works," I replied. Summer would always remind me of getting back with Sutton under a perfect, blue, cloudless sky.

"We're in August now," Dad said. "You've only got a few weeks of summer left."

"It wouldn't have to be this year," Madison said. "Maybe they want to wait."

"I don't want to wait," Sutton said, slipping her hands into mine.

I smiled at the thought of being married to Sutton in just a few weeks.

"And have you thought about where?" Mum said. Was she angling to host another wedding? Maybe she'd been bitten by the bug after having Nathan and Madison's wedding at the house.

"You want to have it in Norfolk?" Sutton asked. "That might be nice. I think I was in love with you already by the time we came here."

A chorus of ahhhs filled the room and then Dad shouted at Dog for bringing a bone in from the garden and ruined the moment.

"Let's do it here at the house then," I suggested.

Sutton grinned up at me. "That would be perfect."

All the decisions we'd had to make since we'd gotten engaged had been so easy—like as long as we were together, everything else slotted into place.

"Are you going to move to Highgate?" Nathan asked. Zach pressed a glass into his hand.

"No," I said, then I realized I wasn't the only one with a say in where I lived now. Sutton and I would decide together. I turned to her. "Unless you want to live in Highgate?"

"I like Hampstead," she said. "The hospital's there and Parker and Tristan have finally found a house they like there."

"No," I said to Nathan. "We're not moving to Highgate." I turned to Sutton. "Are we moving?"

"Not if we're getting married in a few weeks. One thing at a time, right? And I like your house. I'll like it even more when we put the library in."

I pulled her close. "It's our house." I turned to the others. "If she calls it my house again, we'll move."

Mum raised her glass. "To my eldest son and my newest daughter. May you be as happy as your father and I have been. May you be as loyal as Zach, as lucky as Beau, and as rich as Nathan and Madison."

I clinked glasses with Sutton. "Welcome to the Cove family."

Want to read more about the Perfect Cove brother, Zach? Read **Dr. Perfect**

Did you miss out on Nathan and Madison's story? Read **Private Player**

Love work place romances? Click **The British Knight**

BOOKS BY LOUISE BAY

All books are stand alone

The Doctors Series

Dr. Off Limits

Dr. Perfect

The Mister Series

Mr. Mayfair

Mr. Knightsbridge

Mr. Smithfield

Mr. Park Lane

Mr. Bloomsbury

Mr. Notting Hill

The Christmas Collection

14 Days of Christmas

The Player Series

International Player

Private Player

Dr. Off Limits

Standalones

Hollywood Scandal

Love Unexpected

Hopeful

The Empire State Series

The Gentleman Series

The Ruthless Gentleman

The Wrong Gentleman

The Royals Series

King of Wall Street

Park Avenue Prince

Duke of Manhattan

The British Knight

The Earl of London

The Nights Series

Indigo Nights

Promised Nights

Parisian Nights

Faithful

What kind of books do you like?

Friends to lovers

Mr. Mayfair

Promised Nights

International Player

Fake relationship (marriage of convenience)

Duke of Manhattan

Mr. Mayfair

Mr. Notting Hill

Enemies to Lovers

King of Wall Street

The British Knight

The Earl of London

Hollywood Scandal

Parisian Nights

14 Days of Christmas

Mr. Bloomsbury

Office Romance/ Workplace romance

Mr. Knightsbridge

King of Wall Street

The British Knight

The Ruthless Gentleman

Mr. Bloomsbury

Second Chance

International Player

Hopeful

Best Friend's Brother

Promised Nights

Vacation/Holiday Romance

The Empire State Series

Indigo Nights

The Ruthless Gentleman

The Wrong Gentleman

Love Unexpected

14 Days of Christmas

Holiday/Christmas Romance

14 Days of Christmas

This Christmas

British Hero

Promised Nights (British heroine)

Indigo Nights (American heroine)

Hopeful (British heroine)

Duke of Manhattan (American heroine)

The British Knight (American heroine)

The Earl of London (British heroine)

The Wrong Gentleman (American heroine)

The Ruthless Gentleman (American heroine)

International Player (British heroine)

Mr. Mayfair (British heroine)

Mr. Knightsbridge (American heroine)

Mr. Smithfield (American heroine)

Private Player (British heroine)

Mr. Bloomsbury (American heroine)

14 Days of Christmas (British heroine)

Mr. Notting Hill (British heroine)

Single Dad

King of Wall Street

Mr. Smithfield

Sign up to the Louise Bay mailing list www.louisebay/newsletter

Read more at www.louisebay.com

Made in the USA
Coppell, TX
14 September 2022

83145586R00166